WEREWOLVES DON'T CRY

WEREWOLVES DON'T CRY

JIM MILLER

Hydra Publications

Also by Jim Miller

Heavy Jets – This is the tale of the first jet transport aircraft, the C-141, and the rowdy men who flew it. They were a breed apart, operating beyond the reach of 1960's communications. Alone and fiercely independent, they were every commander's nightmare.

Counter Intelligence – As World War II enveloped Europe, the Army Counter Intelligence Corps was tasked to cripple Hitler's military machine. They were first-in, last-out of every operation, living or dying by their wits and bravado.

Vienna – In the war's aftermath, 1946 Austria was divided among the Occupying Powers; America, France, Britain and Russia. But the dawning Cold War made cooperation impossible. The city of Vienna became a lawless, violent stage for intrigue, kidnappings, assassinations and endless spying.

Stealing Ho Chi Minh's Gold- Three airmen shot down over Laos manage to hijack several North Vietnamese trucks and escape back to Thailand. The trucks turn out to be full of gold, tons of gold. But it will take almost fifty years and cost many lives before the survivors smuggle the loot back to Hawaii.

Kentucky Weed – A retired Marine, abandoned by his wife and child, goes back home to rural Kentucky seeking peace and solitude. Instead, he finds two drug dealing clans locked in endless warfare - and he is related to both.

Terror on the Tundra – In this prequel to *Terror in Appalachia*, giant creatures, superbly adapted to the Arctic, come out of the ice fog to terrorize a small Alaskan village. The Army and Air

Force try to destroy them, but a young paleontologist from the University of Alaska vows to save the species – or die trying.

Terror in Appalachia

Giant wolf-like creatures prowl silently in the dark woods – hungry and desperate. The townspeople see them as horrifying monsters that must be killed at any cost. But, to the wolves, humans are merely obstacles to their own survival, and obstacles must be destroyed – utterly destroyed. Check out J. Esker Miller's debut masterpiece, Terror on the Tundra – In this prequel to Terror in Appalachia, giant creatures, superbly adapted to the Arctic, come out of the ice fog to terrorize a small Alaskan village. The Army and Air Force try to destroy them, but a young paleontologist from the University of Alaska vows to save the species – or die trying.

Terror in the Smokies

When giant wolf-like creatures appeared in the remote Kentucky hills, Forest Ranger Craig James and the townspeople fought back and chased the monsters off. A year later Hollywood has come to the Great Smokey Mountains where they hope to recreate the story, but in an area with greater tourism potential. They hire Craig as an advisor to ensure realism, but they wind up getting more realism than they expected, more realism than they can handle. The wolves have followed Craig and they now prowl North Carolina mountains rich with deer, elk, domestic cattle, and sometimes, even humans. Their numbers have grown and their appetites seem insatiable. The Cherokee people vow to protect their land and people. Local farmers are livid at the loss of their livestock and blame the movie-makers. National news outlets come alive at the drama unfolding in the hills. Soon, the place is overrun by State Police, National Guardsmen, and a bunch of good old boys who call themselves the "Carolina Cryptid Research Associates." .

Ranger Craig meets with a college-educated Cherokee Medicine

Man who tells him that he, Craig James, is the only one who can cause the wolves to leave. Craig has no idea, no plan, no hope, but he decides he must go to the wolves. He must try to communicate with them, or die trying.

ISBN: 978-1-948374-45-3

Hydra Publications

Goshen, Kentucky

www.hydrapublications.com

Awakening

J ohn Wagner sat ramrod straight and looked down the conference table where seven men sat and focused intently on him. He wasn't at all sure what was going on, but it probably wasn't good. Why was he even there? Newly hired, barely in-processed and, now, summoned to the executive conference room and seated at the end of the long table; no one offered any explanation. Was he about to lose yet another job; he had barely even started this one?

Louis Sypher, CEO of Digital Nation Inc. entered the room, and everyone stood. He was a muscular, tough-looking man with eyes as dark as polished obsidian. When those eyes met John's, they drilled right into his soul, and the new employee suppressed a little gulp. This could really go badly.

Sypher sat and remained quiet for what seemed like an eternity before he spoke. "Mister Wagner, you have been care-fully chosen for membership in this very select community. You were selected, not by us, but by your own DNA. You, and all of us here, share a very special genotype, one that is outside the defined Homo Sapiens parameters." Sypher leaned forward, and those black eyes seemed to grow larger. "You see, Mister Wagner, you're not quite human."

John made a sound halfway between a cough and a laugh. Not human? "What? Sir, what on earth are you saying? I am as human as any of you."

Sypher's eyes were steady, unblinking. He put an elbow on the table. "Yes, that is quite true, exactly true. Look around you at the men at this table. Look carefully at each of them. Note their physical resemblance to each other, and to you. We are all powerfully built and big-boned, with heads a little too large for our bodies, and we all have the same dental anomalies, specifically, a longer jaw and outsized canine teeth. We, you and I and the rest of us here, are different from ordinary Homo Sapiens in significant ways."

John Wagner exhaled, folded his arms, and sat back in his chair. Fear was being replaced by skepticism. His look was more than just skeptical; it was dismissive, almost defiant.

Sypher continued. "We know from our background investigation that you're a well-read man who, I'm certain, is familiar with the Neanderthal and other Homo species: *Erectus, Ergaster, Heidelbergis, Habilis,* and others. You, and we, represent yet another unacknowledged offshoot of the family tree."

John sat back, becoming bolder, almost sneering. This seemed like total bullshit. "Another offshoot? So, what exactly are...*we?*"

Sypher cleared his throat. "*Homo Lykanthropis.* The name is derived from the mythical werewolf."

John threw up his hands. No longer intimidated by the big boss and senior staff, this all seemed just too absurd to deal with on a rational level. "Are you serious, *werewolf?* Have you *people* lost your minds? I thought I worked for a company of clear-thinking businessmen who dealt in hard reality, not mythology and magic. Do you expect me to believe you change into monsters during the full moon, or whatever? Do you think *I* turn into a monster?"

Sypher scowled but kept a steady voice. "I know that this is a lot to deal with but, down deep, you're not surprised by my words. You already knew, have always known, there was something about you, something you couldn't really identify. You felt it as a child, and you feel it now. The DNA clearly shows it. You're not fully human."

Sypher sat back in his chair and continued in an almost paternal tone. "And DNA is what our company does: DNA analytics for police departments, government agencies, commercial enterprises, and individuals. Many genealogy companies outsource to us. That provides enormous access, and the capability to comb the population data to identify our own kind. That's how we found you. That's why we gave you an unsolicited job offer. That is why I am going to offer you something even more special today."

John shook his head. "You're actually serious about this? You think I'm some kind of monster. Why should I believe any...?"

Sypher still sounded patient. "Consider this. We all know women have monthly physical and emotional cycles. Do you have a monthly cycle? Think about it. Do you become aggressive, irritable, and hyperactive on a regular basis?" He paused, "Now, understand, we aren't saying there's anything magical here.

"We don't morph into wolf bodies, grow hair, or walk on all fours, but we do have a monthly cycle where we become hostile, even dangerous. We've looked at your police records, your expulsion from college, your failed marriage, and your history of psychotherapy. We know, and you know, you're *not* a normal Homo Sapiens."

John sat back, still sulking, but no longer adamant. "Okay, so why do you even care? What do you want from me?"

Sypher made a thin smile, but his eyes remained cold and locked. "Here is our offer. We want to welcome you to our family, guide you, and protect you. You see, you are truly one of us. You'll come to understand all that means, and you'll rejoice in your new family, for we have a destiny to fulfill."

John felt his heart beating. *This was totally unbelievable and, yet...*

Sypher continued, "You'll become a vital part of that movement, that revolution. The day will come when we do not hide, or pretend. For we are inherently Apex Predators, meant to be rulers, as you shall be no longer be the misfit, the bully, the embarrassing relative, the unloved, the unwanted, the untrusted loner; you will become one of the masters."

Now, the boss's voice became intense. His lips parted to reveal glistening, oversized teeth. Those dark eyes seemed to flicker, as though revealing some inner fire. "But you must agree to give up your old life in exchange for a new realization of what you are; what you can become. That is our destiny, your destiny. Accept my offer. Do not shirk from fate."

There was a long moment of silence. Every eye in the room still focused on John.

He realized that he wasn't breathing and tried to relax, but that wasn't possible. His pulse pounded in his neck. He cleared his throat and was surprised at how quiet, and controlled, his voice sounded. "Okay, how does this work? If I say 'yes,' what will happen now?"

Sypher gave an approving look. "Vladimir Petrov, the man to your right, will become your mentor. He, along with others, will teach you our ways. Pay attention. You must learn fast because we believe there is a time of conflict fast approaching and we will need warriors like you. The battle looms, and we must all be ready."

With that, Louis Sypher rose from his chair, as did everyone else. Even John, stood. The big man paused for one final glance, nodded, and then was gone.

The others filtered out, all except Vladimir.

John eyed him with an antagonistic look, almost a glare. "So, Vlad, you're supposed to be kind of like my teacher, or drill sergeant, or something. Is that right?"

Vladimir Petrov was taller than John but lacked his new student's in-your-face brashness. In fact, he avoided eye contact and sounded almost apologetic. "Okay, first of all, call me Val. Vlad, well, that freaks people out. Anyway, you're correct. I'm here to show you the ropes, although, I gotta be honest, I've only been aware for a couple of months myself, and I don't quite get all that goes along with this thing. But I'll do my best to answer your questions, or find someone more experienced."

John grabbed his new friend by the arm. "First things first, do you really believe this shit? Do you think you're some kind of monster?"

"Monster? No, but special. We are truly special." He brushed John's hand off his arm, took a breath, then seemed to struggle for words. "The full moon is in four days. In the meantime, we'll work through a lot of information, and even some exercises. You've got to learn fast. See, you've spent your whole life ignoring your special abilities, being embarrassed, even ashamed of them.

Now, you're free to accept and develop, to feel their power. It'll be great. You'll see. We'll begin tomorrow by opening your senses, by experiencing the world around you. Once you allow yourself to be immersed into a different consciousness, a different reality, you'll be amazed."

John still wasn't convinced. "Listen, if we're going to be out late, I need to call my girlfriend. She'll be worried."

Val scowled and shook his head. His voice was stern, exasperated. "No. You don't get it yet, do you? You're done with your old life, your old girl, your old job. Everything before is gone, erased. That whole world is dead to you. In fact, as we speak, you are being reported as drowned. A death certificate is being prepared. A bogus life insurance policy will give two hundred thousand dollars to Gretchen Jones, your live-in girlfriend, and another smaller sum to your mother. They will be notified within the hour."

"And what if I say 'no'?"

Val looked uncomfortable, shrugged and held his palms up. "Then, I would guess the death certificate would become factual. But don't dwell on that. Your mother, your girlfriend; they're just ordinary people. Now they're in your past. You're free of them. We are your people, no one else. You've just walked through a door into a whole new world.

"If you accept Mister Sypher's offer, by midnight tonight, every trace of your old life will have been erased. Your dull, misfit human experience will just evaporate. From this day forward, you have no past, no history. You have just been reborn as a wolf-man and must live up to your destiny."

John's shook his head. "I'm dead? But, I can't just…"

"You can," Val snarled. In an instant, his whole demeanor changed. No longer the insecure newcomer to the wolf clan, he was something else, something intimidating. The taller of the two, he stood over John, snarled again and then, with a Spiderman-like move, leaped high, high enough to touch the conference room ceiling and somehow brace himself between the ceiling and wall.

That gravity-defying pose looked impossible, as though he had adhesive hands and feet. He hung there for only a moment, teeth bared. His huge canines were curved and vicious-looking.

After a few seconds, Val let go and landed on the tile floor, but softly, cat-like. Then, he rose to stand face-to-face with John, just inches apart, tilting his head as his lips formed another wet snarl. This was clearly just a demonstration.

John didn't think; he just reacted to the aggressive challenge by reflex, grabbing handfuls of Val's suit coat, lifting the bigger man and hurling him back against the wall. The impact shattered the wallboard and sent glass picture frames crashing. Then, John made his own snarl and started toward his opponent, like a lineman going after a quarterback.

Val stopped, seemed to collect himself and raised a hand of surrender, along with a sly smile. "Okay, okay. I just pissed you off. But look what you found within yourself. It's been there all along but, now, you feel it. You're a dominator, truly are one of us." He beckoned to John. "Come, let's find more surprises within you."

———

Vladimir Petrov didn't feel as confident as he could have been, should have been. He and John left the office building, seeking the privacy of a public place where strangers would pay no attention. After the physical exchange in the conference room, Val decided to be more careful and not rush things. His own knowledge, after all, was still limited. He was struggling to adapt to his new identity as a wolf-man, but he would do his best. He would try to be a good teacher. Training John was probably one of the most important things he would ever do. He *would* get it right.

Madison, Wisconsin was blustery and cold on that March morning. They came to a sidewalk café with outdoor seating.

Wrought iron tables had large beach-type umbrellas rolled and tied, waiting for a warmer season. The cold gave the two men privacy. No others dared brave the chill by sitting outside in frigid wind.

A waiter in a black vest, long apron, and wind-whipped tie came outside and eyed them as though aggravated for having to be out in the cold. He presented menus and poured coffee without asking questions. His apron flapped in gusty wind as he stood with his order pad ready.

Val waved the man off. Then, John's mentor leaned forward and used his coffee cup as a hand warmer as he decided how to begin his duties.

"Okay. Tell me about your early life, from your first memories."

John shrugged and slumped back in his cold metal chair. He, too, cradled his cup in both hands and began slowly. "I was an unwanted child. That is not speculation. My mother told me almost daily how much she regretted my being born. My father seldom spoke to me and, even when he did, it was mostly grunts and threats."

Val tried to look interested. "Did he show any of the signs; the big head, the teeth?"

John thought before he answered. "No. He was a good-sized man, fairly athletic before heavy drinking destroyed him, but I recall none of the characteristics Mr. Sypher mentioned."

"Do you know much about your family background, nationality and so forth?"

"Yes, my father's people were all English from the north close to the Scottish border. He was proud of his heritage. My mother was a refugee from Hungary brought to America as a child."

"Hungary? That's interesting. Hungary is just about the

epicenter of our kind." Val considered for a moment and then opened a binder. "I should have already known all that. I have your dossier right here." He thumbed through and read for a minute, nodding to himself. "Okay, I'll tell I you what I see about your lineage."

He spent another moment scanning and then looked back at John. "The man you grew up with was almost certainly not your biological father. Your unique genotype traces to a very small area in the Balkans, where many of our family trees originated." He turned a page. "Your mother's ancestral home was not far away. Whoever made her pregnant while she was married, it was definitely not Mister Wagner, the man who raised you as his son."

John sipped quietly. "So, how does that matter?"

"Confirmation, that's all. It makes perfect sense. You make perfect sense now that we have taken the British stepfather out of the genetic picture."

"Okay, Val, tell me about this *genetic picture*. Who, or what, am I, and what can I expect?"

"Sure. But understand I'm a novice at this. I have only been aware for a couple of months, myself. The recruiting has been ongoing for a year or more, but I'm a newbie, still trying to get my head around the whole thing. So, here is the deal to the best of my knowledge."

He wet his lips and looked John in the eyes. "There has always been a small, hard core of our kind who understood exactly what they were but tried to pass as ordinary people. They knew, intuitively, that ordinary humans around them could be a danger. The Sapiens could never, would never, understand us or accept our abilities.

"Sometimes, lone Lycans recognized each other and joined together, tentatively forming small packs for self-support. But most led solitary secret lives, always pretending to be normal, always suppressing their needs, always biting their tongues when secretly they wanted to be out biting throats."

Val sat back, lost in his storytelling. "Those associations, or packs, usually proved disastrous. When humans discovered them, it was like the old Frankenstein movie, you know, the villagers with pitchforks and torches, or whatever. The Church, in particular, was always ready to exterminate 'demons.'

"The man-wolves were often murdered, tortured, and butchered by the most cruel, barbaric means. Afterwards, the humans involved usually covered up and explained away those incidents. The Church saw to that. They wanted no taint of monsters in their own backyard."

Val closed his book and looked off into the crowded street. "We have, for hundreds, maybe thousands of years, lived isolated, secretive, fearful lives, never really knowing just what we were, but always understanding the danger if others found out."

John clenched his fists. "Okay, great history lesson, but answer me this, just what are we? What is really going on with me, with us?"

"Well, Louis Sypher is the expert, but I'll give it my best shot. We are more than a ninety-nine percent match to Homo Sapiens' DNA. That's more than a Chimpanzee, Bonobo, or Neanderthal, even more than Denisovans.

"Our one percent is unique among the Homo species. It affects our physical structure, obviously, but it has an even bigger influence in the function of our brains and nervous systems. In school you were probably a whiz in math but hopeless in foreign languages and poetry, right?"

John shrugged. "I guess. I really wasn't much of a student."

"But athletic, strong and fearless, right?"

John sat back. The tension went out of his shoulders.

"Yeah, that was the only good part of high school." He smiled at the memory. "In football, I was a lineman. They called me 'Bone Crusher.' I was competitive for a heavy-weight regional title in weight lifting but got thrown off the wrestling team for hurting too many opponents. In my senior year, a pro wrestling scout offered me a job, but my father, the man I thought was my father, absolutely refused to permit it."

Val smiled. "You've heard of the warrior gene? Well, that is a genetic indicator that, somewhere back in a human's family tree, there is a remnant of our kind, but only a remnant, a trace. You and I, we have almost the full genome. So now you understand that you are special, but you don't know yet how special." Val watched John, trying to decide just how hard to press, how hesitant John might be.

"All mammals have pretty much the same senses. Ours are similar, but sharper. You have a predator's vision. If an optometrist ever bothered to test closely, you would probably have 20/5 vision. Your hearing is likely more acute than normal by a factor of three. You already know about the strength part.

"But you have an even more powerful sense, one that is almost impossible to describe. It is the ability to feel a sort of ether that flows all around us. Unlike normal humans, you can sense it, like a wind of destiny. You will come to know when something is about to happen. It is kind of like The Force in the old *Star Wars* movies. You are sensitive to fate, or whatever you want to call it. That sense peaks with the moon."

They sat for a long time in silence. The cold wind ruffled John's coat collar and hair.

He seemed to be trying to take it all in, to make sense of it. Finally, he said, "What about this coming event Louis spoke of. What's that about?"

Val drew close as though sharing a secret. "There are religious groups whose leaders have known about us for eons. Their interest has recently been revived, possibly because of our efforts to educate and protect our fellows.

"In particular, there is a sect of Catholic monks from Italy, who have made it their mission to learn about us. They have created a secret cadre dedicated to ridding themselves of unholy monsters, demons, they call us. Even the Pope is fully on board with this plan to exterminate our kind.

"He has provided money and resources to these Bible-thumping thugs. They have spies and surveillance teams all over the world gathering information and their goal is simple, to kill us all. That's one reason Sypher created the corporation, to fight back. That's why you *have* to commit. We're organizing, recruiting, finding our fellows and preparing them for the coming conflict."

Val tried to control the anger in his voice. "In order to survive, we must eviscerate this Army of fanatics. We, *Homo Lykanthropis*, must survive. You and I and the rest of our kind will seek out and slaughter the real demons, those God-fearing fanatics, and send them to their own version of hell."

It took a while for Val's emotion to subside. They continued to talk, but he was still agitated. He needed to get away, burn off some energy. Maybe a walk would do it. He made excuses, left a tip, and buttoned his overcoat all the way to the chin. His hands were shaking, and not just from the chill.

He dropped a brown envelope on the table in front of John. "There's an address written on the front. Inside, there is a key and directions. It's a cheap downtown rental. Go there and await further instructions. Do not attempt to contact anyone from your old life. Oh, there's also money and contact phone numbers." He hesitated. "And a contract. Read it, but don't sign until I'm there to explain how it must be done. That will be necessary for your training to proceed. I'll see you tomorrow."

He gave John a stern nod and walked off into the crowd of pedestrians that flowed along the sidewalk, like an endless train chugging along, puffing out clouds of foggy breath. He looked around at them, these ordinary humans, and felt disdain, even pity. Vladimir Petrov puffed up his chest and snorted his own cloud of condensed breath, like a bull asserting himself in a pasture of cows.

Ahead, he saw a man scurrying in his direction, a man dressed in a black hood, cloak, and robe. He was a priest, one of the hated Catholic tribe? Val stepped to block the man's path.

The priest muttered something apologetic and attempted to go around.

Val moved sideways to again block.

The priest looked confused and started to say something that included the words, "My son."

Val leaned close and opened his mouth wide to display that jaw full of impressive teeth. He exhaled a great long hiss.

The startled priest stumbled backward, tripped, and sprawled on the concrete. He held his hands up, as though shielding himself from a bright light.

At that moment, Val wasn't sure what he felt; power certainly, dominance maybe, but also a touch of arrogance. He didn't really want that. As a kid, he had often been accused of being a bully. He remembered being shunned, feared, distrusted, and alone. The memory still stung.

As an adult, he tried his best to be humble. He looked down and regretted his unprovoked aggression against the puny priest. Val reached out to help him back to his feet.

The priest accepted, but with a tentative soft hand.

Val held that plump little appendage and resisted the urge to crush it.

The priest seemed unsure how to react.

Val shrugged his overcoat back in place and walked away, head high, without a look back at the bewildered priest, who stood looking confused and talking to himself, or maybe to his God.

Luppo Mannaro

"Soon, this magnificent garden will burst forth into bloom in God's glorious springtime awakening. All winter rot and spoilage will be cut off, dug up, and replaced. Beautiful new colors and shapes will emerge in a rebirth, full of vitality." The big man spread his arms and exhaled a cloud as he turned in a full circle taking in the labyrinth of stone walls and paths. Behind them a cathedral spire rose into gray sky. "But I think we here shall not see the spring reincarnation quite as early as your neighbors back in Sicily, Monsignor Antonio."

The smaller of the two men who walked gardens paths wore a simple hooded brown robe with a rope for a belt. He used a deferential tone as he spoke to the larger man dressed in a business suit, heavy overcoat, and Homburg hat. "Yes, Your Grace. By this time of year, the people of our little island will already be smelling the delicate flowers... And the hills, the hills will come alive with color. You must visit us sometime."

Bishop Helsing, the larger man, tugged on his kid leather

gloves. "Perhaps I shall, someday. But, now, you and I must deal with a more pressing issue. You have heard reports of the re-emergence of demons here in our country. Apparently, these are not simply demon-spirits, they are physical beings, some say like werewolves."

"Yes, Your Grace. I believe that is precisely why you requested *my* visit. I must say that you here are not alone. All around the world, we hear increased reports of sightings, attacks, sacrilegious activities, even desecration of relics. Evil is spreading across the land, and wickedness is growing within the hearts of men. The appearance of the wolf is simply more evidence of the moral drift."

"Yes, yes, it is so." The Bishop nodded vigorously. "And I am told you have a group whose sole purpose is to eliminate them all."

Father Antonio was quick to respond. "In the Monastero Arcadia, we have a truly dedicated group of monks who have sworn an oath to kill all demons, or die in the quest. They are from several countries, mostly European, all ex-military, all combat veterans, all true servants of the Lord."

"And how soon can they be made available? Our need seems urgent."

"They are already here, Your Grace. They accompanied me. We will, of course, need your help and your influence to procure arms and secure cooperation from local agencies but, believe me, my monks stand ready to go into battle now, within the hour, if necessary."

Bishop Helsing took a deep breath and added, "With the Cross of Jesus going on before."

Both men made comfortable smiles.

John Wagner couldn't sleep. He paced in his underwear and looked out the window of the small apartment he had been given. Below, a run-down inner-city neighborhood still bustled at 2:00 in the morning. Like every city, Madison had its night people; druggies, hookers, drunks, and vagrants.

He clenched his fists and gritted his oversized teeth. *Why did he accept this werewolf crap so easily?* Well, he didn't really accept it; he just went along with it. Sure, he saw his resemblance to the other men. It was creepy, but undeniable. But why should he agree to give up his life, his home, his girlfriend, without more resistance? He needed more... More what? More evidence, facts, what?

On the battered table lay a simple contract. He expected that it would be full of legal gobbledygook and multi-syllable words. When he finally quit pacing and read it, he was surprised at how brief it was.

"I, Johnathan Wagner, swear to protect all members of the Therio Lycan Society and to be at peace with them always. I hereby abandon all previous alliances and obligations and devote myself, my heart and soul, to the obedience of my leaders and service to my fellow members. I take this oath with clear mind and shall adhere to it on pain of death."

It was a pretty vague document. But it implied that he was agreeing to give up his life, everything he owned, every association he ever had, not that there were many. And, in return... what?

He tried to work off the tension, punching the air, flexing his muscles, feeling a bit foolish as he did. John ran fingers through his course black hair. *Okay, enough of that.* He had to pull out of the funk, try to accept the weirdness, maybe learn to feel that sense Val had talked about.

He forced himself to relax, let his shoulders sag, and lifted his chin, as though seeking a gentle breeze. Nothing. He tried again, shoulders back, arms loose, mind clear. Still nothing.

But the concentration did make him aware of faint noises in the building, and smells. There were funky odors of mold, garbage, beer, dust, and cooking grease, and cooking, even at 2:00. And there was something else. He wasn't sure but, as he relaxed even more, the sense of it got stronger. *Violence,* something violent was about to happen. Somehow, he knew.

Still in his underwear, John walked out into the dingy hall and heard voices, arguing voices, from around the corner. He turned the bend to face three men, gang-members, judging by the looks of their tattoos and clothes.

They held another young man down on the floor as he sucked air and made frantic noises. Blood ran from his nose and facial cuts. He had already taken quite a beating.

One of the tormentors turned and sneered. "What the hell you want, mister. This ain't none of your damned…"

John hit the man once, but hard enough to make him collapse into a pile.

The other two stood and began drawing hardware from under baggy clothing. A single punch to one jaw, and a back-swing that planted an elbow in the other man's face, and the discussion was over.

He extended a hand to the bloody man, more of a boy really, and helped him stand. "You okay?"

The response was tentative. "Yes, sir. Thank you, sir." The boy ran his hands down the front of his chest, as though making sure that all his body parts were still intact. Then, with a quick leap over the three bodies, he took off with churning arms and bolted down the stairs.

John made a little chuckle and looked down at the three unconscious men. He poked one with his foot and received a groan in response. Then, as he started back to his room, he heard soft crying. No, he didn't really hear the crying, he felt it. *Could this also be the sense Val talked about?*

It came from the room directly across from his. After a moment's hesitation, he tried the doorknob. It was unlocked. The door squeaked and opened into a dingy room lit by a single bulb in an unshaded lamp. An old woman sat on the side of her bed rocking and moaning.

"Ma'am, what is wrong? Are you all right?"

She jumped at the sound of his voice, turned to him and spoke in a shrill voice. "Who the hell are you, and why you standing there in your underpants? You some kind of pervert, or something?"

"No, ma'am. I just heard you crying and thought…"

She held up a hand in a halt gesture. "Ain't nothing you can do. They took my grandson. Said they was gonna kill him if he didn't pay them what was owed. They was drug dealers. I'm sure of it. My boy's good as dead."

"No, ma'am. I chased them off and the young man, your grandson, I assume, ran off as well. I think he's probably safe for the moment."

Her response was soft, hesitant. "Why you do that?"

John shrugged. "He needed help, that's all. I was there, and I helped him, simple as that."

Her "thank you" was a whisper.

John admonished her to keep her door locked and went back to his room, mumbling to himself, "Well, I might be a monster to some, but I'm still capable of kindness. Does that make me less of a wolf-man and more of a human? Guess I'll find out in time."

Once inside, his thoughts turned to Gretchen, his girl-friend. What exactly would they tell her? They would say he was dead, of course—didn't Val say drowned? How would she take it? He wanted desperately to call her, but that could lead to so many complications. He would find a way to check on her, but it would have to wait until morning.

With that decision, he finally felt fatigued enough to try sleeping, but it would be a fitful sleep with wild dreams, monster movie dreams.

———

Mister Vrykolas was a shaggy man. Most of the Lycan group at Digital Nation easily passed for ordinary humans and could move unnoticed in everyday life. Vrykolas could not. He shaved enough of his face, neck, and hands to get passport and driver's license pictures, but there was no hiding the hair, fur really, that covered most of his body. When he went out among the American public, he wore a wide-brimmed hat, overcoat, and gloves, regardless of temperature.

Vladimir Petrov knocked and waited as the surveillance cameras scanned him. A buzzer sounded and Val entered a dark room filled with a library's worth of books. The air was thick with a musty antique smell.

Vrykolas - if he had a first name no one knew it - sat waiting. "How did he do, this new trainee of yours?"

"Sir, it is too early to say. He has the physical requirements. The man is a brute. He seems receptive, but he's upset about leaving his old life."

The hairy man wore a wrinkled shirt and suspenders as well as a clerk's eye shade that hid most of his wire-brush eyebrows. He scoffed. "His old life. He had no life. His records say he was a failure at everything he ever tried. His marriage didn't last. Still, he has enough of the human in him."

Vrykolas held up his hands. "His appearance, his voice, his mannerisms are all sufficient for people to overlook the characteristics that make many of us immediately noticed. He, like you, can move easily among them. The question remains, can he fulfill his mission? Will he kill when we ask?"

Vladimir hesitated, shook his head and scowled. "Sir, I cannot say, at least, not yet. I lack the experience to see into a man's soul."

"A *man's* soul? That is the question Petrov; is he *man*, or *Lycan*? And how shall we know? There is no time to waste resources on him if he lacks the steel to serve us."

Vrykolas hunched in his squeaky, wooden office chair. "We will give him, and you, a trial mission, something simple, but violent." He thought for only a second. "Do you know of the demon hunter monks, the death squad from Sicily? The local bishop has commissioned them to hunt us down. You and this man, John Wagner, must kill one of then, at least one, to show us you're worthy. If you succeed, we will allow you both to continue in the program. Otherwise…Well, that will take care of itself."

"Sir, how will I inform him about this group of monks? I know little, myself?"

Vrykolas made a hint of a chuckle. "On the sixteenth floor of this building, there is an office door with a sign that says *Archives*. Go and knock. I will send them your clearance information."

"They will schedule an appointment for you and Wagner to be briefed on the operation. His job, your job, will be to put fear into these monster hunters, to send them whimpering back to Sicily with their tails tucked between their legs." He smiled with jagged yellow teeth. "If it is monsters they seek, let us give them monsters."

Vladimir left but paused in the hallway. His blood was running. His heart was beating fast and hard. This would be his first mission as a wolf-man, his first blood. He could barely wait to share this adventure with John Wagner.

The Farm

J ohn hadn't slept, hadn't bathed, and hadn't eaten for a night and a day. His pacing threatened to wear through the carpet in his cheap apartment. He met Vladimir at the door with excited questions. "What's going on? How long do I have to stay in this shithole? What's the next step?"

"Okay, slow down. I have a lot of information, John. Just let me get inside, okay."

"Yeah, yeah, sorry. It's just… I need to know something. Val, can you tell me what happened to Gretchen? How about my mother? And my belongings, how will they—"

Val put a kindly uncle's hand on John's shoulder. "I have all that information, and more. Let's get something to eat, and I'll tell…" He paused and squinted. "What's that on your hand? It looks like dried blood."

John waved an open hand in a dismissive gesture. "Nothing. It's nothing. I broke up a fight in the hallway, that's all."

"A fight? You're supposed to be keeping a low profile.

John came back. "Okay, now about my questions."

"Gretchen, I'm told, was upset but is dealing with it. Your mother put on a big show, crying, disconsolate. I think she'll got over it as soon as she counted the settlement money. Your background information says the two of you were not close. We've recovered your computer and personal files. I have them in the car. Now, let's find a restaurant, I'm starved."

John gave a sigh and followed Val. The old lady neighbor left the chain on as she cracked her door and watched them leave. The room behind her was dark, unlit, not even the small lamp.

As they tromped down the stairs where the young man had bolted the night before, John kept asking questions "We have talked about the male Lycans, are there females? Are there were-women?"

Val laughed. "Of course, but not many. We mixed-breed males can usually fit in fairly well with the Sapiens, but the women don't fare so well. I'm told that they, like us, are robust and hairy, and they tend to be sexually aggressive. Those are not desirable female characteristics in western society. And, then, there is the problem of breeding with Lycan males."

John looked curious.

Val continued. "Males of our kind have no problem mating with female Sapiens women, but there is some physiological problem with human males trying to screw Lycan females. It often results in damage to the guys. I guess they're just not built for rough sex."

Both laughed, and Val continued. "The offspring of Sapiens-Lycan unions are often pale and cuddly and not usually seen as remarkable in the maternity ward. But a Lycan-Lycan baby is dramatically bigger, hairier, and more animal-like. They are, even as newborns, considered abnormal."

"So, what becomes of these purebreds?"

Val hesitated and chose his words. "In the Balkans, they

are killed at birth. Here, and in the other developed nations, I'm told they are neutered and sent to a compound in South Africa to be raised in a community of mine workers. They live out their lives without ever leaving that compound. Their work helps subsidize the rest of us."

He hesitated. "We believe that some are overlooked and wind up living wild. There have been thousands of reported sightings over the years, often described as Bigfoot, or Sasquatch, or some other colorful, cryptid name."

"They live in the wild, like animals?"

"That's pure speculation based on claimed sightings. But I do believe the part about the Balkans and the mining camps is true."

John shook his head. He didn't like that. "So, we actually murder our own kind?"

"Everything I have told you came to me in whispers. I cannot vouch for any of it but, when I questioned my mentor, he simply reminded me of the villagers with torches and pitchforks. I remember his words. 'Better to die quietly by your brother's hand than be torn apart by the zealots. We must survive before we can rule but one day, hopefully soon, we will rise, and the frail Sapiens will bow before us."

John was still shaking his head. "Val, that seems barbaric, killing our own. Why not find a way to live separately? Why don't we all just go to South Africa…"

The taller man made an indulgent smile. "Because it is not our nature to live in peace and harmony. We are the people of the wolf, and our day is coming. Then, it will be the Sapiens who need to go hide in South Africa. We will stand at the top of the food chain and the frail and frightened Sapiens will serve us. We are the dominators and, now, it is time for you to show that you have the strength and will to fight with us, for we, you and I, have been given a mission."

John asked no more questions but thought long and deep as they drove. They got drive-in fast food and headed into the countryside.

Val lectured as they meandered along the rolling hills and sparse barns and houses of farm country. "Digital Nation is a big employer here in this declining agricultural community. The company has almost total support from the elected government, and the citizens. In turn, Mister Sypher donates generously to all kinds of local agencies. In return, he gets whatever he wants, no questions asked."

They turned down a dirt road and came to a long-abandoned barn in a field of three-foot-high grass. "Okay, here we are. Finish off that burger, and I'll show you some things that will knock your socks off."

John jammed the last wad of bun into his mouth and stood beside the car as his jaw churned.

Val grinned like a schoolboy. "See that flat-roofed shed? What would you say it is, maybe ten feet tall? Watch this."

John was still munching and could not respond.

Val seemed to squat deep and then, in an explosive leap, jumped higher than the roof. He hung in the air momentarily, arms outstretched like a free-falling parachutist, and then landed with enough force to drive him to one knee. He turned to John. "You can do that. I'm about to show you how."

John, with mouth full, could manage no more than a muffled grunt.

"So, your actual muscle tissue is exactly the same as a Sapiens, but our connective tissue is different. The Sapiens have tendons and ligaments, and other stuff; we have tensors. That's what we call the special connective tissue that gives us such power. Reach down behind your knee and feel the bands that attach your calf muscle to the bone. They're twice the thickness of a human tendon and completely different physio-logically.

"The tensors are power multipliers and come into play when you fully extend the muscle. We have the same tensors in our backs and shoulders but, for some reason, they only work in pulling actions. You have no abnormal strength when you squeeze your hands together but, when you pull back, you'll have four, or five, times the power of a Sapiens."

Val demonstrated by pushing his right fist into the palm of his left hand. "See, just normal strength. Now, watch." He snapped his elbows back wide. "That motion, the pulling apart, activates the tensors in your back. Lifting activates shoulder tensors, but pushing down does not."

The teacher grinned. "I guess we are meant to be leapers and rippers and grabbers, not builders and stackers. We are predators, not farmers."

Val took John by the shoulder. "Okay, your turn to try. You must squat all the way down on your heels to compress and stretch the tensor. The leap will consist of a normal jump, but use your arms to add momentum, and yell from the gut. It will take practice to find what works best for you. Oh, and the landing; keep your knees slightly bent and your arms spread to stabilize and help keep you upright. Got it?"

John didn't feel completely convinced that this would work. He bent down, and Val admonished him to go lower, to fully compress the tensors, or whatever. His legs weren't used to being stretched so far, and the strain was a little painful.

"Okay, leap wolf-man. Soar."

John jumped with everything he had. He could feel an unaccustomed boost, but his effort was puny, barely four feet high. It was higher than he had ever jumped before, but it was still puny, but still well within athletic human standards. He tried two more jumps, each a little higher than the one before.

Then the leg cramps hit, and he danced in a circle, grabbing his thigh and cursing.

Val sighed and shook his head. "Okay, now, senses. While you're loosening up those muscles, we're going to work on expanding your ability to detect things. You've been taught to depend almost exclusively on vision to perceive the world, but you have other ways. The first thing is learning to calm the static noise all around you and open up to the underlying vibrations. Let's try it."

John's cramp was easing. "Sounds kind of Buddhist, Zen, or something."

"Could be, but that doesn't matter, it works. Just become calm, relax, attend, and feel. Everything has a sound, a smell, a presence. Just experience it."

John was trying, but it seemed all new age hippie, or something weird like that. Still, he tried and, as he tried, he felt relaxed, more relaxed than he could remember. He lost himself in the moment, feeling the breeze, smelling the earth and the grass and hearing sounds of air moving and distant birds chirping as the day's light faded. He heard machinery far off and even voices of unseen people. He was almost startled when Val spoke.

"You heard voices, right? What direction and how far away were they?"

John started to say he had no idea, but he did, actually. He raised a tentative finger and said. "Over there, I think. I have no idea how far away."

"Good, very good. You'll need to practice. It is particularly hard to open your senses when there is a lot of background noise, or activity, but keep working. Are you ready for another jump?"

The cramps were gone, and his next few jumps went higher and higher.

Val nodded approvingly but recommended a hot soak later.

John was feeling really good about the day. He was feeling ready to give up his human life and accept being a werewolf.

Then, Val stiffened and thrust his head forward. "Rabbit! There's a rabbit in the grass. Do you see it?"

John squinted at the ripple in tall grass. "Yes, I see a fuzzy, little, brown…"

"Kill it."

John was taken aback. "What? Kill it? It's just a little bunny rabbit. It won't hurt…"

"Kill it." Val was stern. "Show me you can leap and attack and kill. Show me the wolf."

Despite the cool breeze, John felt a bead of sweat. *Could he actually do it?* He shuffled his feet into a good stance, shrugged his shoulders, concentrated on the movement and then, with a yell, he jumped. It was a good leap that covered ten yards and kept him airborne for two full seconds. He wasn't even aware of the landing, only his catch. He snatched the little bunny in his right hand.

John grinned and held it high.

The little bugger was frantically kicking both hind legs, struggling with all its might.

Val was shouting something.

John didn't pay attention. He focused on his prey. With a fierce grunt, he closed his fist hard and crushed the little guy. It made a crunching sound, but there was no squeal.

Then, John made an involuntary yell. Actually, he bellowed. He looked at the squirming little fur ball, took a deep breath, and surprised himself with a quick swipe that brought the rabbit to his face as he yelled again and then bit off the head.

He was startled by his own violence and quickly spit out

the bloody little ball of bone and skin and long ears. He spit and spit, trying to get rid of the vile taste. Wiping the back of his hand across his mouth, he looked up at Val, who stood frozen and said simply, "Jesus."

After a long silence, Val inhaled and said, "I guess you're going to do okay."

John felt confused, horrified, elated; all mixed with total disbelief. *What had he done? What was he?*

They found old wooden boxes to sit on.

John kept using leftover napkins from the drive-through to wipe his lips, but he couldn't get rid of the taste.

Val brought a couple of beers from the trunk of his car and they sat quietly. Val, the mentor, sipped and grimaced before asking, "What was it like? I haven't killed anything yet."

John just shrugged. "I don't know. It just came over me. I guess it was instinct, or something."

Beers done, Val stood and squared his shoulders. "Okay, let's do darkness. The sun is almost set. Now, I want you to close your eyes and try to feel the world around you. Your night vision is sharp, but you need to get comfortable with your other senses. You need to feel what is going on all around. I'm told this takes most newbies a while to get the hang of. It's a big change in the way you have always perceived, but you seem to be a quick study, so here we go."

The last glow of the sun was fading. Val stood and closed his eyes. For a full minute, he didn't move, didn't even seem to breathe. Finally, he inhaled deeply and flicked his eyes open to look at John. "Do you remember the ether I told you about, the stuff of existence that flows all around us? Well, it's strong here. Relax enough, you'll feel it, tap into it, become one with it."

"More Zen stuff?"

"Just try, okay?" Val seemed to inhale the night. "From this brief moment, I can tell you there are six people very near this field." He pointed. "In that direction are two men working on replacing a fence post. Their flashlight just burned out, and they're swearing. A little farther down the road is a woman in a car, preparing to have sex with a man who is not her husband. Still farther is an older woman sitting on her farmhouse porch with a big dog at her feet. There's a man in the house, but I can't read anything about him."

John still tasted the bitter rabbit flesh. "Is that what you do? You *read* these people?"

"Well, I don't know if that's the best word for it but, yes, I feel as though I'm reading them. Now, you try. Just as before, just close your eyes, relax everything, and allow the ether to flow."

John tried. Once again, he squared his shoulders, shut his eyes, and tried to relax as fully as he could: nothing. He inhaled deep, took a better stance, shook himself, and just let go. He felt the cool night air, took in the musty farm smells, heard insects he could not identify, and let his mind drift. Sure enough, he felt a faint presence. No, several. They weren't images exactly, just an awareness. The woman in the car was crying. The man was apologizing. It was emotional for them both.

He tried again, seeking to connect with the fence-repair guys. No luck. Then, the old woman; yes, he felt her loneliness, even the warmth of the big, furry dog as it rubbed against her leg. John was barely breathing. Somewhere, he sensed danger but could not locate or describe it. He blinked twice and focused back into his physical reality. The barn was still there. The grass was still tall. Somewhere out in the dark field lay a dead rabbit. The bitter taste of its blood lingered in John's mouth.

The experience had been sobering. He realized that this

was no joke, no misunderstanding. He was certainly not fully human—although he wasn't sure just *exactly* what he was.

———

They were six men of six nationalities with six native tongues, but all had a working knowledge of spoken and written English. It was the universal NATO standard language when they all served in Afghanistan, Africa, or Europe. Sure, some words simply did not translate well but, despite their different backgrounds, the combat veterans had no difficulty communicating.

It helped that they were all Catholic, all deeply religious, all true believers in the Church's teachings. They shared beliefs in many things; duty, honor, personal integrity and, above all, God and His infinite wisdom. They were, however, a very unlikely group of monks. Close cut and well-muscled, they greeted each other with shoulder punches and loud grunts. They exercised and ran, listened to raucous music, drank heavily, and argued politics.

They were as different as any six men could be and, yet, they were the same. Interchangeable, expendable tools of war; those were the men you call when things got tough and, now, the Church had decreed that things were getting tough.

Carlo was the informal leader. He was Sicilian, and that was helpful back in their monastery. He could negotiate with locals in their own language, on their own terms. Still, every member had an equal say, and decisions were made by consensus. They were a combat team, a solid, good combat team.

The other monks were an odd international collection of warriors: Benny of Boston; Pierre, a Frenchman with an unpronounceable last name; Dag, a Norwegian body builder;

Hershel, a rare Israeli Catholic; and Robert the Scot. Different as they were, together, they became a fearsome fighting unit, each prepared to die for their cause and for each other. But they had no idea what they were about to face.

The Bishop had arranged for them to stay in a decent motel in the suburbs. It had a decent bar, decent gym facility, and a decent, small conference room where the six, all dressed in brightly colored jogging suits, now sat in a semi-circle of folding chairs facing a small wooden podium.

That was where Father Antonio, still in his brown robe, met them. He took his place behind the podium and held up a stack of papers. "My brothers, here are the documented reports of demonic behavior in this area. It all seems to have begun with the vandalizing of a downtown church spray-painted with hateful graffiti, even one depicting Satan with a huge blue penis."

There was a ripple of suppressed laughter. The priest scowled, but continued. "Two children, twins five years of age, have been brutally murdered, sadistically murdered, in a play-ground behind the Elm Street church." He displayed grue-some pictures. "Mutilation, possible cannibalism."

The men shifted uncomfortably, and Carlo hissed under his breath. "We need to hunt down these sons of bitches."

"Exactly," Father Antonio said as he stepped from behind the podium and leaned close. "Here's what we know. The demons are organized, and have a hierarchy. We have already killed one, a young man, probably late teens. We learned of him when he bragged of being a werewolf. He killed a dog, probably showing off to impress a group of girls. That dog's body was cut open, actually torn apart.

"When police confronted the boy, he attacked by leaping onto them, at a distance of more than ten feet. The police report right here says…" He opened a folder. "The white male in his late teens, had a long history of mental illness and aggressive, delusional behavior." Father Antonio read from the report. "He wore a leather jacket and motorcycle boots and seemed deranged, snarling and acting like an animal. Officers report that it took five shots to stop him."

The priest paused with tight lips. "This boy-monster was wearing a cross around his neck, a cross twisted into a swastika. Things became even stranger in the autopsy. DNA from a hair sample showed unusual genetic traits. No one knew what to make of it. We asked the police to avoid publicizing the incident and play down the horrific nature of the attack. Chief Mitchell has agreed. That man's a good Catholic."

Carlo spoke up. "Okay, we have an unusual attack, but you said the demons were organized. How could you know that?"

"Bishop Helsing said several parishioners have come to their local priests and claimed that husbands, or brothers, or even children have been possessed by the devil and have left to serve him. In each case, they took nothing; no money, clothes, phone—nothing. They left their jobs and family and homes to just disappear.

They were all later reported as killed but, in each case, it was some sort of bizarre death that left no identifiable body; intense fire, drowning and being washed away, getting buried under a concrete spill in a construction accident. Death certificates were filed, insurance paid, and accounts closed. And yet there have been reports, some by very reliable people, of those same men being sighted, still alive and moving among us. That kind of cover-up requires sophisticated staging and organization."

Carlo was nodding as he thought. "Do we have any clues of their operating location? They need a central gathering place, a headquarters, office, den, or something. I'm thinking perhaps buildings closed for the winter, or abandoned." He wrinkled his brow and gestured as though frustrated. "Do we suspect any type of support group that coordinates or directs the demon's behavior? We need some place to start our search."

There was a long silence. Dag, the Norwegian, spoke loudly. "Demons fear the light. They generally act only in darkness. We should consider hiding places where they could hole up in daylight. Also, we should plot out each of the activities Father Antonio has documented. That will center our search area."

Hershel leaned forward with hands on his knees. "Dag is right about darkness. I think we should seriously consider tunnels, caves, and underground storage sites. Has anyone looked into the background of any victims to see if they are somehow connected?"

Father Antonio seemed to agree. "I will ask Chief Mitchell to give you access to all information the police have. I have also made arrangements with a shooting range south of the city who will provide any arms you desire, all pre-paid. You have two four-wheel-drive vehicles waiting outside. There is a box by the door behind you with throw-away cell phones, all with GPS and walkie-talkie capability. Anything else?"

The six men sat silent and resolute. There were no more questions. Father Antonio spread his arms and spoke softly. "Go with God, my brothers. Go, and do the Lord's work."

The Contract

John woke feeling wired. The events of last night's exercises at the farm left him exhilarated. He wanted more; to learn more; to be more. If only he could get the taste of the rabbit's head out of his mouth. His mind was a kaleidoscope of flashing thoughts, memories, ideas, dream-like images of Hollywood werewolves.

He had learned much from Val, but he still felt overwhelmed, almost in shock. He made coffee and stood in his apartment window, looking down at the street below. It was just coming alive with ordinary people starting their day, going to work, grabbing a snack and living their ordinary lives.

What of his life? What would he do? What would he be? He had no answers, only promises. They said he would have a steady income, but not have to work a normal job, but no one ever said how much income. They gave him a place to live, but it was a crummy slum of an apartment. He would have a new untraceable identity, a new purpose. He would be assigned missions, yet undefined missions, and he would work with a team of other…*what the hell should he even call them?* It seemed awkward, even uncomfortable, to say *werewolf*. The whole thing sounded so hokey, so theatrical, so false.

He turned to a mirror and bared his teeth. Okay, they were much larger than normal, but they weren't really fangs - just really big teeth. He held up his open hand, made a fist, and turned it over and over. Yes, it was bigger and bonier than most, but he had seen laborers with hands nearly as thick and powerful-looking. His physique was probably at the upper limit, but still within the range of normal spectrum.

He couldn't help but notice things about himself, things he had always ignored before. In the shower, he soaped a hairy body and realized it wasn't like the normal curly, almost invisible chest hair of other men. It was real hair that flowed in a pattern across his chest and down the center of his stomach. He could have almost combed it. That hair was probably why he always avoided the beach, short sleeved shirts, and summer shorts.

He sighed. There was no getting around it. He was a freak. Werewolf, gorilla, Sasquatch, whatever; he was clearly a freak. He thought about the women he had been with. There weren't that many. Why had there been any? What possessed them to be with such a bizarre man? Okay, scratch that, why be with such a bizarre creature? Could they have known? Could they themselves, have been...like him?

Time would tell. At least, he hoped it would. He was desperate to know more. What lay ahead? And this conflict with the Church, how would that play out? He had been raised in a conservative Baptist church, but his parents didn't take religion very seriously. They attended church every Easter and Christmas, but not much in between. He didn't remember being baptized. He didn't remember much of his early childhood at all.

His family moved often, never seeming to break out of

lower middle-class neighborhoods and society. Both parents worked. Neither talked about work. Neither talked about friends, or family, or the future. He was just sixteen when his father, his English father, died. That, on top of his raging hormones, turned him into a hard-edged loner, social outcast, problem child, loser.

He was expelled from high school but had no trouble finding work as a bricklayer's apprentice. The next fall, he was readmitted to school after making many promises. Now two inches taller and forty pounds heavier, he was welcomed to the high school football team and, with that, academics no longer seemed to matter. Now he was a football hero, the "Bone Crusher." Maybe that's what attracted the girls. Try though he might, he couldn't remember any of their names, except one.

Gretchen was not the most beautiful girl in the school, but she was the only one who didn't seem frightened by him. Many of the others had a brief "bad boy" fascination, but Gretchen actually liked him, stuck by him. Moreover, she wasn't intimidated by his tough-guy attitude. She, far more than his parents, was a humanizing force in his life. She coached him on how to act, what to say, how to get along. She kept him out of jail and in school long enough to graduate.

Then they went off to separate colleges. Without her, he struggled to fit in. Fights, arrests, counseling, and eventually another expulsion left him alone, and adrift. He married a woman, just some woman who was desperate for a man, but it barely lasted a day.

Gretchen heard of his plight; she took a bus and found him.

For the next ten years, she guided him through life, moderating his temper and soothing his endless conflicts.

Now, he was dead - at least to her - and she was lost to

him. *How would he manage the ship of his life without her at the rudder?*

The finality of it weighed heavy. He stiffened and spoke aloud as though that made the realization somehow more real. "I have to deal with today and tomorrow…and forever after." He ran his fingers through his wiry black hair and did his morning routine of one hundred pushups followed by a hundred sit-ups and two cups of black coffee.

He was still breathing hard when Val barged in without knocking. "Get dressed. Hurry. Sypher is on his way here. Come on, get moving."

John was still holding a half-empty cup. "Okay, okay. Just a minute."

He pulled a pair of pants from the back of a chair, where he tossed them the night before, and he had just finished zipping up when Mister Sypher walked in.

"Good morning, John. I understand you're progressing well in training. I just dropped by to see if you had any questions and, to make sure you sign the contract. That is critical before we can move on."

John hesitated before responding.

Sypher's forehead wrinkled, and his cheek twitched.

Val almost panicked. "The contract. I gave you the contract, remember?"

"Of course. It's sitting on the table."

Vladimir Petrov almost leaped across the room to look. His voice was shrill. "It's still unsigned." Val's shoulders visibly relaxed.

John let out a deep breath and looked Sypher in the eye. "Yeah… I want you to know that I'm ready to accept my role and serve you, but I have one problem, and I can't shake it."

Sypher shot a look at Val and those fierce eyes narrowed. "I thought you said he was ready. What's going on?"

"Don't blame Val. It's me. I just can't shake the fear of losing Gretchen forever. She has been my..."

Sypher was fuming. "Your what; your crutch, your lover, your human guide dog? She thinks you're dead, and she's moving on with her life, so must you."

"I know. I know. I can accept everything, except losing her. I will gladly sign the contract, but I need to, somehow, get her back. I never realized before how much I depend on..."

Sypher almost hissed, "How much you depend on a Sapiens. She will distort your thinking, weaken you, eventually abandon and destroy you. I cannot, will not, allow it."

John's voice went silent. He knew that he was committing a sin by Lycan standards, but he couldn't help himself. He wanted Gretchen back.

Twice, Val started to say something but then fell back to grimace and wring his hands, his oversized Lycan hands.

Sypher sat down and stared at John through slit eyes.

Minutes passed, long, silent minutes full of electricity.

Finally, the boss spoke through clenched teeth, but the tone was businesslike.

"Three years. You give us three years and then, if she is still willing, I will reunite you with this girl. That is the best offer you're going to get. Take it or leave it, but be sure you understand the implications of leaving."

John took the deepest breath of his life. His knotted fists relaxed slightly. "Three years?" After a long silence he spoke softly, "Okay, I'll do that. I'll give you every ounce of my body and soul for three years and then, if I'm still alive, I'll bring Gretchen into the fold."

Sypher turned to Val. "Do you have the syringe?"

John looked confused, "Syringe?"

"The contract is only valid if signed in blood."

John sat at the table across from Mister Sypher, rolled up his sleeve, and extended his bare forearm.

Val drew a vial of blood, injected it into a fountain pen, and John signed just below the words, *"On pain of death."*

Now, he was one of them, a full-fledged Lycan - for three years.

———

After Sypher left, John paced and ran hands through his bristly hair. He laughed out loud, but it was an unconvincing laugh. *Okay, so now I am a monster, a real live, no-shit monster. Beware, ye foolish mortals…*

He bolted to answer a knock on the door. There was Val again, this time with another man. The stranger was thick, muscular, and imposing with black wiry eyebrows and a protruding jaw. He was clearly one of them, a Lycan.

Vladimir Petrov introduced the man as Morley. He was to be the coordinator on their mission. Morley, it seemed, was a man of few words and many grunts.

They sat at the well-worn kitchen table, and Morley began emptying folders from his satchel. He spread pictures and maps and then looked at Val, who took over.

"Okay, I guess I'll brief you. Morley here can correct any errors I make." He and John looked at Morley and, seeing no objection, went on. "Here are the players in our little drama. They look like soldiers home on leave from some combat tour, but they are in reality, Catholic monks from some obscure Italian monastery. There are six that we know of. There may be more coming. From what we can discover, these guys are military-trained combat veterans and righteous holy rollers, and they're very good at their job."

Val paused to let that sink in. "They have travelled across

the ocean for no reason except to do us harm. Our task is simple, beat them to it; kill them first, all six."

He fanned the airport camera pictures. We know their names, their history, and their preferences." He smiled with a conspiratorial grin. "We have a snitch in the local bishop's office. She says the monks are holed up in a motel just east of town and, today, they will be picking out guns and weapons from a shop an hour away. That will give us time to scout the motel."

He pointed at the pictures one at a time.

John tried to take it all in. They were an interesting, if fairly odd, bunch for "men of God."

Val selected one picture, a man with tight curly black hair and intense eyes. "Carlo came from a Sicilian Mafia family with a long history of gang warfare. He was sent to the monastery after his father was killed. Unsuited for monastic life, he volunteered for the French Foreign Legion and spent several years in Africa working with U.S. and United Nations troops." Val looked at his two companions. "Now he is back at the monastery, not as a simple monk but as a kind of contract killer. We think he recruited the others."

The next picture was a boyish, red-haired man. Val went on. "Benny had a similar background, but with the Boston mob. He is a U.S. Army vet with explosive ordinance skills who served in Iraq and Afghanistan. He came to the Church seeking redemption and found a comfortable home with the Jesuits in Europe."

Val produced a well-worn map. "Eventually, he retreated to the small Carmelite monastery in Sicily. There, he fit in nicely with the diverse group of military veterans who found it difficult to wean themselves of violence after their Middle East and Africa adventures."

Val actually shook his head in disgust after looking at the

next picture. "Anton Bourgeon was a pervert, a deserter, a fugitive for four years in his native Serbia. Wanted for multiple rapes and murders, he decided to seek God, or at least safe refuge by changing his nationality to French, his name to Pierre, and his piety to the Sicilian sanctuary. He's very good with a knife."

Then there was a picture of a blond man with a movie star smile and pale eyes. "As a young man, Dag was a very successful missionary. He was a compelling public speaker with a warm manner." Val shook his head again. "But multiple allegations of sexual misconduct with young women back in Norway made the Army an easy means of escape. He worked undercover for several covert agencies, using his looks and his language skills. He is handsome, affable and appears to have absolutely no conscience when it comes to even the cruelest, cold-blooded murder."

Next was a thin, hard-looking man. "Hershel is an anomaly. An Israeli Catholic, he has always been a permanent outsider. His Jewish father and Catholic mother separated when he was very young, and he grew up hating everyone around him: Jews, Arabs, Americans, Russians – everyone. He served in the Israeli Special Forces but was treated contemptuously by the Jewish soldiers. Suspected of poisoning his roommate, he fled to remote Sicily. There, the Catholics ruled. There, he was safe. He thinks he owes the Church and will do anything for that Church, anything."

The last was a square-jawed man whose face seemed swollen. "Robert is a morose thug, a mean drunk who is rarely sober. But his love for the Church is real. It gave him sanctuary, despite multiple accusations of violent acts. Even though the Sicilian monastery is far from his Scottish birthplace, it is the church that gave him a safe and accepting home. He seems happy doing God's work, particularly if it means breaking a few skulls."

John looked over the rouge's gallery of pictures. "These men look like a lot of things, but definitely not like monks, or priests. How in the world did they wind up in some remote little Italian village religious cult?"

Morley leaned in. "They were recruited. The Jesuits have long maintained a self-defense cadre of ex-military operatives who can be deployed to aid Catholics in danger, particularly in overseas locations where they are subjected to mistreatment by criminal, religious, or intolerant government groups. The Sicilian Monastery is probably just an offshoot, but the Arcadia monks are more military, more specialized, and more capable. They are all seasoned special operations types who are comfortable with danger, violence and secrecy, and they are truly dangerous."

John took a deep breath and exhaled. This isn't going to be a walk in the park."

———

The motel gym was modern metal and glass with the latest workout devices. The six muscular monks were burning up the machines and intimidating everyone else who even considered using the hotel exercise equipment. They were loud, with their clanging barbells, banging punching bags, huffing and grunting, and even shouting at each other. There was some back-slapping, fist-bumping, and the normal noise of workouts.

A bellman interrupted. "Gentlemen, you have a visitor." The bellman stepped aside, and a trim lady in tweed approached, clutching a stack of binders before her.

The men stopped all noise, except some residual panting, and gathered to face her.

She seemed unsure. "I was told you are monks. Is this true?"

Benny, the American, answered. "Yes, ma'am, we are all brothers from the Carmelite Monastery in Sicily, but we realize that we don't look or act much like most people's image of priests. Don't worry, we're still men of God, and you have nothing to fear from us."

She loosened her grip on the volumes. A hint of a nervous smile flickered across her face. "Well, I'm glad to hear that. I'm Emily Seibert, and Bishop Helsing sent me to brief you on our problem. Would you like to move to the conference room and - uh, do you want to freshen up before we start?"

They looked from one to another.

Carlo shook his head and Benny answered for the group. "No, ma'am, we're fine as long as you don't mind a little sweat."

Emily Seibert relaxed a bit and almost smiled. "I prefer the conference room, gentlemen. Please, follow me."

They did just that with a couple of hoots, shoves, and towel snaps.

In the conference room, the men sprawled over chairs with feet on tables and hands clasped behind their heads. They seemed cheerful, receptive.

Emily cleared her throat and spread her materials on a table trying to be tidy. "Father Antonio asked me to provide you with maps annotated with suspected..." She looked up and said, "Perhaps we should close the conference room door."

Again, Benny jumped to his feet, closed the door, and gave her a thumbs up and a wink.

"Thank you. Now, if you look at your individual map, you will see the locations of suspected demonic activity." She hesitated. "Dear me, that is so difficult to say. Demons in our town.

It's just unimaginable. Nonetheless, you can see the marks. Red indicates a killing, blue, a non-lethal attack, black is simply a possible sighting, and green indicates residual evidence of the demons' presence."

Carlo used his best English. "How are these sightings and attacks verified?"

Emily nodded as though that was an excellent question. "I don't know, but I am confident they have been thoroughly vetted."

Pierre shook his head vigorously. "Yes, yes. You see the two patterns formed by these events. The epicenters of the circles are here and here. That is where we should begin our search." He rose and moved toward Emily.

She took a half-step back.

"Can you tell us, Madame, what are these two places?" He pointed the index fingers of his two hands at the map on laid the conference table.

Emily leaned over his outstretched arms and tried to ignore the man's sweaty smell. Then, she stepped back, straightened her back and announced, "One is an old indoor sports arena that is scheduled for renovation. The other is a warehouse associated with the Museum of Science and Technology."

Pierre punched the air. "Ha. As I said, if we find the center of activity, it will always lead to the lair of the beast. We must go to these places."

Carlo stood. "Agreed. But, first, we need to obtain the arms Father Antonio promised. We will do that now and then split up into two teams to investigate these locations. Anyone have any questions? No? Well, thank you very much, Ms. Siebert. Please, tell the bishop how much we appreciate his help."

Emily nodded with a pleasant, if slightly tense smile. The

group broke up, and she busied herself collecting her maps and books. When she looked up, she was startled to see Benny the American still standing there. He wore a sweatshirt cut off at the shoulders to reveal muscled arms. His scruffy growth of beard spread into a boyish grin. He leaned close to gather a few papers and hand them to her.

"So, Emily, it was Emily, right?"

"Yes, Emily Seibert." She averted her yes and was surprised at the girlish tone of her voice.

"Just wondering if you'd like to get a drink and talk a little about your maps... and things?"

"A drink?" She said in a moment of panic. "You have all taken vows of celibacy, haven't you?"

"Yes-s-s, but you may have noticed we're not your regular priests. We are allowed a bit of - I don't know - latitude, from the normal rules."

Emily squeezed her hands around her books and papers and maps as though that might keep her from shaking. "A drink would be... quite nice."

Benny gave her an all-American smile. "Of course, but I'm sure you know we need to keep a low profile and avoid public areas like bars when on a mission." He looked into her eyes with a steady, unblinking confidence as he slid his room key across the maps and into her hand.

Then, Benny turned and threw a few punches into the air as he walked away.

Emily stood, frozen, and looked at the key. She whispered to herself, *Will I actually go to his room? I'm just not that kind...*Ms. Emily Seibert clutched her paperwork to her chest and quietly hyperventilated.

Robert the Scot's Last Stand

A dreary, gray sunrise tried to shine through monotonous light rain. Three Lycans, Morley, Val, and John sat in a delivery van and surveyed the motel. There were few lights on in the guest rooms, and no visible movement, not even motel staff.

"Good morning to sleep in," Morley mumbled.

John spoke quietly, "Yeah, but I didn't touch the bed last night. Couldn't stop thinking about… whatever we're about to do."

Val shrugged and turned to the driver. "So, you got a plan, or are we just going to sit out here and… what? Val did a bad vocal of *Listen to the Falling Rain.*"

Morley grinned. "I love that song but you ain't no Jose Feliciano." Then, he got serious. "Now listen, you sound as though I'm in charge here. Well, that's not true. This is *your* mission. I was told that you, Vladimir Petrov, and you, John Wagner, were given this assignment as a test. The leadership just wants you to get the demon hunters' attention. This is the first mission for both of you. Sypher and Vrykolas, in particular, want to see how you do."

Val pushed back in his seat and folded his arms in front of him, like a stubborn child. "This is a hell of a time to tell us we're just here to be tested. It's kind of like being invited to a party, only to find out it's a job interview."

Morley shrugged. "I don't see how it matters all that much. You've got a mission. Just do your best, regardless of whether it's being called a test."

John leaned forward from the back seat. He was uneasy about such unfocused guidance. "Okay, let's just get the instructions straight. You said we are to single out one of the monks and kill him as a demonstration, is that right? Just kill a man with no provocation? No more specific guidance than that?"

Morley nodded and seemed uneasy. "Well yes, that's pretty much it. I have a list of their room numbers, if you want it."

Val breathed out hard. "Let's quit wasting time and get to it." He started to open the van's side door but hesitated and gave Morley a hard look. "Any advice?"

Morley shrugged. "Don't get caught, don't leave clues and, you know, be careful. These guys have a reputation for being really mean, even sadistic."

Val pulled up his collar and hunched off into the rain.

Frowning deep, John followed. He wasn't a killer, but he had given his word. He would obey Sypher's orders for three years. But he didn't expect things to be this casual, this loose, this sloppy. It seemed almost amateurish for he and Val to just barge into a motel and randomly pick someone to kill. Even worse, the men they were after were all professional assassins. This could go horribly wrong. The three years of his life he promised might turn out to be just mere minutes.

They splashed through puddles on their way to a side

door. It was locked, but Val had a tool, a long strip of metal he slid into the space between door and frame to release the latch. Inside, they both shook off water and surveyed the hall. No movement, no sound but the steady beat of rain on the roof.

John asked. "So, we just going to go knock on a door, or…"

Before Val could answer, a door down the hall banged open and a man in socks, boxer shorts and a loose-hanging motel robe stomped out, groaned, and rubbed his face. His body was thick, like a side of beef ready to hang in a butcher shop. From his walk, it was obvious that he was suffering a major hangover.

"Is that the Scottish one?" John whispered.

"Yeah, Robert, I think. Let's see what he does."

Both men moved back into the shadow of an alcove.

Val flashed a flicker of a smile and said, "I think I'm about to make this guy's morning a little more interesting." With a deep breath, he stepped out boldly, marched down the hall. Val shoulder-bumped the man in a bathrobe. "Oh, so sorry. You okay?"

Robert the Scot, grumbled, "Yeah, just watch where the hell you're going, dumbass."

Val tried to hide a grin. "What did you say? What did you call me?"

Robert growled and started to say something. Val's punch caught him off guard. The big Scot shook it off with a look that was more confused than angry. It seemed like he wasn't used to being on the receiving end.

Then, with the deep chuckle of an aroused bully, Robert drew back an arm to counter punch, but Val was quicker, also probably quite a bit more sober.

His second punch was square in Robert's nose, and the

flow of blood was immediate. It ran down lips and dripped from his jaw.

Now the Scot's reaction became animalistic. He raised both arms, yelled a primal sound, and grabbed Val by the shoulders. Two more quick punches to the face didn't faze the drunk. Robert head-butted Val and then lifted him off the ground as though he were just a child.

Val was still throwing punches, still drawing blood, enough blood to splash all over his block-headed opponent's shoulders. But the drunken Scot seemed to barely notice. He heaved Val halfway across the hallway and against a wall, just as John had done to him at their first meeting Then, Robert paused, swiped a hand across his bloody face, glared, and made a lion-like roar, as though preparing to charge.

John wasn't waiting anymore. He had to protect Val. He made a Lycan leap clear across the hallway, his best yet. It took Robert by surprise and knocked him off his feet.

The two rolled onto the ground, but John wound up on top. For a moment, they looked at each other, unsure what to do next. John felt all the fear and tension of the past days suddenly explode within him.

In complete rage, he grabbed great handfuls of Robert's face, squeezed the fleshy cheeks into balls and then, with a cry like nothing he had ever done before, like nothing he had ever even heard before, John Wagner used those special tensors in his back to yank his arms apart and rip the meaty flesh right off Robert's skull.

John sat back and gasped at the exposed skull. It was macabre. Covered with wet, stringy strands, flesh dangled and dripped. Golf ball eyes stared from deep in bone sockets. Lipless teeth still moved, as though trying to speak. Fluids of many colors dripped and flowed from the grisly exposed skull bones. Arterial blood from the neck pumped in squirts that diminished with each heartbeat. Blood splattered over Robert's neck, shoulders, belly, and even the carpet, where it pooled and soaked.

John stepped back, panting. His hands were still full of mushy, dripping meat that had once been a human face but now seemed more like a torn rubber mask. That mask had eyebrows above empty openings for eyes and nostrils and mouth. Robert was still alive, still conscious, still trying to talk, to fight, to survive, but only for a moment. He raised a feeble, furtive hand that hovered and then went slack.

Val was beside John now and put a hand on his shoulder. "Jesus, man. I've never seen…"

John's voice came back hard and emotionless. "We have to make this look like an accident. Help me tip over one of those vending machines so it falls on his face."

Val nodded and started to move one of the machines but paused. "His face, you have to put the face back on him."

John seemed numb, but nodded his agreement. He shook the bloody, dripping wads of meat, trying to get them free, but they stuck like to his fingers like glue. With a look of absolute disgust, he used the knuckles of one hand to scrape the other and was able to wipe the two wadded pieces free. Then, he pressed them back into position on Robert's skull. They looked unnatural, like a pair of chicken breasts waiting to be cooked.

John stood back and looked at his hands. They still trailed strings of mucus and human sinew. He looked up and down the hall but saw no bathroom where he could wash it off.

Almost in panic, he ran outside into the rain and knelt at a curb where fast-flowing water poured into a sewer drain. Furiously, he scrubbed one hand against the other as numbing icy water streamed over both. Harder and harder he scrubbed. He couldn't tell if it was tears, or just rain streaming down his checks.

Finally, he stood, shuddered, inspected his hands, and turned his face up into the rain. His hands were now clean. The evidence of his atrocity was gone, washed away by the cold water. He stood there on the curb for a long time. *What have I just done? How could I have done something so...? How could anyone do something so barbaric? What am I?*

John took an unsteady breath and went back inside to help Val position the vending machine. It had to look as though the six-foot-high glass and metal box caught Robert in the head as it tipped over. That would be an obvious explanation of the injury, even if it wasn't totally convincing.

John's hair and sleeves were wet and dripping as he and Val moved the body while trying not to make tracks in the pooled blood.

Then, both men reached up and used their full weight to tilt the machine forward, wiggle it until the angle looked right, and then slam it down against Robert's body. It made a horrendously loud crashing sound as metal bent and glass shattered. Pieces flew in all directions.

One of Robert's arms still protruded from beneath the machine. His curled fingers extended, as though reaching out. Long, triangular pieces of glass had flown all over and imbedded themselves in rug and wall and furniture. A rivulet of blood flowed from beneath the wrecked vending machine.

Val took John by the arm and led him back out into the rain. Both men walked silently, in a post-traumatic-shock fog.

Back in the van, Morley asked, "So how did it go?"

Val looked out the side window and spoke quietly. "We killed the Scot."

Morley started to ask more but, hearing Val's tone, he seemed to understand that there would be no more conversation. It was over, time to move on. He started the engine and drove off into gloom.

———

The drive was silent. John's heartbeat had calmed, but his mind was still replaying the moment when the man's face came off in his hands. He kept wringing his hands, as though trying to wipe away the last microscopic bit of Robert's flesh.

Val finally spoke. "Hey, Morley, where are we going?"

Morley didn't answer. He just looked straight ahead and drove downtown, where he turned off into an underground parking garage, parked in a reserved spot. He got out and beckoned.

Both men silently followed to an elevator that whisked them to the eighteenth floor. Morley inserted a key, and the elevator climbed three more unlabeled floors.

The doors opened into a glass-walled penthouse bathed in pale light from a crackling fireplace on one wall. Sypher and Vrykolas sat waiting, quietly swirling brandy snifters. It was Mister Sypher who spoke.

"Well done. We had a camera feed in the motel, several, actually. Your performance tonight was impressive, most impressive." He paused and might have smiled. "I think we can expect a significant backlash from your mission. If history is any guide, the Catholic minions will strike back, demanding some victim but, without much evidence to go on, they will just be wasting their time and energy."

He sat up. The morning light through the glass walls was too soft to reveal the expression on his face. "Would you care for a drink? It's a wonderful vintage. Our people in the south of France bring some on every visit."

John started to speak, had to clear his throat, and then continued. "Thank you, sir, but I'm not feeling all that sociable."

"Yes, yes, of course. First kill. Quite understandable. Not to worry. It gets easier."

Vrykolas lifted his glass to his nose and closed his eyes, as though consumed with the aroma. He looked back at the two novices. His voice was gravelly. "You have done well; courage and cleverness worthy of a master. I am quite glad to have you, both of you, on our team. We have many challenges ahead, and I expect to be proud working with you."

John gathered his courage to speak. "Challenges? I'm not sure…"

Vrykolas was looking off at the city lights. "We are not the only ones. Did you know there are other clans?"

John looked confused, "Clans of Lycans? Are you saying that we are just one of many?"

Sypher was nodding. "Yes, we have alliances and some strained relations. We consider ourselves to be the most civilized and reasonable group, and we maintain a state of virtual truce with the others, but there are strains, particularly now that they are involved with politics."

John shook his head. "Seriously, politics?"

Sypher nodded slowly, seriously. "We, in our group, only want dominion over our own lives, and our own futures, but there are others who seek more than just power over humans. They have allied themselves with extremist groups who seek to rule, not only humans, but other Lycans like us. We anticipate battles on many fronts."

He leaned forward, and the flickering light of the fireplace illuminated his face. "You… You shall be our warriors, our knights in the coming battles. You have proved worthy."

John hesitated but went ahead and asked. "The contract, sir…"

Sypher looked down into his brandy glass as he spoke. "Three years, I keep my word. You keep yours."

There was a long empty silence before Vrykolas spoke. "You will now be living here, on the sixth floor of this building. You will each have an apartment. This building provides much greater security. You will find your new homes to be comfortable, but not extravagant. You will have ready access to all of our intelligence gathering, our armory, and our experts. Your tasking will come from me, or Mister Sypher, and no one else."

After a long silence, Sypher said, "There are two envelopes on the hallway stand with your names on them. They contain key cards to your new apartments, identification papers, and five hundred dollars in cash. If you need more, go to Barker on the eleventh floor. He won't ask any questions. If you need surveillance, go to Jennings on the same floor. If you need backup, or reinforcements, see Mrs. Parker in the next office. If you have no further questions, I shall say 'good day' and, again, congratulate you both on a job well done."

Sypher stood.

So did John and Val.

After a moment's hesitation, they went straight to the small table, retrieved their envelopes, and looked at each other but said nothing. There was nothing to say. They were in this thing all the way. There were going to be more deaths, perhaps even their own.

John the Assassin

He used his key card, and the door clicked open to reveal a well-appointed apartment. Not quite luxurious, but still very nice. In fact, he had never lived in anything near this quality. Twin leather recliner sofas sat on hardwood and tile floor with plush woven carpets. Real paintings hung throughout, not reproductions, but real hand-painted landscape renderings. He even had his own fireplace with fake logs, probably gas-fired.

It was wonderful, but fatigue overtook him, and he went searching for the apartment's single bedroom. Apparently, he was not supposed to have overnight guests. He laughed at that thought. *Who would I ever invite?* Gretchen was the only possibility and, hopefully, she would sleep in the same—*No. Put that thought out of your mind.* Gretchen would never see this place. For the next three years, assuming he survived that long, she would be no more than a memory.

He that wished he had a drink and, sure enough, there was a small bar stocked with whiskeys and wines, all brands he could never afford. He poured two fingers of bourbon into a glass and admired the sparkle of cut crystal. One sip, and he almost collapsed. Bed, he needed to go to bed. It turned out to be a four-poster king with mattresses so thick that he had to make a little hop to climb on. But, as soon as he stretched out, the whole world faded. He slept in a near-coma - as though practicing for death.

———

Afternoon sun streaming in his window hit him in the face and he lurched upright. John was stiff and disoriented. Still fully clothed, he hadn't even taken off his shoes before falling asleep. The early morning's memories began to come back into focus. He closed his eyes and relived Val's confrontation as well as his own leaping attack. He saw, and even felt, the visual and the visceral action of ripping Robert's flesh.

He snapped out of it and sat up, stiff and sore. His hands were clean now, except for some tiny remnants under the fingernails. John climbed off the bed, stretched, and moaned. *So, this was home for now. He would do fine here...after a shower.* The water was warm and comforting. Water washes away so many stains. He faced into the stream of steaming, cleansing water, closed his eyes. He might have become an assassin but, at the moment, he didn't have a care.

The towels were thick and soft, heated by their metal rack. He took his time luxuriating in the feel, trying to live just in this moment. He knew it would not last. The gladiator should always relish his good fortune knowing it might be his last.

Then, with a couple of quick shakes like a wet dog, he was alive and ready for the day and whatever it held. First, he would explore his new apartment. It was by far, the best place he had ever lived. A thought crossed his mind. The Roman gladiators were well treated, even pampered during their short lives. Maybe he would be also. He roamed, opened empty drawers, clicked on an oversized TV, ran his fingers over freshly polished surfaces, and went to the fridge.

There was a carton of whole milk. He didn't really care for milk. There were fancy bottles of water. Perhaps his Lycan masters thought that plastic water bottles were a threat to the environment. There were frozen meals, enough to last a season. He was okay with microwave dinners and breakfasts.

The closet was empty. He would have to wear last night's same soggy, blood-stained clothes. He went to the table where he had tossed Sypher's brown envelope and emptied its contents. There were fake ID documents, complete with his pictures, all in the name John Rawlins with a mid-town address. How in the world did they create these without his help? They looked authentic enough, even the signature.

There were also bank-wrapped bundles of twenty-dollar bills. He wasn't sure how many, but it would certainly take care of him for a while. His first priority would be to buy new clothes to replace his bloody outfit. He dressed, but he didn't bother to put on his soggy underwear, or socks.

Making note of his apartment number, he took the elevator to ground level and mixed into the sidewalk crowd. He had no coat, didn't know what became of it. The stores were mostly upscale. He needed non-descript, everyday clothes that would make him unremarkable.

Rethreads called itself a Recycled Fashion Boutique, perfect. He bought a good winter coat, four pairs of pants, and four shirts. But the store didn't carry shoes, or underwear. He found those at a nearby Gap store and used their changing room to put them on. Seven twenty-dollar-bills had transformed him from gutter bum to unremarkable city dweller. He threw his old clothes into a dumpster and went looking for breakfast.

He couldn't help himself from humming *Raindrops Keep Fallin' on My Head*. Some things just stick in one's mind.

Mickie's Dairy Bar provided a noisy, crowded, anonymous atmosphere with hearty portions that would last him through the day and night.

All his needs satisfied for the time being, he wandered back to the Digital Nation office building, and his apartment. No one noticed him in the lobby, or the elevator. He was back, safe in his…his what, home? He shrugged. Better to enjoy it while it lasts. Then, a dark cloud blocked the sunshine of his mind. *Could it possibly last three years?*

The Meetings

J ohn was back in his new room, folding clothes and organizing his chest of drawers. He had forgotten to buy socks. Oh, well, another shopping trip.

He answered a knock at the door, and a stranger handed him a note, *"Meeting at three in eighth floor conference room."*

"Conference room?"

The stranger said, "Yeah, the eighth-floor conference room. You know, the soundproof, electronic-shielded room. Must be big stuff. That's where the clan's most secret plans are discussed.

"The clan?" John smiled at the thought that he was now one of them, one of the Lycan monster clan.

At quarter to three, the room was filled. Val was there, along with a dozen other fairly young men. John scanned the crowd, all very fit, tough-looking Lycans. Vrykolas sat at the head of the table and spoke with a creaky but still authoritative voice. "Seats, please, we have much to cover." He touched a hand-held device and one wall became an enormous display screen. It showed the motel in heavy rain.

The old man's voice was horse, but steady. "You all know of the Killer Monks who have come seeking our heads. Two of your comrades, John Wagner and Vladimir Petrov, killed one of them this morning."

The screen flashed a sequence of pictures showing the hall, the confrontation, and the killing. A murmur of approval went through the crowd and, then, a collective gasp as John ripped off Robert's face.

Vrykolas spoke again, "The priest from Scotland is dead, but there are five still alive, and they are coming for us. To make things more complicated, we believe the Madison chief of police is in league with them and using his resources to help find us. Therefore, you will be dispersed. We'll give you encrypted phones, but use them primarily for texts. Texts are much more difficult to track."

Vrykolas looked around the table and seemed pleased with the strength he saw in their Lycan faces. "Our intelligence unit will be providing you information on the monks' movements and, if possible, on their plans. Your task will be to shadow them and, when you see an opportunity, kill them.

"You will operate as independent teams, but keep us informed. Each team will have a rental car. Your armament will be in the trunk. Inside the glove box, you will find a self-destruct switch. If you have to use it, the blast will level a one-hundred-meter radius. Do not allow yourselves to be captured. The autopsy would become too sensational."

He paused. "There is a bag on the floor beside your seat. Verify it has your name on it. Find your teammate, whose name is also on the bag. One of you will have the keys to your car, and its parking location. Your individual safe house address is there as well. No one outside of our intelligence department will know where you will be, not even me."

There was a long silence. No one mumbled. No one

coughed. No one questioned. This was not the time for words, but for action, Lycan action.

Finally, one man at the far end of table spoke in a voice like a growl. "May their God have mercy on the killer Catholics, for they will soon be meeting Him."

At that, they all slammed a right hand to pound on the table and let out a ferocious, reverberating roar. Val and John, the newest initiates imitated their fellow Lycans pounding and yelling. The sound of their fists thundered. The air crackled with adrenaline.

Vrykolas sat back but could not hide the pride he felt in those warriors. As they filed out, each man raised a defiant fist at their elder statesman. He acknowledged with a dip of his head.

The battle was joined.

———

Carlo and the five remaining monks assembled in a motel basement storeroom. They sat on folding chairs and fidgeted as they waited.

When Father Antonio entered the room, his face and eyes were tight, as though holding back anger. He took a breath so deep that it made his chest swell. Then, he faced them for what seemed a very long awkward moment before he spoke.

"¿Brother Carlo, *a cosa stavi pensendo*? What were you thinking, my son? You let the Scot go unsupervised."

Carlo, the iron fisted leader of the killer monks, took deep breaths. "*Non-Loso*. I don't know how it happened." He had an anguished, almost pleading expression. "*Eva Umbriaco*. Robert was drunk. He let down his guard, and the demons killed him."

The priest, in his usual brown robe, cast eyes to the ground and interlaced his fingers as though about to pray. When he spoke again, it seemed carefully worded.

"Now, it seems clear that they know of us; who we are, where we are, and why we are here." He paused. "We have lost the advantage. From now on, we must be much more careful and never, even for an instant, relax our guard. These demons are cunning, and fearless. They have no souls to lose, and they do not value human life. They must"- his voice fairly trembled - "must be exterminated."

There was silence, all heads bowed, all eyes averted. They had failed. Robert may have been the weak link in their group, but all shared responsibility for allowing his death. They were a team, and the team had failed to protect one of their own brothers in faith. Despite all his shortcomings, Robert had been a devout Catholic.

Carlo winced and spoke without making eye contact. "Monsignor Antonio, we shall avenge this monstrous act. We shall find the demons, and we shall slay them. It matters not how many, or how fierce, we will hunt them like vermin and crush them beneath our heels. We, the Arcadian brotherhood, shall have no rest until the earth is cleansed of these monsters. In God's Holy Name I swear an oath to destroy these hellish creatures."

He turned his face upward toward the basement's bare, neon ceiling lights and spread his arms.

"Dear Jesus, give us the courage and strength to persevere against the demons. We humbly ask You to empower us, to protect us, to stand over us as we go forward into battle."

He held the pose for a long moment before he said, "Amen."

Every seat creaked as the demon hunters put their hands together and mumbled their prayers. They sat straighter and taller, clenching fists and jaws. Their eyes said it all. *This was their great quest, probably the greatest of their lifetime. They would give all, sacrifice all, to kill the beasts, kill them without mercy, or forgiveness.* The avenging monks raised their right hands and shouted in unison, "Death to the demons! Death to the beasts of hell!"

Then they calmed and sat back with crossed arms and scowling faces.

Father Antonio also sat, sagged actually, into a chair. He looked weary, defeated. "Pierre, your inspection of the two buildings you suspected to be the monsters' lair; did you find anything?"

Pierre stood respectfully, but kept his eyes downcast. "No, Monsignor, nothing."

The old priest sighed. "Carlo, do you have any leads at all?"

"The Chief of Police has used his resources to get us pictures of men you spoke of earlier, those men who had been reported killed but were later seen alive. The chief is now having his people go through the CCTV coverage for downtown Madison. They have a computer that does facial recognition."

Carlo looked at his priest-leader.

"If it finds matches, he will notify us. He also has a video of a van leaving the motel right after Robert's killing. The heavy rain makes license plate identification difficult, and the most likely match turned out to be a stolen plate so, no help."

Bennie spoke with hesitation. "You know, we gotta consider the possibility that this might actually *have* just been an accident. Vending machines do fall over…"

Every face turned to him with the same blank stare.

Bennie shrugged. "Just saying is all."

Carlo's voice was bitter, "It was no more of an accident than what our vengeance against these creatures shall be."

The room went silent until Carlo spoke again. "Let us all

take a moment to pray." He spread his arms and looked upward as though the ceiling might suddenly part to reveal angels playing harps.

Then, in clear English, "Oh, God, our help in ages past, give us the strength and wisdom to kill without mercy, to eviscerate and dismember these demons. In Your name shall we go forward into battle. In Your name shall we slaughter any who impede our quest."

Every head bowed. There was silence.

Finally, Father Antonio reached to lay a hand on Carlo's shoulder. "Well said, my son."

———

The five monks arrived in a van. They stepped out and surveyed a quaint rural church with white siding, an unassuming steeple, a crumbling asphalt parking lot, and a well-tended graveyard that covered several acres. They were met by Father Edmond Riley, an elderly priest whom they knew had been banished to the hinterland many years ago following charges of improper activity with male parishioners. He was probably anxious to do anything that would help ingratiate him to his bishop and perhaps restore his reputation. Providing a secure hideout for the monks might just help.

Their living quarters would be in the church basement. Five small rooms; each with a bed, a nightstand, a desk, a lamp and a small closet. It was austere but, then, they were monks in contrition. It would be adequate, as long as the Internet worked.

The dimly-lit basement storage area had a faint smell of dampness, maybe even mold. Carlo set up a whiteboard on an easel and then taped photos around the edge. They were stills of motel hall camera shots. In them, Val and John's faces were clear.

As soon as they settled into folding chairs he began. "Okay, here is what we know about Brother Robert's killing. The two demons arrived in a van with a driver. They are intelligent and they act in a deliberate way. They used a tool to open the locked motel door and then hid in shadows. Robert was probably a target of opportunity. They were waiting and used a team attack. The tall demon distracted Robert and the shorter, thicker one attacked with a jump that none of us could hope to match."

He paused and seemed to be carefully choosing words. "We all know Robert, and we know how tough he was. The savageness of this attack suggests super-human strength, along with the viciousness of a wild animal. To rend the man's flesh as it did… Well, it means these things have powers we can't comprehend. If they're not normal, we can't depend on normal tactics. There will be no close-up confrontations. We must stalk and kill them from ambush."

After a long silence before Pierre spoke up. "That is all very fine, what you say, but we cannot ambush demons we cannot find. How do we go about locating them?"

Carlo sucked air through clenched teeth. "I wish I knew. They are obviously intelligent and act in a careful, well-planned way. We have to assume they have us under surveillance. Now the Madison Chief of Police is working on tracking the van, but I think we need to take the initiative by setting ourselves up as decoys to draw them out."

There was a long silence with no sound but heavy breathing. Pierre was tapping a finger to his chin and appeared to be thinking hard. "These two men in the pictures, they appear…different."

Carlo wrinkled his brow. "Different? What do you mean?"

"The hair, the eyebrows, the chin; they are just different." He shook his head as though plumbing his memory. "As a very young child in Serbia, I remember some men in my village being killed for unnatural acts. From that childhood memory, I can still see the dead bodies being hung out for display. Those men, they looked like these two. The people in the village said they were…werewolves."

"Werewolves?" Carlo didn't seem to know how to respond.

Benny made an "aha" gesture. "Werewolves? Makes sense. I've heard that Wisconsin has more reported werewolf sightings than any other state but, I gotta say, while these guys look a little strange, they don't look anything like my idea of a werewolf."

Carlo seemed thoughtful. "Does anyone know what guidance the Church has given on werewolves?"

———

Val drove the rental car, blindly following directions to a preset GPS location. They were well outside Madison and approaching the small town of Livornia when the cheerful computer voice announced, "You have arrived. Your destination is on the right."

Both looked at the row of small, rundown houses. John checked the address of the computer's destination. "Thirty-four Paine Street. It's the faded purple one."

John said, "That's really weird. All the houses in this little town are some shade of purple. Do you suppose it's some sort of religious, or cult, thing? Does the Midwest have cults? I think of California and New York, not Wisconsin, as locations for cults."

Val shrugged. "Maybe there was a sale at the local paint store."

That was worth a laugh.

John backed into the crumbling concrete driveway in order to make for a faster getaway. The front door key worked, and they stepped into a 1950s vintage house with thrift store furniture and faded wallpaper. Everything smelled of dust and age.

John went to the kitchen faucet and ran cold, and then hot, water. Both worked.

Val found the thermostat and increased the temperature setting. He was rewarded by the sound of a furnace coming on and a rush of air from the floor vent.

They set to work unpacking and settling in. That didn't take long. They were traveling light.

John yelled, "Okay, I guess it's livable. Now, let's try the Internet." The signal was strong, but it was secure, and they had no password.

Val pondered for a moment and then started going room to room. It didn't take long. There were only six, two of which were bedrooms. He hoped to find a computer, or some information. No luck.

John checked the pantry and announced, "Plenty of food, mostly pre-packaged meals. You have any dietary restrictions?"

Val shouted back, "Just that I hate Brussel sprouts." Then, he opened a closet door and yelled, "Jackpot, a computer with a sticky note that says, *Password is V's middle name.*"

He sat and turned on the power switch. The logon screen immediately asked for a password. He typed, *"Ivanovitch"* and he was in. There were several messages with contact phone numbers, credit card numbers, and emergency instructions, including an "erase" icon for the computer.

Back in the living room John checked the TV. It was old, no streaming capability. At least they could see local Madison news. They had just settled themselves on the musty couch with a bag of Cheetos when John got a text: *"Check messages."*

Val trotted off to the closet, logged on and read, *"The Sicilian Priest has contacted Bishop Helsing. He wants guidance on the Church's policies for werewolves. The Bishop has reluctantly passed the request up the Catholic chain of command but has so far received no reply."*

John had come in to read over Val's shoulder. "So, they know."

Val shrugged. "At least they suspect."

After a moment's silence, Val said, "This changes nothing. They thought we were demons before. All that has changed is the name they use for us. We still have to kill them."

Planning the War

"Yes, this is Helsing. With whom am I speaking?"

The voice on the phone was breathy, like an old man with asthma. "Good day, Bishop Helsing." There was a long inhalation. "I am Cardinal Skietsky. I have been retired many years, but I have been asked to call and answer some questions. Please forgive my poor English. I have not used it for many years, and I forget easily these days.

"Your Eminence, I am honored that you took the great effort to call me, but I fear I do not know the reason."

Another wheeze. "Werewolves: the Vatican says you may have a problem with werewolves, yes?"

"We think that is a possibility. I am, quite honestly, skeptical but felt I had to investigate."

"Well, I will tell you what I know...and what I believe." A cough. "I know there are creatures out there who can be dangerous. I am from Belarus, and there we called them Lycanthropes. The Church has always used the term Cynocephali. There is much written about them. It is even said that

Saint Christopher, the carrier of Christ, was one of them before his redemption."

The cardinal paused to breathe before continuing. "I have studied the literature and, in my opinion, except for being quite hairy, I have found no real connection between the Lycan and actual wolves. These man-monsters are - what is the word - a mix, some sort of mix. Some are more human, some more animal than others, but all are strong and dangerous. The amount of hair tells you how much animal. They can breed with humans, so there can be many variations, many degrees, of these monsters, these werewolves. Some have skin as smooth and clear as a newborn piglet. Some are as hairy as orangutan, this is the right word, orangutan?"

"Yes, cardinal, I believe so."

"Yes, good. Those with little hair often pass for ordinary people. Sometimes, even *they* do not know what they are, but hear me when I say, they are all still dangerous. They all conspire with the devil and commit vile sins against the Church. You must guard against them, kill them all."

"And how do we kill them?"

"Ah, that is the question. There are many answers, but few have been tested. Some say wolfbane, but I think that is a, how do you say, old woman's tale?"

"Yes, something like that."

"The best is, of course, exorcism and conversion to Christianity like Saint Christopher, but that is unlikely. Others say you must catch the creature before it can change back to human form and nail its hands to a tree, until it dies, or gives up its demon ways. I personally do not believe they actually change. That is just another old woman's tale. No, the only reliable cure is a sacred bullet."

Bishop Helsing came back, "A sacred bullet?"

"Yes. It must be blessed. And some say it must have at least some silver in it. I do not know if the silver is really necessary. I think God's blessing on the bullet is sufficient to make it the necessary instrument of demonic death."

The old man began hacking and wheezing as though desperate for air.

"I thank you most sincerely Cardinal Skietsky. I shall follow your guidance and I pray you…" But the line was dead. The cardinal had hung up.

Helsing sat back and mumbled. "A sacred silver bullet? This is all getting too bizarre."

———

John was bored. They had been hiding out in the little purple house for a full morning. He yawned and realized that he had slept only a few hours in the last two days. He told Val that he was going to take a nap and selected a bed. It was old and soft with a creaky, coil spring mattress and no sheets, but he pulled up the bedspread and was asleep in seconds.

Later he woke, disoriented and panting. *How long have I slept?* He had no idea. It was still daylight outside, but the light was soft, as though sunset was approaching. He sat up to stretch stiff, sore muscles and worked his shoulders trying to get his body mobilized. The bed made complaining sounds.

Coffee… He needed coffee.

The TV was on in the living room where Val sprawled across the overstuffed couch, arms splayed wide and mouth gapping. He did not snore. John stood very still and listened to make sure his companion was still breathing.

Once satisfied that the man was alive, he went puttering around the kitchen to find a coffee maker and coffee pods. They weren't his normal choice of brand or flavor but beggars, after all, can't be choosers.

Once caffeinated, he thought about a shower and walked down the narrow hall past the closet, where he noticed the computer had a flashing dialog box. It read, *"Urgent. Touch here to view video."* He tapped the box and, immediately, a recording of the little house's front sidewalk and steps appeared. He hadn't noticed a video camera there.

An older lady with her hair in a bun approached. She balanced a plastic cake-keeper as she climbed the three front steps and appeared to knock. He could see a man's shoulder come into the corner of the screen. It had to be Val accepting the cake. The lady had an expectant look, as though wanting to come in. There was no audio, so John couldn't tell what was said, but she finally tilted her head slightly, crossed her arms, and forced a thin smile before she turned and walked away, pausing for a quick look back and a nose-high sniff.

He thought that would be the end, but the video continued. The little old lady walked almost out of frame when an SUV drove slowly past and stopped. John could only see the back corner of the vehicle, but it seemed to jostle as though people might be getting in or out.

The video froze and a new dialog box read,

"License plate is Dane County Sheriff's Department. Be vigilant. We are looking for alternate location for your team. Stand by for further instructions."

Should I wake Val? Not yet. He needed his sleep as much as John had. What should he do? He remembered Vrykolas saying, "Your armament is in the trunk." He went to the door and peeked out. There were only a few people outside.

An elderly couple directly across the street sat in a porch swing and seemed to be laughing at something. An older man two doors down watered bushes with a hose. All three of them noticed John immediately. The water-hose guy actually waved.

How would it look to these small-town neighbors if I carry in a bunch of military-style weapons? He smiled and returned the wave.

Then, he fished in his pocket, found the keys, and casually popped the rental car trunk. Inside was a duffel bag that held an arsenal of guns. *Okay, don't act suspicious.* He fished through and found two pistols and several boxes of matching ammo, better than nothing. He remained bent over the trunk and slid the guns under his shirt and into his waistband. The bullet boxes didn't seem all that obvious, so he just held them by his side.

Reaching the top step, he turned, made a final wave to his hose-wielding buddy, and went in. Val was snoring now, and loud. John loaded both pistols and left one on the coffee table where Val wouldn't miss it. Then he went to the computer. There was a new message, *"Get out of the house. Ditch the car. Police are en route. Hit 'erase' on this machine and go, now."*

He ran to the living room and grabbed Val's arm. His companion blinked repeatedly and seemed confused. "What? What's going on?"

"We've been made. Cops are on the way...I think. Anyway, we've got to run. Take the gun on the coffee table and let's go."

Val held up his hands. "Okay, okay. Just let me take a crap first."

"No time, man, we have to go. We'll find a toilet on the way."

"I'm not kidding, man. I need to go."

"On the road, now, move."

Val grumbled. "If I get shot and wind up shitting my pants, I'm going to be really pissed at you."

They hopped in the car and squealed out. As they passed, the cake lady came out onto her porch, fished a cell phone from her apron. She held it to her ear as her eyes tracked the car.

Val sat up, pointed at her through the open window with thumb and forefinger extended, brought the thumb down, and mouthed the word, "bang."

The old woman took a step back and covered her mouth in a look of fear as though Val's gesture had been a real gun.

He winked at her and pointed again as she ran into her house.

He laughed, sat back and said, "Well, where are we going?"

"I don't know. Check the GPS to see if they have downloaded a destination."

"They can do that?"

"Yeah, I saw it on TV."

Val punched keys and shook his head. "Well, maybe somebody on TV might be able to do it, but we got nothing. I say we just head out into the country. But I wasn't kidding about my problem. We need to find a toilet."

Two black SUVs roared by them in the opposite direction and. Inside each, men dressed like a SWAT team looked out. But these were police *not* the Killer Monks.

John said, "I think we just barely made it out of there in time. I hope that cake grandma brought you was worth it."

Val scrunched his face. "How did you even know about that? You were asleep."

"The house had video cameras. I saw you on the computer."

Val shook his head. "Damn, that computer has a whole bunch of shit on it."

John shrugged. "No, I hit the erase icon before we left… And, speaking of shit, I'm turning onto the gravel road off to our right. It looks like it leads down into a heavily wooded area. You can go commune with nature there and then we can take a minute to regroup and make plans."

"Thanks. Man, but hurry, it's starting to rain."

"Oh, I'll bet you're waterproof. You're a wolf-man. You can manage a dump in the rain."

"Yeah, I can do a lot of things I don't really care to."

As he slowed, John checked his rear-view mirror. He spoke slowly, "One black car is turning around." He spoke in a calm voice, but with a hint of urgency. "We need to evade."

"Evade? We're on a farm road - actually more of a farm trail - with nothing but overgrown pastures of grass for a quarter mile, and then it's all trees. Where exactly do you intend to evade *to*?"

John didn't answer. He made a sharp turn off the gravel onto grass and headed for a rise, a gentle mound where tall grass moved in waves as the wind gusted and the sky threatened. It looked more like a stormy ocean than bucolic pasture.

John was breathing heavy. "If we can just get over the crest of that hill, we'll be shielded from view."

"Any idea what's over the hill?"

"Only one way to find out."

There was silence as John drove, plowing through grass now as tall as his car window. The rain became heavier and wind gusts buffeted. A crack of thunder made both men jump. Then rain came in sheets, lashing their window. The wipers could not keep up.

John couldn't see much of anything ahead. He slowed and rolled down his window to poke his head out slightly, but that was little help. Ahead, there were only vague gray shapes, possibly trees. The deluge worsened as wave after wave of the downpour swept over them.

They were still moving, but at a creep. What had been waist-high grass beside them now lay flattened under the pounding rain. His field of view was getting smaller, narrower, closer.

Suddenly, the car pitched forward. The men felt momentarily weightless. They must have crested the mound. The other side felt ski-jump steep. They began to accelerate, almost falling.

Val yelled, "Slow down. We can't see five feet ahead."

John held the steering wheel in a death grip and gnashed his teeth but said nothing. The car kept picking up speed. Brakes had no effect; neither did the steering wheel. They were sliding, slipping, skating over rain-slick grass out of control and headed into a gray abyss. Their vehicle began a slow rotation until it was facing sideways to their forward motion.

The dark form of a mature tree appeared for only an instant before the impact against Val's door. That shock was enough to propel John all the way across the seat to slam his body up against Val. The impact shattered side windows and actually bent the car frame, distorting it into a Chinese fortune cookie.

Dazed by the crash, John took a long, confused moment to recover, at least partially recover. He tried to disentangle from Val, who seemed unconscious. A foul smell told him that Val's bowels had released. His fellow werewolf no longer needed a toilet. No. What he needed now was a bath.

"Val, you okay?"

No answer.

John placed a palm under Val's nose. No breath. He placed a hand on Val's chest. There was no rise and fall. He lay crammed against Val's motionless body, helpless, impotent, and without ideas.

John banged his fist on the dashboard. "Damn it. Damn it.

You can't be dead. I need you. Without you, I'm like a child lost in the wilderness. *Don't be dead!*"

John Wagner, fearless fighter, lifelong tough guy, and recently realized Lycan, began to sob. Between gasping breaths, he whispered to himself. "Damn it, werewolves don't cry."

The rain came still heavier. Water rippled over the spiderweb of fractures in the front window. Vladimir Petrov, his mentor, his guide through the strange new world of the Lycanthrope was gone.

John was alone, and there were people trying to kill him. He sat for a long time, just waiting for the rain to let up, waiting for some plan to form in his mind, waiting for whatever came next.

The Pures

It was almost dark now. That was probably to his advantage since he was still a fugitive on the run. It took an athletic effort to finally disentangle himself from the wreckage of overturned car. Val's body was stiff and cold. He hated to do it, but he put both feet on his friend's shoulder and pushed hard against the man's body to lift himself up across the car now tilted on its side. He was able to reach up to the driver's door. It was jammed. But the car was old enough to have crank-down windows, and he managed, with great effort, to roll his window halfway open.

Then, he twisted, braced one hand against the steering wheel and the other on the headrest, and kicked the window with everything he had. The remaining glass broke out piece-by-piece. He paused and caught his breath. Now, he just had to wiggle through the jagged remnants to be free from the wreck.

The car lay on its right side, two wheels in the air. Eventually, he wiggled clear of the window and plopped down into mud, too slick to stand without grabbing a bent tree limb. He pulled himself against the tree and stood, shivering and trying to collect.

He had to get his head straight: Val dead; SWAT after him; unsure where he was; and he just realized his right leg was bleeding from the window shards. Now what?

He sighed. At least the rain had lightened into mist, a damp soggy mist, but the fog and overcast only intensified the darkness. There were no lights anywhere, and he couldn't see much farther than the length of his arm. Okay, he would just have to feel his way along.

He pulled himself from branch to branch, until he found better footing in the mud. The force of the impact had popped the trunk open. That was a help. He worked his way back to the trunk and used his cell phone flashlight to inspect its contents. There was the duffle bag, still filled with weapons; several rifles, a couple of handguns, a telescope, and some other items he did not recognize. He wrestled it out of the trunk sideways. Once free, the weight of it almost yanked him face-forward down into muck. It was too heavy to carry, but he could drag it through slippery mud.

But, drag it to where? Somewhere? Anywhere? He began to move in almost total darkness, slipping and plodding along, lugging his bag of guns, but with no plan, no destination, except to get away from the wreck. Then, he saw lights above, beams of vehicle lights coming from the ridge above. In the foggy night air, they penetrated like misty, glowing spears.

Had to be the SWAT guys. Who else would drive out into a pasture in such weather? The glow of their headlights enabled him to see just a little of his surroundings. He took stock of the area. The tree the car hit was at the fringe of thick woods. *That could be a good place to hide.* He headed deeper into shadows, still lugging his duffle bag armory behind him like a sled.

From somewhere ahead, he heard voices, shouting voices, military-sounding voices. But he couldn't understand them clearly. So, he stood still and tried another way, the Lycan way. He relaxed, let out his breath, and opened his mind. It was working. He felt the presence of many beings near, very near. Some were likely police, or military, or even the Killer Monks. Their sensations were hostile, but also apprehensive, even scared. *Imagine, those heavily armed troopers were afraid of him.*

But there were others he sensed, and they were not threatening. John stood very still and allowed the flow of feelings. Yes, there were others, very close to him. But, from them, he could sense no words, only emotions. They too seemed to be afraid. He turned in a circle trying to feel more, sense more. As he did, his injured leg gave way, and he fell, making an unintended grunt.

He recovered his balance but remained still for a moment, hands on his knees, catching his breath. His clothes were soaked and heavy with mud. Every movement was an effort, particularly in the soggy woods, but he had to move, to keep moving.

Then came a sound like "Whuh," just a single sound.

Without thinking, without reason, and almost by instinct, he repeated the sound, "Whuh."

After a long silence, a response, "Whuh, whuh, huh, huh, huh."

It was an animal sound but, for some reason, John was not afraid. He forced himself to relax and feel the flow again. There were multiple presences. Someone, or something, was very near and yet, he felt no threat.

He stood very quietly for what seemed an eternity until he saw a momentary reflection. It was just a few feet away, but it looked like...eyes. Yes, it had to be eyes. About level with his own, the creature must be staring at him, evaluating him...

And, *still*, he felt no threat. John reached his left hand out into the void of darkness. It was a tenuous reach, ready to snap back at the first hint of threat. His right hand clutched a pistol beside his leg.

He touched something fur-like. Resisting the reflex to draw back, he held his breath and let his fingers linger. In a few seconds, he felt a hand on *his* shoulder. *Now what?*

John took a footstep closer and he could begin to make out the creature. It was about his height but leaner, and hairier. Its eyes were wide, but curious not hostile. He tried again to feel the flow, still no threat. The creature seemed just curious.

John cleared his throat and said, "Hello."

The beast made a half step back, but his hand remained on John's shoulder. The thing made a soft, "Huh, huh, huh."

John tried to imitate it. "Huh, huh, huh."

He felt the hand on his shoulder relax slightly.

The mist lightened slightly, and car headlights from the ledge above them shown clearly. It was a soft glow, but enough to make out several other creatures closing in around him. He fought the urge to run as they moved close, very close. Now, several hairy hands touched him, patted him, stroked him. A muffled chorus of huffs and hoots came from the crowd.

He did his best to stay relaxed, to stay open to feelings and, sure enough, he sensed something, felt something. *The creatures wanted him to come with them.* He took a hesitant step and all touching stopped. As a group, they moved out quietly, deeper into the woods. The headlights behind them grew faint.

They descended a rocky slope, and several of the creatures reached out to help steady John with his bag. A bit of moonlight finally penetrated the mist, and he could better make out their forms. Erect, but stoop-shouldered, they were about the size of a regular human, a Homo Sapiens. But they were hairy, with short fur, soft to the touch. They moved gracefully, but with a deliberate stride.

He realized how tense he had been and straightened his shoulders. The creatures seemed to sense his increased confidence. He began to get more feelings from them. They wanted to help him, wanted to know him, wanted to care for him. He felt strangely comfortable with them.

Eventually, they came to a large concrete structure overgrown by forest. He thought it might once have been a hydroelectric station, but long abandoned. Once inside, it was dry, and a flickering fire burning behind a concrete partition gave off reflected light.

He could see them more clearly now. His companions were thin and lithe; he thought that was the right word, like furry ballet dancers. They had a larger jaw and more deep-set eyes than a Sapiens but, besides the fur, their most obvious difference seemed to be the bend of their legs below the knees. It looked backward. Still, they moved in an elegant, smooth stride and seemed purposeful in everything that they did.

One of them came to him. She - somehow, he knew she was female - motioned for him to sit on a ledge that might have once been part of an interior wall. She placed her hand on his forehead and then felt his chest and arms. Her hands were gentle as she moved them over his body as though doing a physical. He decided that he would call her Nurse.

Once satisfied, she stepped back and smiled. Yes, it was clearly a smile. She had a faint smell of fresh pine and another scent he could not identify, but it was not at all unpleasant. She turned to a large male and made soft huffing sounds, smiled again at John, and left.

The big male came over and squatted before him, staring eye-to-eye.

John fought the urge to back away. He thought he knew

what the male wanted, but didn't know how to communicate, so he just spoke in English.

"I am John Wagner, and I am half Lycan. Who are you?"

The male bobbed his head and made a humpf-humpf sound.

"All right, I will call you Humpty."

The next sound was clearly a laugh, recognizable by any human, or ape, or Lycan.

All of the creatures laughed.

A couple came over to pat him on the shoulder.

"Well, I guess I'm part of the clan now." John grinned and patted them back.

———

The phone caller was abrupt.

"They killed one, but lost the other. The cops are presently combing the woods but, in this weather, there's little chance they'll find anything."

Father Antonio drummed his fingers. "Thank you, Carlo. Tell me, what will they do with the body of the dead demon?"

Carlo spoke in a clipped tone. "The police chief has given directions that it will be taken to a specific veterinarian's office. It seems they have some sort of agreement about autopsies. There should be no public knowledge of the body, or the results of the dissection."

"He can do this?"

"It seems so, Monsignor. The policeman in charge of the tactical team who killed the demon indicated they have done the same thing before with some gangsters' bodies. I do not know the reason. That policeman promises he will deliver a full report to us within a day."

"Good work, Carlo. This could be very helpful. Tell me,

what do the police know about the demon or demons who escaped?"

"Very little. The police had an informant in the small town. She said that yesterday morning, two men moved into a vacant house in her neighborhood. On instructions directly from the chief of police, she went to the house with a welcoming gift, a pastry I think."

"How could they know where to look for the monsters?"

"I'm not sure. The woman may have already been a - how do you say - informer? I think this house may have been used for drug deals in the past, but I cannot be sure I understood all that was said. The policeman has a very strange American accent."

"It is of no matter, Carlo. Just stay in touch with the police and keep me informed."

"Yes, Monsignor. I am here with Pierre. The others will join us within the hour. With or without the police, we will begin a search of the woods where the demon car crashed."

———

John needed to notify the people at Digital Nation of Val's death. He rummaged through the mud-soaked duffel and found several flip-phones. He picked one and opened it but didn't know the phone number. The call history was empty; it had to be a brand-new phone. Maybe it was in the contacts list? He checked and found several stored numbers but recognized few names. He thumbed through until he found Vrykolas and hit call.

The man who answered was not Vrykolas. He only said, "Yes."

"This is John Wagner. I am alive, but my companion is not." He paused.

The voice said, "Hold on."

The next voice *was* Vrykolas. "Yes, Mister Wagner, the phone is now secure. Tell me what happened."

"We received the warning on the house computer and left moments before a police tactical team got there. They must have spotted us and pursued. I drove into a farmer's field in heavy rain and slid off a ledge, crashing the car and killing Vladimir. I managed to escape, and I am now travelling with a small band of Pures."

"You're what? You're travelling with what?"

"Pures. They sensed my presence in the woods and came to me. We can only communicate in very simple gestures, but I have a good sense of their feelings. They are protecting me."

"This is…I don't know what. It is astounding. I have never heard of a cooperation between Pures and mixed bloods, at least, not in America. This is phenomenal, wonderful. I will send help. Just tell me where you are."

"I'm a couple of miles south of the little town where you sent us, probably a mile or more west of the road in a thick forest of tall oaks. I believe there are still police cars out in the field. I'm safe for the moment. My Pure hosts are quite accommodating."

"Thank you, John. This is so terribly exciting. We will come for you, but it may take a while. We don't want direct conflict…"

"I understand. I'll be patient." John hung up and felt better about his situation. Help would be coming…eventually.

Humpty ambled over and made a beckoning gesture. The others gathered, and so did John. The big guy huffed and gestured, and then they all turned to move out.

The nurse-friend came to him and began making soft noises, as though explaining what was going on. Then, she glanced down and saw the blood on his leg.

Instantly, she became excited, making high-pitched hoots and pointing.

The others gathered. She pushed John and, through gestures, made him understand that she wanted him to sit.

He found a chunk of concrete and plopped down. She bent before him and tore open his pants leg with her hands. *Strong girl.* The wound was more than six inches long and a thumb-width deep. She chattered, and a young male brought her a metal cup of water. She washed the wound and inspected it before making "hoot-hoot" sounds to Humpty.

The big guy stroked his chin whiskers and grunted.

With that, the whole team mobilized. They brought sticks and large leaves that Nurse used to clean and wrap the wound.

He expected her to make a splint with the sticks but, instead, one of the males just handed them to John and pantomimed how to use them like a cane, or crutch.

Now Humpty stood and bellowed.

Everyone else stood and fell into a line. Apparently, they were leaving, trekking off to some unknown destination. *How would Vrykolas' men find them?*

Nurse took John's arm, and they too, headed into the woods, their final destination unknown.

The Killer Monks Ride

The five monks bristled with full battle gear: protective vests, helmets with night vision goggles, handguns, and combat knives, all strapped to their bodies. They carried a variety of assault rifles with laser, telescopic and low-light sights. They were ready.

As they clambered aboard a rental van, all that equipment jangled and bumped. The driver simply nodded. He had obviously been warned and given directions.

This was the beginning of an "op," the point where Carlo usually made a little speech and led a prayer. Today, he was silent.

Finally, Benny from Boston could stand no more. "Okay, boss, where are we going, and what's the plan?"

Carlo's voice had a vacant tone. "We're going out into the country to an accident scene where the cops think they have recovered a demon body. I don't know much more than that. We'll get further instructions." There was frustration in his voice. "I hope they have some more information for us. I sense that the cops think this hunt is really their thing and they don't particularly want us involved."

Benny sat back. "But that's why we're here, right? This is what we do, man. Why do you think they're holding back?"

"If I were to guess, I would say," he seemed to be searching for the right English word, "publicity. They probably don't want foreign fighters operating in their town, or country, and stealing credit."

Benny shook his head again. "But we don't do that. We don't want headlines. We just go after the demons, kill 'em, and move on. Life goes on in happy little Madison, and we go quietly back to Sicily."

Carlo took a deep breath. "You know that. I know that. But I don't think the local Chief of Police here knows that. I think he wants credit for any monsters killed or captured. I think he may be more politician than warrior."

Hershel piped in, "Then, he is a fool. Better to just keep it all quiet. The more people know, the more questions they will ask and the less plausible the answers will seem."

Carlo knit his eyebrows. "*Scuzi*, what means *plausible*?"

Benny held up his hands. "Ah well it means believable, acceptable, reasonable, and not deceptive."

"Ah, like a plausible lie?"

Benny popped back. "Yeah, I suppose. Anyway, Hershel is right. The less publicity we get, the better the cops look, and the more willing people will be to accept the killings as normal criminality."

Carlo thought about that for a time. "That makes sense, but you all know we are better able to deal with these creatures than a bunch of local police. We must just be careful not to take any credit."

Pierre chuckled and looked out the side window. "We

never take the credit. We blow in like the wind, spill a little blood, and drift silently away. That is our life, our *raison d'etre*."

There was silence in the van. They all knew it was true. They were ghosts, albeit holy ghosts. They would live and die alone, anonymously. And yet, there was pride in living a life of high purpose. Like earthbound angels, they extracted God's revenge. It was a glorious calling.

No one spoke for a time, but every chin was held high. Time to steel themselves.

———

John was doing pretty well with his walking stick, but his leg was starting to throb. He didn't know how far they had walked, but night had given way to sunrise and thinning fog. He was keeping up with the clan as they trudged through the wet and dripping woods. They seemed purposeful, sure of their way.

To him the forest seemed endless, and his leg was hurting more with each step. The female he called Nurse came back and checked on him every half hour or so. He looked forward to her quick visits. In daylight, her dark eyes seemed to sparkle. Her complexion was like smooth caramel, with very human lips, and only a little hair on her face. He could understand Sapiens-Lycan mating; he might be willing to try it, himself.

They came to an open grassy area, a *mowed* grassy area. On the far side was a freshly painted house. Humpty, the clan leader, stood tall and hooted. The rest waited.

After a minute a woman, a regular female human, stepped out onto the porch. She was young, mid-twenties, probably. Her house dress looked faded, but John sensed that her shotgun was freshly oiled.

She shaded her eyes and shouted, "Who goes…" and then

lowered the gun. "Oh, Lord of Mercy. It's my Forest People." She beckoned, "Come on, you all. I got a pot of beans on and a fresh side of pork. C'mon, now."

How long has it been since he had eaten?

They went in single file. It looked to John as though the line was in order of seniority. Humpty went first and then the next oldest male, two younger ones, and then his nurse. There was one other female, but she held back, as though timid, waiting to be invited. There must be a lot of rules to this Pure Lycan thing. He remembered the first day of junior high school, so many rules.

John went last, hobbling on his stick. The Sapiens woman looked shocked at the sight of him, a regular white-guy human. She raised her gun again. "And who the hell might you be, mister?"

He tried to smile. "I'm John Wagner, and these good souls have saved my life. I was in a car crash, and they helped me. My passenger died, but they took me in and sheltered me."

"So, you just up and came along with the forest people? You didn't think nothing of it? Them being what they are, I mean?"

He considered before he spoke. *Well, this woman had accepted the Pures. Why shouldn't she accept me?* "The truth, ma'am, is that I am related to them, so it was easy to be accepted."

"What 'cha mean - related?"

"I mean that I am a half-breed, half human and half Lycan."

"Liken, liken to what?"

"No, ma'am, Lycan is short for Lykanthropis. Your friends here belong to that species."

She thought for a moment and nodded suspiciously before she lowered her gun. "Well, I'm Miss Betty Mae. Now, you just come on inside. I got to talk to you."

Once inside the house, she set out bowls and ladled bean stew and poured cups of water. The Pures had no trouble sitting in chairs and eating at a table. It all seemed eerily normal, like a Norman Rockwell painting, only a Halloween painting. There was even a dinner conversation of a sort. The Lycans hooted and snorted and laughed. The laughter seemed very human.

After dinner, the Nurse Lycan came to inspect John's wound. She made some low, mumbling sounds.

Betty Mae watched and seemed to understand. Betty went to a cabinet and returned with bandages and ointment.

The two of them fussed over him for a while. They seemed completely at ease, like old friends, patching up a wandering stranger.

Once his wound was cleaned and wrapped, he sat back and felt the muscles of his back relax. He looked around at the bizarre scene. Everything had settled down. The big hairy Pures were crouched beside empty chairs. They made noises and poked at each other in a good-natured way.

Betty Mae came to sit beside John and spoke in a soft, nervous voice. "You see the tall boy over there? I call him Honey."

"Yes, he seems like a strong young fellow, a real worker."

She made an awkward girlish smile. "Yeah, I think so, too. Well, I like him a lot, and we got close, real close, if you know…"

"I think I understand."

"Thing is…I'm afraid I might be pregnant…and I'm scared to death. What will come out, and how will I deal with it all? I don't want to die in birthing, and I don't want to pump out a monster."

John put a kindly hand on her shoulder. "Betty, look at me. My mother was human, and my father was Lycan. I pass pretty easily in the human world, except I'm way tougher than they are. Your baby will probably be just like me. Some are a little harrier, and some less, but we're not monsters, not any of us."

She hesitated, took a couple of breaths, and then hugged John tight and began to sob. "Thank you. Oh, thank you. I am just so scared."

John had trouble breathing in her embrace. Then a shadow blocked the light, and he looked up to see Honey looming over him. The look in the young Lycan's eyes was not friendly. John held up a palm and tried not to sound alarmed. "It's okay, buddy. She's just grateful. That's all."

But Honey's eyebrows were knit, and his fists clenched. His upper lip quivered, and his shoulders bunched as though ready for action.

"Betty Mae, tell him it's okay."

She pulled back from John, tears still streaming down her cheeks. Once disentangled, she stood and wrapped her arms around Honey's neck.

John realized that every eye in the room was locked on him.

Humpty stood and moved closer. His face was tight, fierce looking. The closer he got, the more his chest puffed, his shoulders squared, and his grunts became threatening.

Betty Mae was rocking back and forth clamped in her embrace with Honey. She paid no attention to Humpty's threat posture.

Okay. John decided that he was on his own. If there was going to be a fight, he was going to put up a good defense. He clenched fists and crouched, ready for action. He had been in a lot of fights, and he knew how to handle himself.

Humpty came at him, and John threw a roundhouse punch to the jaw.

It stopped the big guy cold. He shook his head and stumbled back with a confused look.

Betty Mae finally came out of her tangled embrace, stood, and put hands on her hips.

"Now, you two, cut that out. I don't allow no fighting in my house. You boys hear me?" For such a small woman, she had a Mother Superior authority in her shrill tone.

John was taken aback.

The young one she called Honey looked confused.

Humpty grumbled, as though he didn't know what to do about this little screaming Sapiens female. There was a lot of tension. Somebody had to defuse the situation.

John stepped close to Humpty, bent his good knee, and bowed his head before the big Pure Lycan. He was now completely vulnerable to attack and he knew what a risk he was taking.

Humpty considered for a long moment, huffed, and then placed a fatherly hand on John's head. *Crisis averted.*

John struggled to stand, and Nurse came to help him.

Humpty made low grunting noises, but they didn't seem threatening anymore.

Nurse smoothed John's hair and patted him on the neck and shoulders. Her breath smelled sweet like honeysuckle. He felt his heartbeat slow.

Yes, he could absolutely understand interspecies breeding. He only hoped that his advice to Betty Mae had been wise.

————

Chief Mitchell looked up from his desk as the breathless young policeman burst through the door and held out several sheets of paper. "Sir, we have the initial report from the veterinarian, Doctor Dean. He says his initial findings are…" He looked down and read the single word, "Unremarkable."

The police chief sat back in his chair and extended his hand. "Let me see the document." After shuffling through the pages, the chief looked up. "What is this company he recommends that we contact?"

"Digital Nation, sir. It's just a few blocks from here. They do DNA stuff, you know, like where your ancestors…"

"I know what DNA is. Do we have a point of contact there?"

The young cop looked pleased with himself. He produced a business card. "Yes, sir, the CEO is a Mister Louis Sypher. That's his private number there on the card."

The Chief nodded. "Good work," He looked at the man's name tag. "Good work, Billings."

Now alone in his office, Chief Mitchell read through the six-page report and repeatedly raised his eyebrows. "The unidentified body was a big guy, six three, and two twenty. Oversized canine teeth and muscular anomalies. Scars indicate a history of injury, possible evidence of violent behavior. Recommend DNA analysis."

He threw the report onto his desk. "Damned vet. He's a dog doctor; what the hell does he know, anyway? The only reason we use him is to keep our investigations private. He probably does the same kind of stuff for crooks…and DNA analysis, what the hell will that do for us?"

The chief sat, drumming his fingers and scowling. Finally, he yelled, "Dumb Ass, get in here now."

The slight man who responded had a facial tic and a defeated look. He entered the office but did not speak.

Henry Dumas' father pronounced their last name "Doom us." He always said it was English. His mother, on the other hand, was sure it was French and insisted it be pronounced

"Dew Mah." It didn't matter. From his first day on the job and forever after, he was Henry *Dumb Ass* to the chief and everyone else in the department.

Chief Mitchell was looking out the window and barely seemed to notice the assistant, even as he spoke to him. "Dumb Ass, we have a dead body with some physical anomalies. The autopsy was inconclusive, and Doc recommended a DNA analysis. I want you to contact a Mister Sypher at a company called Digital something or other and get one."

Dumas cleared his throat and said, "Yes, sir, the company is Digital Nation. It's physically located just a few blocks from here. They do DNA for those genealogy people like '23andme' or whatever it's called."

The chief was still staring outside as he rocked in his chair. "I want you, without arousing suspicion, to get a sample analyzed. It needs to be done in a hurry, and with a guarantee of confidentiality. Can you do that?"

"I think so. I've dealt with the people there on some rape kit questions, and they've been very helpful. If I emphasize that *you're* the one asking, I think they'll cooperate."

"Okay, then. I'll have the sample delivered to you in an hour. Take care of it."

Dumas said, "Yes, sir," and was out the door.

The chief turned back to his desk and muttered, "Faggot. That guy Dumb Ass gives me the creeps. Hate having to work with people like that, destroying the fabric of our society with their unholy behavior. Why can't I just have some good-looking secretary with big tits, like the old days?" He sighed and turned to his desktop computer to type *"Digital Nation"* into the search engine.

———

Henry Dumas waited patiently in the outer office until Louis Sypher swept in with a big grin and a hearty handshake that engulfed the smaller man's hand. "Mister Dumas, I remember you from the Walton case, is that right?"

"Yes, sir. You provided the critical DNA information that led to the release of a man named Todd, and the apprehension of a cousin of the murdered Miss Walton. It was a minor embarrassment for the department, but thankfully, justice was served."

"Well, I hope our information will be as helpful this time. Come on into my office."

Once seated inside, Sypher's tone became much more serious. "Okay then, what exactly is your department looking for? I don't see anything really remarkable here in this blood sample. The man's name, we believe, was Vladimir Petrov. He was the grandson of Russian immigrants from a small town in northwest Siberia that is noted for producing very tall men, many of whom excel in basketball. He had a predisposition toward a specific type of lung cancer and was likely to suffer depression. Beyond that, he seems quite ordinary. Are we missing something?"

Dumas sat back. "I'm not sure. The man is dead of course, killed in an automobile crash. The chief seems to suspect there is more to it than a simple wreck." Dumas shifted forward in his seat and spoke in a softer voice. "My boss has a lot of strong opinions, particularly ethnic opinions. I think he may be looking for some hint of racial, or cultural, factors that could be used to explain deviant behavior."

Sypher sat back and let his shoulders reveal a little chuckle. "Well, DNA doesn't help find excuses for bigotry. I'm afraid your boss is on his own to support his bias. This man, as far as his genetic makeup is concerned, was a perfectly normal Caucasian."

Dumas looked thoughtful. "Okay, I really appreciate your expediting this analysis and for keeping it confidential." He grimaced. "Say, before I go, can I ask a silly question?"

"Yes, of course."

"Well, my boss is always saying he thinks gay men should be 'neutered,' that's the word he uses, to prevent them from breeding. I don't bother to point out to him that gay men don't naturally breed. But please, if you would indulge me, is there actually a 'gay gene,' or whatever?"

Sypher laughed openly. "No, there's nothing like that. There are clusters of traits that are associated with sexual orientation, but the predictive value of those clusters is very, very low. We hear all the time that someone was just 'born that way,' but we can't find any solid genetic correlation that would lead to such a predilection."

He hesitated and seemed to consider his words. "And I think that's a good thing. Genetics is a framework to build on. It is not an absolute determinant. I fear the day when babies can be classified and sorted by characteristics. That *Brave New World* that would be terrifying to me. It would lock in a social class structure that stifled creativity, progress, and hope. Let's pray it never happens."

Dumas stood and offered his frail hand again. His smile was earnest. "Thank you, sir. I'm very pleased to have met you, and I appreciate your help."

The Morning After

Father Antonio arrived at the crash scene, and the police escorted him to the ledge where he could peer down onto the car's wreckage. He grimaced and asked, "May I go down for a closer look?"

The young policeman seemed reticent, as though intimidated by the robed priest. He shrugged. "I don't think that's a good idea, sir. It's real steep, and pretty slippery. That car dug some pretty deep ruts on the way down and ripped up all kinds of rocks and tree roots, and branches, and other stuff. I think it would be dangerous to even try. Your guys in the military outfits have already been down and looked over the car. They're the ones who pulled the body out." He gestured to a group of parked vehicles. "They're standing right over there behind that van. Why don't you speak to them and see what they can tell you?"

Father Antonio smiled his standard public smile and turned to make his way across muddy grassland. The monks saw him and immediately assembled, almost snapping to attention. They stood straight and stern in their layers of battle gear.

"*Salve*, my brothers," said Antonio. "What have you learned?"

Carlo scanned to be sure that none of the police were within earshot. "The dead man in the car is one of the two demons in the pictures of Robert's murder. He seems to have died as a result of a broken neck caused by the impact against a tree. The other demon escaped. We can see his tracks for only a few meters.

"Beyond that, the rain has washed everything away. His initial direction was west, but that may have been just because he was following the tree line. These police are all from downtown Madison. None of them is familiar with the local area. The sheriff's men are coming soon. They may be more helpful in tracking the second man, the second demon."

Monsignor Antonio paused for a moment. "So, what do we know for certain?"

"Well, the Madison police have enlisted the local sheriff to inspect the hideout used by the two killers. The sheriff's people are doing fingerprints and going through trash. They found a computer there, but its hard drive is blank, erased. Still, the tech people think they may be able to trace some message traffic originating from that machine with the help of the internet provider. That is about all I know at this point."

The priest raised his foot from the muck, inspected it, and then lifted the soggy hem of his robe with a disgusted grimace. Turning back to his men, he said, "You know the task. You know the importance. Continue to do God's good work, and find these creatures. Keep me informed."

With that, he gathered his robe above pale thin knees and slogged off gingerly into the field of standing water, tall wet grass, and mudholes. He mumbled and cursed under his breath with every slip and stumble.

––––––

John woke feeling disoriented and panicky. Slowly, he focused. He was lying on a wooden floor in the corner of the main room. Betty Mae must have given him a pillow and blanket to sleep with, but the floor was hard, and his back ached. He sat up and took stock.

No one seemed at home, but there was a smell of coffee in the air. Just what time was it? He struggled to straighten the watch on his wrist. It was 2:00 and, judging from the bright sunlight, that would be two in the afternoon. He had no idea how long he'd been asleep. He stretched and groaned.

The house seemed vacant, peaceful, and quiet. He stood and twisted his aching body, shoulders and neck. Everything was stiff. He spoke aloud, "Okay, where the hell is everybody? Betty Mae…anyone?"

No answer.

He took a deep breath and inhaled the coffee. Thank goodness, coffee. He followed his nose to an old-style percolator cheerfully bubbling away and spreading heavenly aroma. John found a cup and savored the first jolt.

Once his synapses began to fire properly, he tried to recall yesterday's events. The computer's warning, the dash out of town, the black SUV's, the chase, the storm, the crash; it all came back so vivid and real that he couldn't help but experience the emotion all over again, even the last image of Val's crumpled body.

Vladimir Petrov, his mentor, his fellow, his friend, now dead, crushed by the tree that T-boned their vehicle. His lanky arms and legs were left a tangle of twisted flesh. His face was frozen forever in a pale, bloodless look of shock, mouth gaping like a fish gulping air. It was an image that John never wanted to see again and, yet, he was sure he could never erase it from his consciousness.

Along with the horror, there was guilt. John was the driver. He was ultimately responsible for the crash. Could he have done anything differently? *Of course.* He could have done a hundred things differently. But, in the moment, in the rainstorm, in the chaos of an out-of-control car sliding sideways down a steep drop off…what could he have *reasonably* done?

The coffee was bitter. He sighed and began a search of the house. It was a large cottage with at least four bedrooms, two stories above ground, and a full basement. He opened the basement door and was hit by an unmistakable smell of marijuana curing.

"Well," John spoke out loud, "I guess that's how she makes her living, and why she's so far out in the woods." He went looking for food and found a supply of pre-packaged, dehydrated packets, enough to make a Mormon survivalist envious. He tore open a bag of dried something-or-other and went for more coffee but paused at sounds from outside. Distant voices, male voices; they were shouting, clipped, and businesslike.

He was unarmed. Then, he remembered his duffel filled with weapons. But where did he leave it? He made a quick tour of the ground floor and deck, no duffel. Then, he bolted down the outside steps and raced around the outside; no one there, nothing. The voices were becoming clearer. He needed to run, but in which direction?

"Okay, okay, I don't know where I am. I don't know where the others are. I don't have any kind of plan. I don't even know what direction to head…aw, screw it all. Here I go."

Without any real direction, he set off into the woods. Behind him came the distant sound of a baying dog, then another. Bloodhounds maybe? He fought to control his breathing. *Okay, don't panic. Make good decisions. How do I escape from dogs?*

It only took a second for the gears of his mind to turn. *Water! I need to find water. Water will mask my scent. In a forest, you almost always find water at the low point of terrain.*

Without hesitation, he began a headlong run that turned into a mudslide down the wooded slope. It was steep to begin with, and it grew steeper. Leaping from one handhold to the next, he fought to keep his body position as he plummeted down the hill, slipping, sliding, bumping, and bouncing, getting muddier and muddier.

He could no longer hear the dogs, but that didn't mean they had lost his scent. Maybe they were just being more careful as they picked their way down the forest's steep incline after him. He grabbed a bush and held tight as he caught his breath and paused to listen: no dogs, no sound at all. The ground was firmer here, and the slope not quite as steep.

He stood and let his breathing settle. There was absolutely stillness. No birds, no sound but the soft breeze rustling the tops of eighty-foot-tall pines that made groaning sounds. John looked up and inhaled the damp smells of the forest. But there was another smell. It took a moment for his brain to process.

He took a step back, squinted, and craned to look up so high it made him almost lose his balance. He stumbled backward until he bumped something solid. It wasn't a tree. He turned to face Humpty just inches away. He was eyeball-to-eyeball with the big Lycan clan leader.

Humpty grinned and wrapped big arms around John. It might have just been a welcome but, if so, it was a crushing welcome that forced air from his lungs.

Behind Humpty stood the rest of the clan, including the one he called Nurse. They made soft, nervous hoots and glanced all around.

Humpty released John and headed off. The others fell into line.

Nurse took her half-breed friend by the hand and led him, as though he were a child.

In just minutes, they came to a fast-flowing stream.

Humpty stood aside and pointed the way.

One-by-one, the Lycan troop forded the rushing water.

Nurse held back and made little hand flaps goading John to go next.

He stepped into frigid water and suppressed the urge to yell. Step-by-step, he sloughed through the current. His legs felt numb, and his teeth began to chatter just a little, but he made it. Nurse was just a few feet behind.

Drenched and freezing, he hauled out on the far shore and paused to catch his breath. But there was no time. The rest of the group was already moving out, climbing through dense brush, almost hand over hand.

After a hundred feet or so up the hill, they came to an outcropping of granite and paused to rest.

Humpty was vigilant, as always. He leaned over the rock ledge and pointed down. Below, John saw two separate groups of humans. A uniformed police squad moved in a zig-zag pattern as their dogs sniffed and raced left and right. The other group of five men had no dogs. They wore military fatigues and moved in a slower, more deliberate way.

"The monks," John spoke through clenched teeth. He had killed one of them and, from what Vrykolas told him, he could expect some kind of cruel vengeance for that. *Well, let them come.* He would be waiting, and he would show them what vengeance really felt like.

He began to sense feelings from his Lycan companions. They were empathizing with him, experiencing his anger, feeling his emotions. He stood and spoke to them. They might not understand his words, but they would understand his meaning. He was sure that they would understand that one of his mixed-breed clan was dead. There was a debt to pay.

Below, the police dogs howled and sniffed as they made furious pokes into the brush, sampling smells. They were close to the spot where the Lycans forded the stream. But there, the dogs hesitated and seemed confused. They began spinning and quarreling with each other.

The handlers shouted and yanked on leashes, but the dogs would go no farther.

From his perch high above, Humpty made a mocking laugh from deep in his throat. All the others imitated him. Then, they turned and headed off with a determined stride. John, still shivering from the cold water, struggled to keep up. He would have welcomed a little more of their fur right then.

The afternoon light faded as they made it back to the old power plant shelter. And there, miraculously, was John's duffel full of guns. He felt a wave of relief. It seemed like a safe place, a refuge. More than any of the houses and apartments where he had lived during his chaotic, vagabond life, this ruined old concrete structure felt like home.

He looked around at the hairy, grunting monsters around him and had an unexpected revelation. *They were family.*

John's hands were still trembling from cold as he opened his duffel.

The crowd watched with total concentration, almost fascination, as he selected weapons and strapped on webbed equipment, belts and suspenders with holsters and sheathes, and a variety of small containers for ammo and grenades and other tools of war. Once fully outfitted, he stood for inspection.

They sniffed him and fingered items from his fifty-pound military hardware ensemble. They seemed to find it all very interesting

He started out of the shelter. The whole clan fell in behind. But John stopped and raised a hand. "My duty," he said. "My task. You have been good to me, and I thank you, but this is my mission, and my mission alone."

With that, he trudged alone into the dark forest.

The other Lycans all seemed to understand his anger. They did not interfere with his departure but turned instead to focus their minds on other things, possibly the men who hunted for John and, possibly even for them.

———

The monks had moved far ahead of the police canine unit. They crossed the stream and began a systematic sweep of steep woodland. It was wet and cold and tiring, but no one complained. They came to a clearing where an orange sunset flamed above them.

Carlo commanded, "Five-minute break, then we'll go to night vision goggles. He looked up the steeply sloped forest that stood before. "They have to be up there on the high ground. That's where I would go, and these things seem to be smart, really devious bastards. But it will do them no good. We're pretty damned devious, ourselves."

No one responded. They had been plodding through mud and wet brush for hours and, now, they were all cold, wet, and weary. The five-minute break was welcome. Just to sit and stretch and breathe easily felt great.

Hershel sounded thoughtful. "We're making wide arcs back and forth across the hill. Suppose they took off in a straight line? We know we were very close to them back at the little river, but they might have put some distance between us by now. Have we received any recent position data, drone, or helicopter, or anything?"

Carlo shrugged. "All these evergreen trees make it hard to see from above. They also muffle sounds. Is this the right word, muffle?"

Hershel made a confirming nod, and Carlo continued. "So, we must depend on tracks, or visual contact. The tracks will be more difficult to see once we're on goggles, but these trees are full of water drops that shine, making it very easy to see movement. Every branch they touch will sparkle, and the goggles are very good at detecting that. We must depend on our eyes. The highway patrol has people stationed at crossing roads, so it's unlikely they'll get out of the woods unnoticed. They're boxed in, so we just have to keep combing until we find the nits in the beard of this forest."

Hershel didn't sound satisfied. "Maybe we should split up. Pierre and I could go toward the south, and the three of you go north. We could cover more ground…"

Carlo held up a hand. "What do the rest of you think?"

Dag said, "Sure, why not? My only concern is that we don't know how many we are up against. We've killed one, and one escaped, but there may be others out there."

Benny chimed. "Yeah, but we need to find these bozos. I'm confident that even two or three of us will still have enough firepower to take care of a whole herd of supernatural creepy things. I'm for it."

Carlo didn't seem convinced, but this was a group of equals. Everyone's opinion had the same weight. He stretched. "Okay, break's over. Hershel and Pierre to the south; the rest follow me. Check in by radio every ten minutes. Let's move."

———

John's body had yet not recovered from the chill stream water, even an hour later. Numb hands made it difficult to strap on his night vision goggles, but he managed. Only after he snugged the headband straps did he realize that he didn't know where the goggles' on/off switch was.

It took a full minute of groping and feeling and pushing before he felt it and flicked on a glowing phosphorous green world, a panorama of monochrome images that smeared if he moved too quickly.

Judging depth was a challenge. He would have to learn fast, beginning with how to walk using the goggles. It took a full five minutes before he could step confidently with some expectation of when his foot would touch the ground on each step.

He could no longer hear any sound of dogs. In fact, there were few night sounds in the forest. One distant owl seemed to hoot a warning. As John looked up, bats zipping all around him seemed to flicker as bits of fluorescent yellowish green light reflected off their bodies. Even small movements of tree leaves and bushes seemed exaggerated in the glowing green world.

There was much that the night vision gear could not penetrate. Shadows remained an impenetrable black, so John tried to rely on listening almost as intently as looking. The stillness of the forest was an overpowering, dead quiet. But then, a distant snap of a branch, a muffled sound, and other noises, possibly even snippets of human speech. He held his breath and fine-tuned his senses. Something, someone, was out there. He could barely make out words, "Tangle of barbed wire...on the right...watch your step."

John smiled. The voices were headed in his direction. He slipped the assault rifle from his shoulder and inspected the mechanism. That was challenging with the one-dimensional green glow of his goggles with focus set for distance. He found the rifle's automatic fire selector but couldn't locate the safety.

Where would they put it? Had to be close to the trigger, where it could be selected by thumb. Sure enough, he clicked off the safety, selected full-auto, and held the gun ready.

Then, on impulse, he took off his goggles and laid them on a fallen log. He would depend on his own senses, not the artificial light of some toy. His senses were working great, filling him with information, images, and sensations. He must have found the sweet spot in the ether, the exact wavelength of his enemies' being. It was as if he were seeing everything from a remote camera - no, a whole series of cameras. He could even sense the tension in the two men who stalked him.

A moment of doubt. He had only killed one man in his whole life, and that was almost a protective reflex. Could he actually kill in cold blood? The image of Val crumpled into a pale, bloodless mass hardened him. Yes...he *could* kill. *Let the bastards come.*

———

Hershel raised his hand in a halt gesture. Pierre didn't see it and bumped into the smaller man. The Israeli sounded irritated. "Careful, man. When you're on goggles, you have to scan constantly to make up for your limited field of view."

"You don't have to tell me how to use the goggles. I lived on the goggles back in the Syrian hills."

Hershel took a breath. He had never been completely comfortable with the big Frenchman, if he really was a Frenchman. "It's just that visibility is really limited in the woods, and you need to keep your scan going constantly to avoid tripping, or bumping…"

"Okay, okay, I got it. Just walk a little faster, okay. Move your stubby little legs so we cover more ground, that's all."

"You think I'm too slow? Do you want to lead?"

"Sure, why not? Think you can keep up with my stride?"

"Sure thing, big guy…"

Hershel froze, zeroed in on something and said, "What's that ahead? It looks like a light, a green light."

Pierre leaned close. "Of course, everything in the goggles is green." But then his voice changed. "Okay, I see the light. It seems to be glowing green, the very peculiar green of our own goggles. Is it possible that we are looking at someone else's night vision device, a scope or something?"

They both stared before Hershel said, "I think you might be right, but who would be out here using goggles?"

Pierre thought. "Could be the police, but I doubt it. They don't like to hunt in the dark. They said their dogs could be injured." He made a sarcastic laugh. "I'm not so sure it was the dogs they worried over."

Hershel came back. "You know, it could be our guys, Carlo and the others."

"No, they would never be so sloppy as to let light escape from their devices. This is someone else. Is it possible - could it be possible - that the demons have such things?"

"Who can say? We don't know much about them. We just have that one body from the car, and it looked pretty normal. We know they have technology, phones and computers. Maybe they do have night scopes as well."

Pierre was silent for a time. "If we can see their devices, then they must be able to see ours. We must be very careful."

Hershel spoke slowly as though considering his words. "You know, I'm staring at you right now and I can't see any light leaking from your goggles. You look at me and check out my emissions."

Pierre made a childish laugh. "Your emissions? That sounds really crude." He grew serious. "But I can see no light around your face. I'm sorry, my friend, you will have to wait for your halo."

Both laughed but only for a moment. Hershel said, "Okay, so this someone, or something, is sloppy with his gear. Let us use his light as a guide and close in on him."

"Him…or it?" Pierre chuckled, "I agree. Let's go kill it. Let us always be guided by the light."

Hershel shook his head at the pompous Frenchman. They were back on the hunt, and even more serious now that they felt close. They moved with great care, silent and sure. Gun barrels swung left and right. Every step was carefully placed to find solid ground but break no twigs. Eyes scanned like the predators they were. Every sense was on edge; every nerve as tight as a violin string.

———

John knew that they were close, probably less than fifty feet away. As still as a statue, he controlled his breathing; he didn't turn his head, or shrug his shoulders. His night vision goggles lay on the ground ten feet in front of him. He intended them to be a lure and hoped to attract the right fish. He slowed his breathing and lost himself in the ether. He was one with the forest and the wind and even the small creatures of the night. He was just there, just waiting, just being. He had all the time in the world, maybe even the rest of his life.

It didn't matter if he died. He needed to avenge Val, his Lycan brother. The sound of a single footstep told him it was time. He reached to pick up the goggles, closed his eyes to prevent losing his night vision, and tossed them high across the open wood. Then, with a soft exhale, he raised his gun to his shoulder and waited.

He sensed that the hunters were very close, no more than twenty feet. John held his gun barrel straight out before him.

It was Pierre who yelled. "There, something is…"

Two shots in less than a second; the Frenchman fell, gasping and rolling.

Hershel fired back and began spewing blind fire in the general direction of the glowing goggles. He must not have seen John.

Then, he quit firing. Several long moments passed with no sound but Hershel's desperate breathing, more like sucking and blowing, really.

John waited until he was certain that he had the man's position fixed in his mind and fired twice more. The Israeli fell with no sound except his body hitting the ground like a sack of potatoes.

John sat still until he was sure that he heard no breathing. Then, he gathered his things and faded into the night, like a ghost.

And Then There Were Three

The car's two-way radio blared. "Brother Carlo, this is Three Charlie Eight, do you read, over."

There was a slight squeal in the background.

After a thirty second pause, the response came. "Three Charlie Eight, this is Carlo. What can I do for you, sergeant?"

"Yeah. Well, first, do you really want to keep using that 'Brother Carlo' call sign. It's a little unusual?"

"It's fine. Now, what do you want?"

"Okay. The boss told me to keep you informed of our activities. Well, we have a gunshot recognition system in some of our cars. It uses time delays between different cars that pick up the sound of a gunshot and then triangulate the shooter's position. Well, we have just had a total of four gunshots register. The approximate location of the gunfire is Square 32-19 on that grid map we gave you. Check it out."

"Yes, just give me a second. Okay, yes. I see the Square you are talking about. It is perhaps two hundred meters south of the river's bend, yes?"

"A meter? That's like a yard, isn't it?"

"Yes, quite close."

"Then, yeah. That's about right. Anyway, we got a couple guys headed that way. I'll keep you informed."

"Thank you, sergeant. Two of my men are in that area. Hopefully, those were their shots."

"Well, like I said, we'll keep you informed. You take care, Brother Carlo."

Carlo used his earbud radio and lapel mic. "Pierre, Hershel, do you read me?"

He waited and tried again. "Hershel, Pierre, come in."

Benny approached and Carlo said, "Do Pierre, or Hershel, have trackers on them?"

"Just their cell phones."

"That will work to locate them, yes?"

"Should." Benny grinned. "Just give me a minute, and I'll use the *Follow Me* app." He punched numbers. "Okay, I have a good location on Hershel. Pierre is always turning his phone off. So, let's see…Hershel is down by the river, and his signal looks pretty strong."

"Can you call him?"

"Sure." Benny dialed and waited. He sounded cheerful. "It's ringing. He waited and pursed his lips. "Still ringing."

Carlo and Benny both shared a look.

After a dozen rings, Benny lowered the phone. "No answer."

Carlo nodded. "Get Dag. We're not done for the night."

———

Louis Sypher looked up from his desk. It was Jennings, his assistant.

"Sir, you asked me to find a suitable gay person to do

undercover work. Well, I think I have the right one. Would you like to meet him?"

"Yes, certainly. But, first, what's his background?"

"Kevin Holbrook is an I.T. specialist working on a program to correlate several unique markers for susceptibility to uncommon diseases. He was a high school cheerleader and has a blog for gay men struggling to succeed in the business world. I have spoken to him, in general terms, about your request. He has qualms but is willing to consider it as long as we don't ask him to - as he put it – to prostitute himself."

"And he is one of us?"

"Yes, sir. He is a dedicated and dependable Lycan...just a little softer than the most." Jennings smiled. "He's very like-able. He just broke up after a lengthy relationship and is hesitantly considering getting back into what he calls 'the current dating scene.' I think he's a good candidate."

Sypher shrugged. "Okay, when can I meet him?"

"He's outside. I'll bring him in."

Kevin Holbrook was taller and more muscled than Sypher expected. He could have been a running back on his high school football team. His smile was genuine, his handshake a confident thrust. As Jennings said, "very likeable."

They sat, and Sypher went straight to the point. "There is an unhappy man who works in the office of the Madison chief of police. We know that he, and many others on the force, are involved in an effort to kill several of our operatives. To that end, they have recruited a small group of professional assassins from a Catholic order in Sicily. We need to know how deep this conspiracy goes. Does the mayor, or anyone else in government, approve of this murder-for-hire plan? We just don't know."

Kevin's eyebrows wrinkled. "Wow. So, how would I be able to help?"

"The unhappy man I spoke of is named Dumas. He patronizes a local pub called the Swan Dive near the river; goes there every night and orders one frozen daiquiri. If no one approaches him before he finishes the drink, he leaves. Otherwise, he meets people and socializes. He is apparently very selective in his relationships and, consequently, has few."

Sypher watched the expression on Holbrook's face and, seeing no disapproval, continued. "We would like you to befriend Mister Dumas and get to know him. Don't rush it, and don't be too aggressive, but do get him to talk about work. We need to know who our enemies are."

Holbrook sat back and blew out a stream of air. "Well, yes, I am perfectly willing to meet Mister Dumas and get to know him." After a breath, "I must admit I was afraid you were going to ask for much more than that."

Sypher sat back, and his leather chair squeaked. "I don't want you to do anything questionable, or uncomfortable. Just try to find an opening into the opaque world of the Madison Police Department."

Holbrook seemed thoughtful. "Okay, this little fishing expedition, could it be dangerous?"

"As far as we can determine, Dumas is not being specifically watched. Unless you raise some red flag, I don't think you have to worry about your safety. Dumas will certainly not share anything of his personal life with the Neanderthals he works for."

Holbrook sat back with a relaxed smile. "Neanderthals; that coming from a pioneer of genetic classification."

Sypher shrugged and made a little grin. "Just trying to be poetic."

———

Sunrise was a gray pall on the cloudless horizon. John was back at the power station ruin. The Lycan clan was gone. His duffel bag was gone. He sat on cold, damp concrete and realized that his eyes were tearing up. For the second time in as many days, he admonished himself. "Damn it. werewolves don't cry.

But he was only part werewolf, and he had just killed two people, people whom he knew were acting on strong belief, thinking what they were doing was right and honorable. But so was he. He was fighting for the survival of his kind. *Certainly, that was as noble as mindlessly following some religion that demanded blind obedience to medieval doctrine.*

Enough. He was too tired to think. John wandered into the damp woods, found a dry spot under low-hanging cedar branches. With his backpack for a pillow and two rifles cuddled like a security blanket he was asleep in seconds.

He woke to an unseasonably warm, sunny Wisconsin day. Birds celebrated Spring, and what sky John could see above the trees was a flawless blue. He stretched sore muscles and took a ritual pee. It seemed like a normal day. Except, of course, that he was being hunted like a rabid dog.

Okay, what's my plan? He was on his own. The Pures had left. He wasn't sure of his position, and he was afraid to use his phone, for fear of detection. So, without any real ideas, he began to walk and, as he walked, he opened his mind and tried to take in the sense of the ether around him.

He sensed the dog handlers. They were close, less than a mile. But they were tired and irritable, being harsh with the dogs. They too probably had little sleep in the dank forest.

He kept trying to relax, to sense more. He got no hint of the remaining monks. That seemed odd. But, then, there were only three left. He knew their names; Carlo and Dag and

Benny. *Would they have given up?* No. Never. They were the demon hunters. They would die first.

John made a little smile. Yes, they would *die first*. He would see to that. He felt the energy return, rolled his shoulders, and resisted the temptation to throw his head back and howl. No longer the prey. John Wagner was now the hunter.

———

Kevin Holbrook was waiting outside Mister Sypher's door when he returned from lunch. Sypher held the door open, and they sat. Kevin perched on the edge of his chair and seemed a little nervous, but eager to begin.

"That was much easier than I expected. I met Dumas last night. Just as you said, he was finishing his frozen daiquiri when I approached. We made small talk for bit. Turns out, he is a very decent guy, quite likeable, and totally out of place in the macho world of law enforcement."

Holbrook seemed intent. "I bought a couple of drinks and assured him I was new in town and just interested in a little company. We had a pleasant conversation, and I slipped in a question about the monks from Sicily I heard were working with the police."

Sypher was focused, elbows on his desk, eyes locked on Jennings.

"Dumas said there was a small group of high-ranking police officers they called the Catholic Mafia, who believed Church doctrine supersedes secular law. These 'Mafia' guys report directly to the chief when there is a conflict, and they seem to be protected from any internal, or external, pressure. Now, in Dumas' opinion, the mayor and the rest of city government is not actively involved, but they pretty much take a hands-off approach to policing the police."

"So, how reliable do you think the information is?"

"No idea at all. I spoke to the man for less than an hour. He seems stable and forthright, but I can't guess his motives, or even the accuracy of what he said. I do know this; he doesn't trust the chief. He wouldn't share details, but he thinks his chief is a little obsessive, and not a hundred percent rational."

"How about the monks?"

"I think he knows something, but he was reticent, and I didn't want to press him and blow my cover."

Sypher sat back and steepled his fingers. "So, do you intend to see him again?"

Holbrook shifted in his seat. "I don't know. Like I said, he's a very decent guy. I feel a little uneasy trying to create a phony relationship just to use him as a spy."

"The relationship would have to be phony?"

"Yes, I'm afraid so. We are very different people. I don't see any long-term promise to it. Eventually, he would find out what I am, and I don't think he could handle it. I see it as a dog and cat relationship. We could coexist comfortably, but that cat won't ever sleep in my doggie bed."

Sypher couldn't help but laugh. "Well, that's a colorful way to describe it."

Kevin Holbrook sat back and seemed strangely comfortable speaking to Sypher, a straight Lycanthrope. "No more colorful than your comment about the 'Neanderthals' he works for."

John closed his eyes, inhaled deep and, once again, felt the ether. There were men, many men, and they were fairly close. He tried to pick up thoughts but only got emotions. They were the ragged emotions of tired, frustrated seekers. And there was anger in their thoughts. That wasn't surprising since he had just killed their companions, Pierre and Hershel.

John focused on relaxing. He seemed to be more receptive when relaxed, but his own fatigue and the tension of the hunt made it difficult. He tried to hum, like a Tibetan monk meditating, or something. That didn't help. He was still only getting bits of sensory information. Then, like an electric jolt, he picked up a distinctly non-human vibe.

It was the dogs. They seemed charged up with adrenaline, or the dog equivalent. And they were coming for him. They had his scent, and they were furiously charging through the woods after him. Somehow, he knew that they were running free—no leashes, no handlers, no restraints; coming at him like the hounds of hell.

Trying to outrun them would be foolish. Shooting them would only focus the whole herd of men who hunted him. The monks, the police, the dog handlers; all of them would converge on the sound of gunfire. How to escape? He scanned the area: mature trees, little underbrush, bare dirt; no place to hide.

He could actually hear them now, close enough to hear them barking and howling. They were very close. John laid down his rifles and took a fighting stance. His jaw tightened, and he worked his fingers getting ready for action.

The dogs exploded out of the underbrush, shoulder-to-shoulder with furious, wide-eyed faces. Too many to fight at once. Without thinking, John squatted so deep that his butt touched his heels and then, made a heroic leap high over the charging pack. It had to be twenty feet high, amazing even to him.

The dogs stopped in mid-stride to watch him sail overhead. Their looks were confused - or maybe impressed. Either way, all aggression seemed to evaporate as they watched the human pass above them. But, in his panic, John hadn't considered the trees. He crashed through layers of limbs and was bashed and slammed and whacked by one branch after another.

Finally, he came to a stop wedged in the branch of a good-sized limb that swayed back and forth. It was a regular amusement park ride.

The dogs below sat with faces turned up, looking both confused and fascinated. Every dog nose pointed at the exact same angle. Every eye followed intently on John as he swayed in the tree.

For long minutes the standoff continued, John gently moving back and forth in the wind and the dogs sitting patiently; their heads perfectly synchronized with the movement of his swaying branch.

How long could that go on? John was gaming out his options when a shrill whistle alerted the dogs. In an instant, they were gone. John wiggled his way free and hung for a moment before letting go and bracing for the impact of a ten-foot drop. He handled it well, landing with a roll.

After a quick inventory, he decided that nothing was broken. Then, he gathered his guns and backpack and headed toward higher ground. He had no real reason to climb, but it always seemed better to go high.

The trees on the hill were all massive evergreens that shaded the forest floor, a deep mat of fallen needles that softened noises and cushioned his steps. The lack of undergrowth meant little concealment. He picked up his pace, even though he had no destination. Desperately, he concentrated, trying to figure his position, direction, maybe even a plan.

But he was neglecting his Lycan senses. Suddenly his mind flooded with overwhelming sensations. The dogs were back. He turned to face them. Now there were six. Not bloodhounds, these looked like German Shepherds, similar to wolves.

No shelter, no place to run, John made a thunderous yell, dropped his baggage, and braced himself for the fight. They were on him in a flash. He swung, smacked one so hard he heard its ribs break. He was being bitten all over but had no time to bother with that. He grabbed an attacking dog in each hand and spun with all his might to hurl them high and far.

The other three hesitated. He came at them, swinging, yelling, and grabbing two more by the neck. Again, he spun and tossed them. One struck a tree and fell to the ground where it lay still, probably dead.

The last dog chose discretion and trotted off with tucked tail and quick looks back.

John was breathing hard, sweating slightly, and bleeding from bites on his legs, arms, and torso, but he could still walk. Using one rifle as a crutch, he set off in the opposite direction from the one the dogs came from.

But still, he had no destination, or plan.

The Silver Bullet

Kevin Holbrook rushed by the secretary and knocked on his boss's open door.

Lou Sypher looked up with a wrinkled forehead.

Kevin closed the door behind him.

"I just got a call from Henry Dumas. He is really concerned that his boss, Chief of Police Mitchell, is becoming completely unhinged. They are in the third day of the manhunt in the woods north of town. Dumas doesn't know any solid details, but he thinks it's a witch hunt, *for real witches*. He did not mention, or even suggest, any hint of werewolves. Still, he's convinced they think they're dealing with something supernatural."

Sypher leaned back. "Okay. That's not a huge surprise."

"The interesting thing is that they have withheld all this information, the manhunt, the dead policeman, even the inclusion of some crazy Italian monks. I have no idea how the hell the Italians are involved. Chief Mitchell has not told the mayor or anyone on the council what's going on. He is dealing directly with Bishop Helsing, even getting manpower to support his search operation from church members, particularly dog handlers."

Sypher said nothing but he put his pen down and his eyes were intent.

"Now," Kevin Holbrook went on, "They are having silver bullets cast, and they have asked the bishop to bless these bullets."

Sypher's mouth gaped and he leaned forward. "Are you serious, silver bullets? What is this, the fifteenth century?" He shook his head. "Next, they'll break out wolf bane and wooden stakes."

Holbrook held back and seemed to choose his words. "Boss, I may be out of line here but, if these clowns are truly wrapped up in all that medieval stuff, they might be less rational and more unpredictable than you expect. Dumas thinks his chief has gone completely - to use his term - whacko."

Sypher steepled his fingers as Holbrook went on. "The chief has been railing about evil permeating Madison. He thinks the local 'Freedom from Religion' group is in league with demons. He has undercover cops trying to infiltrate Wiccan groups, Democratic politicians' offices, and even the Unitarian Church. He just seems obsessed with imposing Catholic doctrine and suspects anyone who opposes him as being a *Servant of Satan.*"

Sypher stared for a long time. "And, yet, he has deep support both within the police force and the community. We must make sure he doesn't get to parade around a Lycan body to support his Holy Crusade."

Holbrook grimaced. "You know, they already have the body of Vladimir Petrov."

"Yes, but I don't think they're smart enough to capitalize

on that. We here in Digital Nation have already told them Petrov's DNA is not remarkable."

Holbrook was silent for a long time. "But, if they discover that the body actually *is* Lycan, that could cast suspicion back on us."

Sypher seemed to be having an internal conversation, deep in thought, nodding to himself, silently mouthing words. Finally, he turned back. "Get hold of the mole Dumas and have him see if Chief Mitchell has any other weird ideas that could be used to discredit him. We need to become more active, not just to rescue John Wagner and avenge Vladimir Petrov, but to protect all the rest of us from these fanatics. Let's make them look impotent, and foolish."

"Yes, sir." Kevin Holbrook's voice was resolute, almost military, as though preparing for war.

———

Vrykolas was placed in charge of dampening Chief Mitchell's enthusiasm. He summoned the Stumpf brothers, Ben and Bart, and prepared to brief them in his office. Before speaking, he paused and looked them over.

Sypher often spoke of the Lycan genetic presence in Sapiens as a percentage. Everyone involved in the genetics analysis knew that wasn't really accurate and still, it was an effective way to classify members of the group. By that standard, the Stumpf brothers were about as pure as any who could pass as normal in the greater Sapiens society.

Ben and Bart Stumpf both had thick black hair and eyebrows. Their dark eyes set deep in faces that seemed to project a little too far forward. They were muscular and tough looking, just the type you might want as enforcers.

Vrykolas began. "Here are the pictures of Police Chief

Mitchell and his family. Also, in the folder are addresses, phone numbers and general information about his friends, his family and his church associates." He paused to let the two review.

Ben was the one who spoke. "Okay, we will have no trouble finding them. So, what is our objective?"

Vrykolas, the hairy old man, sat back and made a shrug. "We want them to be aware that injury to us will result in a backlash. That is your role: to scare the pants off all of them. You have the experience to avoid being caught. So, do *not* get caught, but still do things that leave no doubt the Mitchells are not safe. No real serious injuries mind you. We just want them convinced that terrible things are possible if they continue to harass us."

Bart pondered with a bobbing head. "No *real* serious injuries you say? How significant do you want the injuries should be?"

"Well, circumstances alter cases. I expect you to use judgement. The more resistive they are, the more forceful you must be. We must implant fear and destroy any sense of security. I know you, and I trust you. Make them tremble. Scare the shit out of them."

Ben, the quiet one spoke. "Do not be concerned, sir. After our visit, the police chief's family will never again sleep in peace."

Vrykolas made a quick nod and slammed his fist on the desk.

The other two slammed theirs even harder.

"Let it be done," said the old man.

————

John half-slid, half-tumbled down the slippery bank of a fast-flowing stream. The pain of his wounds was wearing him down. But he kept moving, dragging one stiff leg, bleeding from all the dog bites, groaning with every step.

The water would, once again, mask his scent and, perhaps, slow down the dogs and their handlers. At least, that was his hope. He knew that he could not keep going forever on his damaged body. He felt weakness creeping over him like a fast-moving rash. It moved from his calves to his thighs and then into his arms and back and neck. He had to rest.

But, first, he had to cross the stream. Spring rains made it a surging white-water rapid. *Would he have the strength to fight such a current?* Only one way to find out. He planted his left foot into the icy flow. A chill shot up his leg all the way into his brain. He was panting now, shivering and unsteady. He took a long stride and thrust his right foot out into the torrent.

Instantly swept off his feet, John floundered and splashed with flailing arms as he was carried along, bobbing and bumping against rocks. He tumbled, alternately submerged or surging up and almost out of the flow. He saw swirling, flashing colors as the current plunged him alternately in and out of water. There was blue sky, then gray-brown cloudy water, then white foam before momentarily glimpsing fast-moving green trees. It went on and on. With every turn that brought his face above the flow, he desperately sucked in all the air his lungs would hold.

Then, the stream made a sharp bend and spit him up onto a beach of pebbles and smooth stones. Gasping and barely able to control his hands and arms, he lay freezing, soaked, and shivering uncontrollably. His only comfort was knowing the dogs could not possibly follow him to…wherever he was.

He stood on unsteady legs and fought to control his breathing. That was a challenge. All energy seemed to be used up by the shivers that racked his body. But he persevered, straightening to stand and put one foot before another. His hands were cramped, useless balls gnarled up by the cold. His boots made slurping sounds with every step and his breath looked like he was sending smoke signals, maybe even Morse Code. Long shuddering exhalations were followed by a series of puffs. Di-di-dit; dah-dah-dah; dit-dit-dit. *SOS, someone save me.*

He picked up the bag that has washed up alongside and plodded off without direction. He had to keep moving. Moving generated body heat. He didn't even look ahead to see where he was going. *Just go; keep moving. Moving is life. Pause and you freeze to death.*

Time meant nothing. His surroundings meant nothing. He limped, hunched and shivering and making desperate little noises in his chest. And, then, the sunlight broke through. For a moment, he was blinded, but then the wonderful warmth on his face made him sigh and lift his chin to bask in the wonderful, warming light.

Slowly he was able to focus. Before him a farmer's field spanned his entire field of view. *Civilization - perhaps help.* He stiffened and stood almost upright. With renewed energy, he began to tromp across frost-covered plow furrows. His boots were still soaked, but the sogginess was being warmed by his skin. It was bearable. No sign of people or buildings. He plodded with the sun on his face. That sun made his clothing steam.

He followed a dirt road for what seemed like a full hour before he saw a building. It wasn't much of a building, but it was something. An abandoned farmhouse, its windows were mostly broken, and the wood siding was in a state of rot, but the roof was intact. Inside, a massive stone fireplace offered hope of warmth.

He hobbled around gathering armfuls of branches and small pieces of wood. A shed behind the building still had rusted tools hanging on pegs. From it, he took an axe and file.

Back before the fireplace, he snapped the driest branches into twigs and struck the file against the axe to make sparks that soon produced a crackling fire.

John lay on the bare floor and let the warmth flood over him. He was going to live. He was going to dry out and survive.

———

It was broad daylight, but the sky was gray with lingering light rain. It seemed quite normal that two men would be wearing hats and clutching their overcoat collars against the wind so that it was impossible to see their faces.

They split up. One went around behind the neat, very middle-class suburban home. The yard was well-kept with daffodils and crocus just beginning to open. Bart was careful as he rounded the side of the house. He saw no one in the windows. The eight-foot-high wood privacy fence had a padlocked gate. That didn't slow the dark-suited man a bit.

He drew a large pair of bolt-cutters from under his overcoat and snipped the latch free from its chain. Then, he eased the gate open and was confronted by a drooling, barking dog, a Boxer that alternately charged and then backed up to wag its stub of a tail.

Bart squatted and made little clucking noises as he spoke to the slobbering guard dog. "Here, boy. Come here and see the treat I have for you. Oh, nice boy. Come see."

The dog was unsure. It glanced nervously toward the house and back. But it also smelled the meat Bart held out; fresh meat, still bloody from the butcher shop.

The dog took one faltering step after another, hesitating, backing up, then coming closer. Eventually, it was near enough to snatch a chunk of red meat and retreat.

Bart was patient. He dangled the remaining strip of meat and waited.

In the meantime, Ben stepped up onto the front porch and rang the doorbell. He shoved his hands deep in the pockets of his long black overcoat after snugging down his hat. With his upturned collar, he looked very much like a detective in an old black and white movie.

Mrs. Mitchell cracked open the door but left the chain on.

Ben rocked from foot to foot and made clouds of steamy breath. "Ma'am," he said with a muffled voice. "I just wanted to let you to know your security camera has been damaged."

She removed the chain and opened the door just enough to look up at the camera over the door. Its wires dangled, ripped loose from the camera.

"Oh, my goodness," she placed her fingertips to her lips. "Who on earth would have done such a thing?"

Ben placed his foot in the door and grinned. "Oh, I did, ma'am. Just wanted you to know that now, no one can see anything that goes on…"

She tried to slam the door, but Ben put his shoulder against it and shoved hard. She made an anguished cry, fell back onto the floor and held the back of her hand against her mouth.

He smiled at her, but it was a frightening smile that did not involve his eyes. "Now, you have a panic button around your neck. Do not use it. You see, if you cooperate, no one will get hurt. If you go all Wonder Woman superhero… Well, then I'll kill you… And, after that, I'll find your daughter at Sacred Heart College, and I'll kill her. Your son will be fine. At the rate he's using drugs, he'll die on his own within the year. So, you see, all you have to do is cooperate, and nobody gets killed." He thought for a second. "Except, of course, your dog."

At that very second, the mournful wails of her Boxer

guard dog turned to panicked shrieking. Ben reached and yanked the pendant that held her panic button. The chain bit into her neck before it broke.

"There. Now we can both relax and speak freely. You see, we need your help. Your husband is being a complete ass, and we need you to have a heart-to-heart conversation that lets him know the effect of his continuing 'demon hunt.' If he doesn't relent, we will kill everyone you have ever loved, or even cared about. Every…single…one."

She was shaking now, clutching her arms tight and looking away.

Ben grinned wide to show off his canine teeth. "You see, we aren't demons, but we are killers, and we can take out anyone at any time. If your husband doesn't relent, you'll be the first to die, but we'll keep on. And don't think for a minute he can stop us. We'll let him live while we pick off one after another of all the people in his life. But we'll never kill him. We want him to die of old age and regret that he ever lived."

Bart came through the back door carrying the limp dog body. Its legs dangled in unnatural angles. Its tongue hung out the side of its mouth, and its blank eyes stared into emptiness. "Ma'am, where should I put the dog?"

She was shaking too badly to answer.

Ben smiled politely and said, "The dining room table will be fine." He turned back to the woman, still sitting on the floor. "We'll be leaving now. You'll try to call your husband, of course. But that won't work. Your landline, even the hard-wired connection to his command post has been cut. We'll take your cell phone, and we'll damage your modem, so no Wi-Fi. You'll be all alone. You can't call anybody. Of course, you could try a neighbor, if you want to put them in mortal danger but, if I were you, I'd just sit tight until daddy gets home."

He looked around. "Well, I guess that's it. Nice meeting you."

The brothers walked out as Mrs. Mitchell's sobbing became uncontrollable. She still knelt on the floor weaving back and forth, clutching herself and gasping for breath.

Ben shrugged and turned to Bart. "I think she took it pretty well, considering the circumstances."

Bart raised his eyebrows. "Yep, she'll be okay. She's a trooper."

Both laughed.

The Chief's Problem

The police car radio blared an unusual announcement. "Uh, Bailey in car forty-five, call dispatch on the secure line."

Sergeant Bailey, who was riding right seat answered, "Okay, roger."

The driver looked at him. "What do you suppose that's about?"

Bailey shrugged and used his personal cell. "Dispatch, this is Sergeant Bailey riding shotgun with a new officer. I have been directed to call…"

He sat back and listened intently before responding. "Roger. I understand. No sirens, nothing to alert the neighbors. Yes, sir, we'll report arriving. Car forty-five out."

The patrol car driver gave a questioning look, and Bailey shrugged. "Well, this is interesting. A neighbor reported hearing loud screams and crying from the house next door. That's Chief Mitchell's house so, we're going to investigate. Now, be on your toes. Everything we do or say could get back to the chief. We'll go low key; no siren, no hero stuff, just casual business-as-usual cops visiting the boss's house."

They pulled up and a woman ran out of a nearby house to meet them. "I'm Emily Johnson. I live there next to the Mitchells. About an hour ago, I started hearing a commotion. The dog, their hateful slobbering dog, started barking, like there was an intruder, or something. I didn't think much of it. That animal is always such a nuisance. But then I heard crying, it sounded like crying, anyway. I didn't pay much attention, but it kept on, so I went to the door and knocked. Nobody answered, but I still heard the crying from inside, so I called you. I hope that was the right thing…"

Bailey put on his caring professional face. "Yes, ma'am, you did exactly the right thing. We'll take it from here…and thank you for being a good citizen."

The neighbor glanced around nervously before retreating.

Bailey went to the Mitchell home door and knocked with authority, a cop's "open-up" knock.

No response.

The driver, a new cop in training, pointed up at the damaged security camera.

Bailey tried the knob, and the door opened. Immediately, he heard the sobbing; breathless exhausted sobbing, like a disaster survivor. He turned to the new guy and spoke quietly, not quite a whisper.

"Take out your weapon and have it ready, but not in sight. Be alert. We're going in."

The entryway showed no sign of trouble but, now, they heard the woman's cries more clearly. Two steps and Bailey blurted, "Jesus Christ, what happened here? Who killed your dog? Are you okay? What did they do to you?"

Mrs. Mitchell looked up. Her face was pale and streaked

with dried tears. Her voice was shaky but calmer now. "They said…they said they would kill our whole family. They said this was just a warning."

"Did you know them, know who they were?"

She shook her head. "No, I only know they asked me to tell my husband, the chief, that he must stop the 'demon hunt,' or they would kill us all, everyone in our family."

The two policemen helped her stand. She was weak after kneeling on the floor for so long. The younger officer brought her a glass of water, and she made a timid, but appreciative, smile.

When she appeared a little calmer and more settled, Bailey stepped into the hall and called on his private phone. "Yes, hello. I need to speak directly to Chief Mitchell, no one else… and do not monitor the call. This is urgent and absolutely 'close-hold.' Yes, I'll wait."

Sergeant Bailey took a deep breath and planned the words he would use. One thing was sure; after this conversation, all hell would break loose.

———

Father Antonio was breathing hard. "I have just learned of the attack on your wife. Does she know how many creatures were involved?"

Antonio was silent as he pressed the corded phone to his ear and frowned. "But does she know how many?" Again, the priest endured a long explanation with silent tight-lipped nods. "I see, just the two and they appeared as normal men, yes? Did she give a good description?"

He looked into the distance, perhaps hoping to find clarity, or truth…or something. He repeated, "Thick dark hair and eyebrows, muscular, with big jaws; they sound very similar to the two on videotape at the motel, the two who killed my man. Could be the same two…or, it could be we are dealing with a family, or a pack? I have heard that wolves are intensely connected to their pack. If these are werewolves, as we suspect, could this be their 'normal' appearance before they change in the full moon?"

The priest continued to pace and gesture as he stretched the phone cord to its limit. "I see. You are now thinking they undergo only a partial change and do not completely become true werewolves. Then, perhaps, we are seeking the wrong kind of monster. If they kill while appearing to be almost normal men, they will be more difficult to track…"

They talked for another half-hour before ending the call. Then, Antonio called Carlo, who was still out in the woods.

"Yes, Monsignor."

"I have just spoken to the Police Chief Mitchell. He is expanding his search. His wife was threatened by men who look very much like the two you fought. We may not be hunting traditional werewolves at all. The descriptions being drawn up by police sketch artists will be distributed soon.

"In the meantime, expand your target description to anyone with thick dark hair, big muscles, and a long face, like a monkey. The chief will have the DNA of the one dead creature reexamined with a much more, *what is his word*, expansive filter. Yes, I think that's right."

They spoke for another ten minutes until Antonio felt that he was current on Carlo's demon hunt. Finally, he closed with a simple, "*Dio sia con voi*, God be with you."

After hanging up father Antonio stared. Then, he spoke aloud and with conviction, "We are the hunters, but they have the advantage. They can lie in wait. We must lure them into the open, into our gunsights." He sat back and smiled at the prospect.

———

John wasn't doing so well. Most of his bite wounds were beginning to scab over, but two were still swollen and oozing. Infection, he thought. What could he use against infection? There were many cabinets in the derelict house but most labels on the bottles and cans had either dissolved in the dampness or simply faded. None were legible.

He tried twisting off caps or puncturing cans to sniff the contents. No use. *Perhaps in the tool shed.* He limped outside, still toting both rifles, and a bag of other weaponry, although the bag was lighter now after losing much in his slalom ride down the rain-swollen rapids.

The shed held paint cans of rock-hard, dry pigments. But there was also a rusty can of turpentine. Would that work? What did he have to lose? He poked a hole with an old screwdriver and braced himself.

Now John Wagner had always thought of himself as a brave man, a former football player, and tough bar fighter. But the first trickle of solvent onto an open wound made him scream like a woman in labor. He bent over, shaking and gasping air.

"Okay, one down, four to go." Methodically, he drenched his pants legs and his torn gut with the vile fluid. "God, I hope this is worth it," he huffed and trembled in pain. It took several minutes before he was able to stand; several more minutes before he was brave enough to put his full weight on his damaged legs. The smell of blood and torn flesh mixed with harsh solvent would have made an undertaker gag. But John overcame the revolting smell, the fierce burning of his wounds, and the fatigue of the chase. He had to.

It was time to move. Staying in one place for too long was suicide. At least, he thought moving would be the safer option. Lugging his gear, he began a leg-dragging struggle back into the woods. Thankfully, the rain was gone. Sunshine warmed his shoulders and neck. Exposed ground was still slippery mud, but grassy areas were drying out.

He was barely into the tree-line when he saw a military-style vehicle splashing along the puddled road. The letters *"MPD"* were painted on its sides. John settled behind bushes and watched. The men deploying from the vehicle looked like a SWAT team in camouflaged body armor, military helmets, and all manner of small items strapped to their bodies. But, thank goodness, they had no dogs who would have immediately picked up his scent.

The police scurried around, looking confused, or maybe just a little panicky. He watched the flak-vested, helmeted warriors walking patterns around the building, yelling and pointing. He only hoped they ignored the fresh marks made by his dragging leg. He stretched out to a prone position and rested one rifle on a branch as he snuggled a cheek against the stock. He really did not want to hurt these guys, but if it became a matter of them or...*well, he'd just have to see how it played out.*

Through the telescopic sight, he could see their faces but could not hear them, or even read lips. They looked serious, pointing and pacing, searching the grounds and probably discussing just how they would corner and then kill the demon.

John Wagner was determined. He would not die easily.

———

Humpty may not have been able to speak like the humans, but he was acutely attuned to the emotional vibrations of their minds and bodies. He and his clan had been feeling hints of police and demon hunter movements for almost an hour. He sensed the danger and knew it was focused around their new mixed-blood friend, John.

The Lycan tribe had followed their senses for hours, trying to catch up and help John. When they left him back at Betty Mae's house, they expected the approaching humans would treat him with kindness, but that was not the case. Dogs had come after him, yelping, and snarling. Men with guns had scanned the forest.

Humpty and the rest of the group sensed the danger, but then they were well into the woods, too far away to help John even though they were aware of the armed Sapiens closing in on him.

Now the clan gathered in the dark shade of a wooded hill and peered down from their vantage point. Humpty stood tall, sniffed the forest air, and felt the vibrations. The uniformed police, the dog handlers, and the small group of foreigners below were all hostile. He and the others of his clan watched with cautious curiosity as the SWAT team hustled and shouted in a flurry of seemingly pointless actions, running around, piling wood into makeshift barricades, and setting up defensive positions.

Humpty knelt behind a tangle of branches and let the ether flow over him, filling his senses. John, his wounded friend, was close. He sensed that John was injured and needed help, but he also knew how deadly the humans' weapons could be.

Carefully, softly, he and the other males wove their way through brush and trees inching closer to the SWAT team.

Like stalking wolves, they moved in stages, ghostly vapors passing through the dense vegetation.

In the clearing ahead, the police seemed to have abandoned building barriers. Perhaps they were making other plans. They seemed on high alert, as though anticipating an attack.

Honey was the first to sense John's location. He closed his eyes and concentrated hard. The others soon picked up his thoughts and followed them until they could almost smell the noxious mix of turpentine, blood, and sweat. They found John, lying prone under an umbrella of bushes, with his rifle still aimed toward the house.

When Honey reached out and touched his leg John recoiled by reflex and tried to jerk his rifle around. It took a second for him to recognize the smiling young Lycan hovering over him. John was confused and too breathless to speak. But speaking wasn't important. Honey and the others actually understood very little of his spoken English. But the Lycans clearly understood his emotional vibes and Honey tried to project a thought to him, *It's okay, I am a friend.*

For a moment, John seemed confused, and disoriented. Then, Hefty appeared out of the bushes and slapped a rough hand on John's shoulder.

Nurse crowded close behind and used a gentler touch to stroke his cheek and make cooing sounds.

As they hovered over him, John began to cry softly, but every sob brought another wave of racking pain. He put an arm over Nurse's shoulder and drew her close.

Honey snorted displeasure.

Humpty, meanwhile, had returned to watching the SWAT police. One was shouting. The others looked in the direction their leader pointed, probably giving directions.

The big Lycan hunched and stroked his soft facial hair as

he watched. After a minute, he turned to Nurse and made a series of hoots.

She seemed to understand.

Nurse and the other female helped John stand. Each of them took an arm over their shoulders to take some of the weight off his battered legs. They began to walk him back into the forest. John protested, but they ignored him.

The Real Lycans

The sun was now directly overhead, minimizing shadows. Ordinarily, the Lycans would have used shade for concealment.

Humpty scanned through branches and trees but could barely see the abandoned farmhouse and the surrounding grassy area. He needed a better view, so he stepped back, squatted deep, and then exploded skyward in an incredible leap that took him well above the trees and brush. At his highest point, he hung for a moment, like someone at the top of a trampoline bounce. That moment was enough.

The leap had been elegant and athletic. The landing was not. He hit with a thud and rolled before standing to shake it off. But that quick glimpse was worth the effort. What he saw was a wide field of tall grass that he and his two male companions would first have to cross if they were going to attack this gang of Sapiens. They would be exposed and vulnerable over a wide distance. But he saw no option. The men at the house were a threat. He had seen what they did to John, one of their own kind - well, almost one of their own kind.

Humpty sat back and cleared his mind to take in the flow of images. His Lycan sense was not precise. It was a fuzzy, often indistinct awareness, sometimes images, other times just emotions. It was a sense shared by almost all living things, to some to a small degree. But, for the Lycans, it took a much more vivid form that allowed premonitions, imprecise feelings of impending events. It was a semi-reliable warning system of things to come.

His awareness even included some of the humans' thoughts and feelings. He felt the SWAT men's anxiety. He knew they had completed reconnaissance of the house, which included kicking in doors, going room to room and shouting, lots of shouting. Now they gathered on the front porch for a tense meeting.

The SWAT team must have seen Humpty make his great leap, but it didn't seem to register. To them, he probably looked like a dark form that appeared for a few seconds in the treetops and was gone - confusing, but not unsettling. They certainly didn't react to the airborne entity as a living creature. After all, what animal was capable of such a feat?

Humpty's thoughts were interrupted by the other two males, Honey and No Name. Both joined his thought stream and instantly understood the plan. It would be like circling and killing deer. They were ready, resolute and fearless. Their warrior blood was surging, and their bodies tightening. They would go in with fury.

The three moved silently on all fours. Humpty led. Honey was several yards to his left, and No Name to the right, as they went slinking into the grass. As they neared the house, they began to move faster until in a near-gallop. Their calloused knuckles were well-adapted to act like front legs, but only for short bursts of speed. In addition, the four-legged, dog-like profile made it easier to move undetected through tall grass.

As they drew closer, they heard the SWAT leader yelling. His other team members were barking responses to their Alpha leader, their attention focused on him, not on the open field. Then, they shouted in unison, a team shout, like the breakup of a football huddle.

Humpty concentrated hard on the humans' vibes. They were preparing for something, some kind of action. Whatever it was, it made their hearts race and their breathing quicken. They were intent, ready for action, but anxious.

Humpty was still on all fours, scrambling as fast as he could, barely able to see over the tall grass. He sensed an image of the SWAT men jumping off the front porch and spreading out into a loose circle around the house. They were still shouting back and forth, louder than necessary. Perhaps this was just pre-battle jitters and bravado. That was good. Distraction made them less likely to hear the Lycan's approach.

It took less than a minute for the SWAT policemen to move into positions evenly spaced around the house, one every thirty feet or so. That would give them excellent overlapping fields of vision, but it would also limit their ability to concentrate fire.

Mistake, Humpty thought. Between grunts of exertion, he hooted softly to Honey and No Name.

The two males acknowledged their clan leader with confident, aggressive growls, but subdued volume. The physical demands of the run limited their sensitivity to extra-sensory communication.

The big Lycan barreled along feeling his companions' energy, trying to see into their souls. What he sensed made him confident. They could be counted on. They would obey. He stopped running and rose, head and shoulders above the grass. He looked first at Honey and then at No Name. They intuitively understood, nodded and then took off, moving into position.

The cops still stood spaced far apart. They scanned constantly, rifles before them, but they were concentrating close in and did not notice the three Lycans moving stealthily around the tall grass perimeter.

The SWAT men were sweating, nervous, and jumpy. That made Humpty smile. A little bit of fear was good in an opponent. It made them prone to overreact.

Now it was time. Humpty rose out of the grass stood to his full height, spread his arms, and bellowed long and deep.

The three humans around the front of the house saw him and froze for a moment to process what they were looking at. They expected a human-looking entity, not a hairy monster.

But Humpty didn't hesitate. After that single shout, he ducked back down and scrambled away.

Frantic, the cop leader shouldered his rifle and panned the tall grass where, just an instant before there had been a creature. The leader's face was pale, and his hands unsteady as he jerked his gun left, then right. He heard nothing: no sound, no motion, no chirping bird or waft of breeze. The sunbaked air was dead.

Humpty crouched motionless in the grass and heard the two closest policemen come at a run. He sensed that the two behind the house had heard a commotion but would probably be momentarily unsure what to do. They would eventually make a decision to head around front, but they were hyper-vigilant and would come slowly, carefully. Humpty thought they were brave men. He had to respect that, but he would still kill them.

Just as the two rear guards were about to round the house corner, Honey and No Name bounded out of the grass, leaping high to hover for a second at the top of their arcs before pouncing, smothering the two policemen in their ripping grasp. The men each got off one shot but, with no time to aim, their bullets went wild.

That struggle was brief. Honey grabbed one man's head, yanked and twisted until he heard the spine crack. No Name bit the other man in the throat, tearing away a fist-sized chunk of flesh. Blood spurted like a fountain. Those two cops were out of the game for good.

The two young male Lycans stood, panting over the bodies, relishing the victorious moment. Blood still trickled down No Name's chin. That part of the fight over, they disappeared back into the grass.

Once safely concealed, Honey and No Name moved with exaggerated stealthy steps until close enough to peek out and see the remaining three policemen now gathered shoulder-to-shoulder in front of the house, each looking in a different direction. The men were breathing hard, mumbling incoherent Sapiens talk.

The SWAT leader was still shouting directions, but his confidence seemed to have faded. He pointed first one way, then the other. Did he know that two of his men were down?

His two remaining cops moved closer to stand almost back-to-back with him. Their conversation was clipped and high-pitched. They were brave - but scared.

Humpty again rose up out of the nearby grass and stood still as statue for a long, tense moment. The policemen froze until their leader whispered the words, "Okay, boys, no fast moves. Just ease your guns into position and let these mother…" He was just starting to aim when Humpty leaped, high and fast, coming at them like a freight train. The Lycan's move was so quick it overwhelmed the leader, deflecting his rifle and knocking him flat on the ground.

The actual act of killing was pure instinct. Humpty simply

grabbed the man by the throat and squeezed hard enough that his fingers sank in up to the first joint. He thrashed the SWAT leader's head left and right. The man's body flailed like a limp rag doll, mouth gaping, arms dangling.

The other two SWAT men jumped back, momentarily in shock. It was a full second before they were collected enough to aim. Focused on Humpty, they were completely unprepared for the two Lycans that came crashing down onto them. Both humans were dead in seconds, body parts broken and ripped apart. One man's head rolled a good ten feet across the grass leaving a trail of stringy wet flesh. The other flopped around on the ground like fresh-caught fish on a dock. The thrashing slowed to twitching, and then…nothing.

The fight was over.

The three male Lycans walked from policeman to policeman, sniffing each and poking their lifeless bodies.

Humpty made a low rumbling sound that seemed sad, almost remorseful at the killings.

Honey snorted as if saying, "Job well done."

Then they all jogged away on two legs to rejoin John and the females.

———

"Chief, we have a report from the field."

"Yeah, what is it, Dumb Ass?"

Henry Dumas clenched his jaw but went on. "Well first, about your home invasion, we have now temporarily moved your wife in the Camden Suites hotel. She's on the fifteenth floor with a twenty-four-hour guard detail in the hall. Forensics is going over your house." Dumas hesitated before delivering the bad news. "But sir, I must report that our SWAT personnel…ran into trouble. They're all dead."

"What? All dead? How? Where?"

"All five highly-trained special weapons and tactics officers were killed…brutally killed. The attack must have been so sudden they only got off a couple of shots. The location is an abandoned building, approximately six miles east of the woods, where that one fugitive was injured by dogs."

The chief deflated. "Five dead? Few shots?"

"Yes, sir, we have some body-camera video. I haven't looked at it yet, but I can run it for you."

Chief Mitchell nodded, speechless for once.

Henry Dumas inserted a thumb drive and hit a few keys. The attack footage lasted a minute and forty seconds. Five men down in less than two minutes.

The chief sat silent and focused. When the image of Humpty lunging right at the team leader's body camera flashed onto the screen, the chief jumped back, knocking over his office chair and gasping. He stood still for a long time, almost a full minute, after it was over. When he did speak, his voice was raspy as though having trouble getting enough air.

"Jesus H. Christ, did you see those things, those monsters? Furry, dark, fangs like a damned lion, or something. If I ever doubted that we were actually dealing with demons, that's over. These creatures must be exterminated, wiped off this earthly plane, banished back to hell."

Henry Dumas stood quietly before he turned off the monitor and removed the thumb drive.

The chief sat back down, put his face in shaking hands and sagged. "They died valiantly." He sounded as though trying to find some honor, some sense in the deaths of his people. Or maybe, it was just shock, like battle fatigue, or PTSD.

As Dumas left, he heard the chief mumble, "Have to tell the mayor. What to say? How can I spin this? Five fallen heroes; monsters on the loose; dark forces at play? What will sell before the city council?"

Henry stopped in the doorway and looked back as his boss slumped in his fancy office chair. He was looking out into space with an open mouth blank expression. As much as he disliked the man, Henry felt sorry for the chief.

Henry Dumas went back to his small desk and dialed Kevin Holbrook's number at Digital Nation. As it rang, Henry scanned to see who might be within earshot. There was no one. Then, he covered his mouthpiece and whispered, "SWAT team, five men dead south of Livorno. I'll send video. Expect a request for new DNA analysis. Keep this strictly close hold."

Henry Dumas hung up and sat stiff and straight. *What was going to happen now?* The corner of his mouth twitched, just a hint of a smile.

———

John was regaining some of his strength. Almost a full day of walking with the two females had a healing effect on his body, and his morale. He wasn't as good at projecting thoughts as they were, but he was starting to get the hang of it.

He understood the females concern for their clan's males, and he understood their concern for him, poor weak human that they took him to be. He had to smile. He had always been the meanest, toughest hombre around, but these females saw him as a weakling, a soft, pampered sissy who slept in a bed in a heated apartment and ate food killed and processed by others.

But still they accepted him, felt protective of him, and overlooked his largely hairless skin and undeveloped musculature. Once nicknamed "Bone Crusher," he was, by their standards, just a wimp. Again, that made him smile.

They reached the rock overhang, not really a cave but a large covered space. There were seven individual mounds of grass that looked like beds. Old tables and chairs must have been stolen from Sapiens' houses, or maybe provided by Betty Mae. Strings of dried peppers and other vegetables hung from the overhead rock alongside skinned rabbit, deer, and coyote carcasses. There were clay pots and some assorted utensils.

This must be their base, their semi-permanent home. It was a good location, relatively well-protected from the elements. It had good visibility of the woodlands below. They could see any enemy approaching and then take one of several escape routes. Best of all. it was far from the Sapiens' population with their guns and vehicles. Here, in this safe place with his two companions, he could heal.

———

Louis Sypher had summoned Mister Vrykolas to review the video with him. They sat in a darkened room and watched the drama of the SWAT team being killed. The body camera footage was jumbled and chaotic, but it was enough to see physical details of the Lycans as they attacked.

Sypher took a deep breath. "Did you know about them? Did you know they were here?" Without waiting for a response, he said, "Now, how in the hell are they involved? This could be a catastrophe for our kind."

Vrykolas sat back and shrugged. "I do not really see this as having such a dramatic effect on us. We have known, for many years, that these more-or-less pure Lycans existed in the wild. Encounters are rare and, when they do occur, the press almost always refers to them as Sasquatch, or Bigfoot, sightings. Only occasionally are they called 'werewolves' or 'wolf-men'. Now, seeing the power and violence of these creatures." He hesitated. "I guess it is reasonable to call them *creatures*. Anyway, I don't see any way they can be associated with us."

Sypher interlocked his fingers on the desk. "Really? Well, I'll tell you how. Those Italian Killer Monks, those idiot Demon Hunters; they will link this animal attack with the killing of their man, Robert. They will say there are monsters walking among us, monsters just waiting to attack, to kill children, drink blood, or whatever stupid superstition they can sell. They will likely circulate pictures of John Wagner and say he is a werewolf who didn't fully change shape during the attack. They will make this a rallying cry spreading fear throughout the community and calling for vengeance."

Vrykolas waited until Sypher had calmed slightly. "I think you may be overreacting. If the monks' involvement is exposed, it will lead to many embarrassing questions: who asked them to come, who gave them the information to hunt us, who authorized them to use deadly force and who determined that these creatures were supernatural entities?"

Vrykolas sat back. "I don't think the Chief of Police Mitchell, or the local Bishop Helsing, are prepared to answer such questions without incriminating themselves. Remember, Petrov is dead. Wagner may also be dead, and *they authorized their killings*. If the police and the diocese make wild claims, they will very likely be forced to admit involvement."

Sypher looked pained but he nodded as though considering his options. "The Bigfoot angle, do you think it will sell?"

"Americans love their Bigfoot stories. To my knowledge, there has never been a substantiated claim of harm from these creatures, but I understand that Wisconsin has more reported sightings of hairy man-like creatures than almost any other state. I think this could even be a boon to the Chamber of Commerce drawing tourists and adventurers and who knows what else. It could be a defining local image, just like Paul

Bunyan and his blue ox, Babe. Perhaps, 'Wisconsin, Land of the Smiling Sasquatch'."

Sypher allowed a tiny laugh. "You certainly know your American legends."

Vrykolas shrugged. "If you are to swim far, you must learn the currents and go with them. I have tried to learn about this country and this state. I will never be accepted as a native, but I don't want many people to know just how different from them I truly am."

The Digital Nation CEO leaned back as though a little more comfortable. "The video, can we get it to news media?"

"Your man in the police department has already done so. He managed to get copies to several news agencies. It will be really interesting to see how the police and the Church respond. That will tell us much about what we must do and, quite frankly, I don't think we'll be very involved at all."

The Great Monster Hunt

Monsignor Antonio fumbled for the phone beneath his robe. When he finally managed to retrieve it and hit answer, he sounded frustrated and maybe a little angry. "Yes, hello, who is calling?"

"Reverend Father Antonio, this is Carlo."

"So, Carlo, have you found the man, the killer of Brother Robert?"

"No, Father, but I have some information about him. Do you remember the house where he was hiding? When we arrived, the house was empty, but we found some strange evidence."

"Strange evidence? How strange?"

"Well, the house deed shows the owners as Mister and Mrs. Goethe. They have not been seen for several years, but their daughter, Betty Mae Jones, has been living there. Her husband, Richard Jones, is wanted on narcotics charges and has gone on the run. Neither the Madison police, the Highway Patrol, County Sheriff, nor the contract dog handlers who inspected the site seem to have noticed the marijuana farm behind it. Maybe they have a reason not to see."

"Is that relevant to our problem?"

"Only so far as it shows that their search for Wagner has precedent over everything else that may be going on in the area."

"Precedent? Excuse me, I don't think I know…"

"It just means high priority, like *precedente* in Italian. If they are willing to ignore a major pot growing operation, they must be really desperate to catch Wagner."

"Ah, thank you, Carlo."

"Sir, there is more. The police found some samples of hair and footprints that are not human. I believe the demons, including the one called John Wagner, were actually hiding in that house. The dog handlers say they caught up with Wagner, and their dogs injured him severely, but he escaped. They also reported that the others with him were in werewolf form, not human like Wagner."

"I see. But how does that help us find him?"

Carlo hesitated before he answered. "Monsignor, I think the answer is the woman, Betty Mae Jones. We have her cell phone number, and we are trying to track her. She has her privacy settings…"

"Carlo, I do not know of such things. If you think this is the best plan, by all means, do what you need to do. But we must, at all costs, remember our purpose here, *uccidere le bestie*, kill the beasts."

"Yes, sir, I shall pursue the woman and try to make her lead us to them. *Dio sia con voi*."

"God be with you as well, my son."

———

He was just about to go on camera. Chief Mitchell was fuming. "Dumb Ass, get in here."

Henry Dumas took a deep breath and mumbled, *Here we go again.* He grabbed a notepad. There were always tasks to be listed. He marched into the Chief's office and stood. These days, he didn't feel quite as intimidated. In the back of his mind, he felt sure that Chief Mitchell's handling of the *Bigfoot Battle,* as it was being labeled in the media, would be a disaster.

"Dumb Ass, I tasked you with getting those DNA samples from the SWAT victims' bodies analyzed. What's taking so long? I need something to feed those reporters out there pacing, like damned hungry lions, just waiting outside my door. They want blood, my blood."

Dumas consulted his notepad. He didn't really have anything written there, but he thought it seemed more authoritative when he checked the notepad before speaking. "The lab says it will take 48-hours to process." He was making that up.

The chief took a deep breath, stood, and straightened his tie before marching to his office door. Another deep breath and he turned the handle to face the mob. Television, radio, and newspaper reporters and bloggers lined the hall, shouting, pushing, demanding answers.

Chief Mitchell forced a smile, thought better of it, put on his concerned face and stepped out into the midst of the surging hoard. The chief, normally combative and loud, seemed to shrink before the onslaught. He held up his hands in an almost apologetic way.

Then, with a roll of his shoulders, he stood tall, cleared his throat, and tried to look tough for the camera. It worked for a few sentences, but the reporters didn't care about his prepared statement. They began yelling over him, thrusting microphones at him. The chief's tough-guy attitude began to fade. Questions came flooding from all directions.

"Do you know exactly what these animals are?"

"We've got top men working the evidence even as we speak." His voice cracked slightly.

"Why was your SWAT team even out at the farm?"

"We had reports of criminal activity, possible Satanic rituals." The first bead of sweat appeared on his forehead.

"You sent a SWAT team to investigate possible devil worship? What were you afraid of?"

"The reports indicated human sacrifice might be involved." He coughed, and his face reddened slightly.

"Seriously, human sacrifice? Where did these reports come from? How did you confirm them?

"I cannot divulge confidential sources." That sounded good. He breathed easier. *At least one good answer.*

"So how does that relate to the Bigfoot killings? They don't seem to have anything to do…"

"It's a very odd case. Certainly, our boys were not prepared to face anything like the monsters they encountered. They were ambushed, eviscerated…but they died bravely, every man a hero." He was getting it together, sounding a little more statesman-like.

Dumas, back inside the office, listened to the interview on a local TV channel. He smiled openly. His boss wasn't going to come out of this looking even remotely competent. "Serves the bastard right," Henry Dumas said out loud, but still in a quiet voice.

———

In the office building of Digital Nation Corporation a few blocks away, a crowd had gathered in Mister Sypher's conference room to watch the televised interview. They were all intent, trying to read into the Police Chief's every word.

The head of the analysis branch entered with a stack of papers in his arms. "Boss, you need to see this."

Sypher held up a hand. "It can wait. I want to see this sideshow unfold."

"No, sir, it can't. This just might change everything."

Sypher walked over to stand eyeball-to-eyeball with the analyst. "All right, you have my attention. Make it fast, and make it good."

The analyst was not intimidated. "We have always talked about the existence of, more-or-less, pure Lycans. We expected them to be primitive, like wild animals. We expected them to have no, or, at least limited Sapiens' DNA. These samples obtained from the SWAT autopsies indicate the creatures involved in the attack are not Lycans with some Sapiens' DNA; they are Sapiens with some Lycan DNA."

Sypher scowled. "That makes no sense."

"I agree, sir, but the genetics are clear. They are basically humans who, at least thirty generations ago, bred with Lycans. They are anything but 'pure.' The basic Sapiens' DNA they display is archaic, similar to Clovis American Indian. The Lycan contribution is Asian Kurtadam, not European Lykan-thropis. In short, these are truly unique creatures and we can only guess at their attributes."

Sypher put his knuckles to his chin. "I don't see how this really changes anything."

"It just means we can't know what to expect from them. They're a whole different breed from our European Lycan-Sapiens mix. We have no basis for any estimate of their capabilities, or their intelligence."

Sypher stood and paced. "You also have samples from many local encounters with alleged 'wolf-men,' or "Sasquatch,' over the years. We have previously assumed they were just primitive 'Pure' Lycans. Isn't that true?"

"Yes, sir. That is true, but the samples are all very poor quality, usually obtained from the encounter site days after the event. The police don't usually allow access before that. By then, weather, the police, and swarms of curiosity-seekers have contaminated everything. Our DNA database of confirmed specimens in the wild is haphazard and spotty at best. Even worse, we can't validate any of it without access to living specimens."

Sypher shook his head and thought for minute. "Okay. Okay. Let's go back to the body-cam video and take a fresh look. Now that we know these creatures are unique, let's try to get a sense of them, figure out what we can about their physiology and intelligence. We need comparative measurements, so examine the range of their movements and behavior. Pay particular attention to their problem-solving ability. We need to know their capabilities."

Vrykolas, who had been quiet, scanned through a stack of papers and looked up. "We've already had people matching the body-camera timeline of events and specific actions. The SWAT attack appears carefully planned and executed. That suggests these Pures, or whatever you wish to call them, must be capable of complex planning and are well organized."

Someone at the far end of the conference table touched his earpiece and broke in, "Sir, I have just been notified of a cell phone intercept. We've been monitoring the Italian monks' conversations. They believe these Pures are protecting John Wagner. The monks think the SWAT team was killed specifically to protect him."

Someone who had been watching at the conference table added with a chuckle, "These things are not only bright, but they're some bad-ass mothers. Look how easily they wiped out that whole team of law enforcement professionals. If he's under their protection, I'd guess John Wagner is in good hands, even if they're very hairy hands." The man laughed briefly, but everyone else remained silent, serious.

The conference room television was still showing the interview. Chief Mitchell was holding up his hands, shaking his head, and turning away from the pursuing crowd of reporters.

Sypher scanned the men around the table and spoke carefully. "The police department will almost certainly overreact to the SWAT killing. They will see the dead men as their brothers-in-arms. They will think of them as family. When family is threatened, all animals strike out. We must pay close attention to our own security. We don't know what may be coming."

He paused with an uncomfortable grimace. "John Wagner seems to be the center of this storm. Is there *any* way in hell we can locate him? I want to see him safe, of course, but I would also like to meet these Pures who risked so much to protect him, if that is, indeed, what they're doing. Any ideas?"

The room remained silent.

————

By 6:00 p.m. Eastern time, the attack video and the police interview had gone nationwide, and then international. More important, it was viral on the Internet. Madison, Wisconsin was now the focus of world attention. The offices of Digital Nation were on lock-down. No reporters or curiosity-seekers or even government officials could get in. Still, the phones rang incessantly.

Somehow, word had leaked that his company had identified the DNA samples of saliva from the SWAT attackers. Wild stories of Bigfoot, Sasquatch, the Swamp Monster, and all the other colorful names attached to regional versions of hairy monster-men were being put forward to explain the creatures.

For Louis Sypher, this was both a curse that brought unwanted attention, and a blessing that guaranteed a flood of new business and he was, after all, a businessman. His board of directors had been in continual session since the attack. They turned their attention away from avoiding exposing the true nature of the Lycan attackers, to an earnest effort to monetize the publicity.

And it truly was an absolute bonanza of free publicity. Sypher had turned down a dozen requests for interviews with news outlets around the world. He did release a carefully worded statement that explained the difficulties involved in accurate assessments of poorly curated DNA samples. He went on to say that the results were definitely not human, or any other known animal, but he could be no more specific than to say they were mammal, probably of the family Hominidae, possibly of the genus Homo. That is to say, man-like.

He knew his story would produce a storm of speculation, and his name, and his company would become world famous. His legal department was already on the phone with existing clients renegotiating contracts.

Louis Sypher felt a little regret at being the focus for an effort that could lead to the hunting, and probable killing, of fellow Lycans in addition to the Pures…or whatever they were. On the other hand, he would become richer and more able to help those of his own kind. Both aspects made him seem destined to become more powerful.

He could live with that.

———

John Wagner slept on the straw pile bed for half a day. He woke groggy and confused. Only after shaking his head, wiping his eyes, and stretching his neck did he begin to realize where he was. The cave-like overhang was illuminated by sun low on the horizon. It made the rock almost glow in warm yellow and reddish light.

He was alone with no idea where his Lycan saviors had gone. He stretched and stood, still wobbly and sore but able to put weight on his chewed-up legs. The dog-bites to his stomach were scabbed over but no longer seemed infected. In fact, nothing was infected; not the wounds on his legs or his arm or even the torn flesh on his scalp.

Whatever treatment Nurse or the other Lycans had done; it had been effective. He took a few steps. No wounds opened. No muscles cramped. No pain shot through his body. He felt whole and well. He even stretched his arms high.

It was good to feel human again. "Well, okay," he said out loud, "part-human." That made him laugh. He was suddenly hungry and went to his ragged backpack. It still held a couple of pistols and boxes of ammunition. It also had one last package of freeze-dried rations from Betty Mae's house. He was grateful that she was a survivalist.

He dug into the pouch, but the food inside was powder-dry. He needed to find water. Using his one remaining rifle as a crutch, he set off slowly, testing his strength with each step.

Once out from under the ledge, John felt the sun on his face, smelled the damp odor of evergreen trees, moss and wild flowers. He lifted his chin to bask in the solitude of nature, if only for a briefly.

He started walking, limping actually, in search of water. It was a brief search. After just a few minutes, he heard the rush of a small stream tumbling down a rocky bed into a waterfall about as high as his shoulder.

John sat on a wet rock and laboriously took off his boots. He intended to undress and wash off in the waterfall but, when he looked down at his mud-caked clothes, he decided to just jump in. The shock of cold water took his breath away and yet, it felt wonderful. Somehow it seemed to be cleansing more than his body and his clothing. It washed away the whole string of memories, the fear of death, and the uncertainty of his predicament. It renewed him completely.

After a few minutes soaking, he was too cold to tolerate any more. He climbed out, undressed and laid his clothes on the rock to dry. Then he stood, shivering, spreading his arms and turning slowly, trying to let the little bit of remaining sunshine warm him front and back.

After a few pirouettes, he looked down at the wounds to his flesh. They were many, but none seemed to be draining. Whatever the Lycans had done for him made them heal faster than he could have expected.

He remembered the food, the reason he had come looking for water. The package, still in his pants pocket, was soaked and falling apart. He was able to save two power bars and a plastic container of some kind of paste he could not identify. He scooped with his fingers and ate it, anyway.

Cleaner and somewhat better nourished, he sat naked on the cold hard rock and tried to come up with a plan. He could not stay with the Lycans forever. He needed to get back to civilization if, for no other reason, to let Sypher and the others know what had happened to him.

His clothes weren't quite dry when he heard a movement in the bushes. He grabbed his rifle, quickly checked to be sure it was loaded, and stood ready.

It was the Lycan troupe returning. He let out a deep breath.

They saw him and stopped with a series of welcoming hoots.

John stood tall and waved to them for a moment before he realized that he was stark naked.

They came closer, looking curious, downright nosey. They circled, looking him up and down.

Nurse reached out and ran the back of her hand along his smooth chest.

The other female was less bashful. She took his genitals in her hand and inspected them.

John took an embarrassed step back, but she still had a handful of his balls and didn't seem inclined to let go. He felt foolish, standing bare-assed naked and holding a rifle while the hairy gang circled and fondled him like a curiosity in a side show.

The older female bent over for a closer look. She hooted, and Nurse also joined her close-up inspection. Now the real embarrassment; their handling gave him a partial erection. They made rumbling noises to each other, as though comparing notes. He pulled back but the older female was not about to let go. He reached down and forced her hand away. She did not look happy.

The whole tribe began to hoot in a way that he had not heard before. He thought that, maybe, they were laughing. He, on the other hand, was breathing deep, a bit of anger mixed with humiliation. He lowered his rifle and yelled, "Okay, that's enough."

Humpty seemed to agree. He made a barrel-deep grunt and they all stepped back.

John stood like a statue of a militia rifleman, a bare-assed naked militia refleman. To make matters worse, his erection was now fully developed, and that did not escape notice. The Lycans moved back from him, but with trailing stares and soft hoots. He exhaled like a steam engine and began to don his damp clothes.

Humpty gave him a long look. Then the big Lycan bellowed and motioned toward the woods.

The clan obediently turned and walked away with quick glances back at their pale, hairless friend. Nurse's eyes lingered longest.

His first inclination was to follow them back to their den, but that might not be safe for them, or for him. No. He would try to find his own way back to civilization. He needed, above all, to tell the rest of his kind exactly what had happened so that they could be prepared.

John had no way of knowing how much, if anything, the Digital Nation people already knew about the conflict in the woods. Even he did not know all the details, but he understood that there had been a battle. The three males of the Lycan group all had fresh blood on their furry arms. He had noticed clumps of coagulated blood on their backs, the top of their heads, their knees and elbows. The battle must have been a big one. With no obvious wounds, Humpty and his buddies seemed to have been decisively victorious.

Done with the awkward task of pulling wet clothes over strained and damaged limbs, he set off with only a vague sense of the direction. At first, he tried to retrace the route he thought he had taken to arrive at the Lycan den.

It wasn't long before he realized that nothing looked familiar but, somewhere off to his right, he heard noise of cars on a road.

In minutes, he came upon a paved country road. Walking openly would be risky, but what choice did he have? With a deep breath, he set off limping, leaning on his rifle with every step.

Before he had taken ten steps, a battered pickup truck stopped. The driver peered at him from a weather-wrinkled face beneath a straw hat. The man's coveralls bore evidence of hard work done close to the earth. "You okay, young fella?"

John tried to smile, even though the man probably couldn't tell in the fading sunset's light. "Yes, sir, I had a little accident is all. I was just out shooting, and I fell down a steep rock face. Busted up my leg and arm a bit." *Was he overdoing the accent?*

The old man leaned over with one hand still on the steering wheel and stretched to open the passenger door. "Hop in. I'm heading to Petersburg. I'll give you a lift that far."

"Thank you most kindly, sir."

The drive was thankfully short with little conversation.

In the Petersburg town square, the driver, whose name was Billy Parker, leaned over and yelled as though John were deaf. "Far as I'm going. Hope this was a help to you."

John slid out of the seat and waved, "Goodbye." He was grateful to be in farm country where no one thought it at all strange to see a man walking around with a gun. Now, what was his next plan? He had none, so he just started walking. Maybe some new option would present itself.

One block away from the courthouse lawn, the town turned dark and quiet. Rows of single houses on small plots were all painted white with matching picket fences. Every porch had a swing. Cars in driveways were mostly older sedans.

A postal service vehicle moved in spurts, stopping at each mailbox, making later-than-normal deliveries. The postman's delivery van waited as a well-polished old Ford pulled out of a driveway.

Under the street light, John could see the driver, a gray-haired man with a stern expression, and an equally dour woman seated beside him.

Once the postman was gone, John scanned to be sure that there was no one else on the street. He opened the mailbox, took out a letter, and held it under street light to read the address. Then, he replaced the letter and wandered around behind the house.

No one locked doors in rural Wisconsin, and Petersburg was definitely rural. He entered the house through a back porch screen door. Inside, he found a tidy, sparsely furnished time capsule from the 1960's. Among other antiques, he found a corded phone. Relief; a cell would have required a password, or fingerprint, or something to unlock.

He thought of calling for a Lyft, or Uber, but that required an app. There on the stand was a thin, dog-eared paper phone book. John risked turning on a table lamp and thumbed through yellow pages for taxi listings; there were only two. The first number returned a "not-in-service" message. The second was Larry's Cab Service.

Larry answered on the second ring. His television in the background was loud.

John gave him the address from the letter.

Larry said the ride into Madison would cost forty bucks.

John agreed. He was just grateful to find any ride from so far out in the country.

Larry said that he would be there in fifteen minutes, or so.

Now, his next problem, how would he pay? His wallet was long gone after the white-water body surfing. But he remembered putting the plastic-wrapped pack of twenties in the calf pocket of his cargo pants. He fumbled. It was still there, but the wrapper had leaked, and the bills were soaked. He picked through to find the least soggy and laid a couple of Andrew Jacksons on the kitchen counter while he went searching for a hair dryer. Luckily, the gray-haired lady had not one, but three hair driers. He wondered why, but it didn't matter.

It took more than half an hour for his ride to come. That

was enough time for the bills to dry sufficiently to handle. Thankfully, the old couple had not returned home.

When he saw the van with Larry's logo pull up, John walked calmly out into the street, carrying his rifle and bag.

The driver, probably Larry, looked at the rifle and frowned.

John bent to talk into the driver's window. "It's a hunting rifle, and it's not loaded." He pulled back the bolt action to show an empty chamber. "I'll be happy to pay an extra twenty for the *cargo*."

Larry hesitated and looked his potential customer up and down. Dirty, disheveled and carrying a rifle, John probably looked like pretty risky passenger.

"Forty," Larry said with nervous, knit eyebrows.

"Forty, really?" John shook his head and fumbled in his pocket before producing a couple more partially dry twenty-dollar bills.

Larry checked those bills, turning them over and over before he nodded approval.

John climbed in. "Okay, like I said on the phone, I need to go to downtown Madison."

Larry was still busy smoothing the money. He spread it on his passenger seat to continue drying. Then, he looked in the rear-view mirror at his passenger and nodded agreement.

"Great, I'll need you to drop me off in the lower level parking garage of the Digital Nation office building."

Larry nodded again, and they were off. John sat back and tried to relax in the rear seat, but his wounds began to speak to him. It was not a friendly conversation.

It took a good fifteen minutes before Larry seemed comfortable enough to start a conversation. "So pretty exciting stuff, this monster hunt. You got anything to do with it, what with that rifle and all?"

John hesitated. "I've been out in the woods hunting. I haven't heard any news. So, what's going on?"

"No kidding, you don't know? Five cops were killed just about five miles from your little town. The news is saying it was Bigfoot, or something."

"Seriously? Cops killed that nearby. That's pretty damned scary."

"I'll say. I've limited my pickups in that zone. You're lucky I picked you up. Your town is just outside my no-go zone."

John suppressed a laugh. "Yeah. I guess I really am lucky. So how long ago did this happen?"

"Just this morning, but it's already taken over the news. There ain't nothing else on the TV, or radio, or even the Internet. It's like this is the only thing going on in the world. Pretty cool, huh? Our local town, Madison, Wisconsin, has the story of the year. We're like world famous. They're calling it the Bigfoot Battle."

John had to careful. "So how do they know it was Bigfoot and not some other wild animal?"

"Pictures, man. The cops got body cameras that recorded the whole thing. It was really something seeing those hairy monsters killing cops, and not just regular cops; these were SWAT guys with body armor and fancy guns and all."

"There was more than one Bigfoot?"

"Yeah, a whole bunch of them. It was awesome, man. These things are huge, maybe seven feet tall with teeth like a sabre-tooth tiger and hair like a bear or something. It was enough to give me nightmares…and I'm an Iraq Vet."

John sat back and thought. When the Lycans had returned from what he thought had been a search for him, the males had blood stains on their fur. They acted distant, as though not really wanting to be around him. But why would they kill policemen? How would they know he was in danger, or even where he was?

Could they have just sensed all that? Was their telepathic ability that comprehensive? And why, when they returned from their mission or whatever it was, why did they seem cool to him? None of it made sense. They had fought to protect him, or he thought they had and, yet, they left him naked and alone in the woods. Nothing made sense anymore.

He tried not to think about it, not to think about anything. He just wanted a warm shower and a clean bed, but that little voice in his head, his own telepathic sense made him uneasy, as though there was danger nearby. He went back to alert status.

Traffic increased as they drove into the city. John leaned his head against the side window and tried to ignore the pain of his wounds. He saw pedestrians walking by, living their lives, being normal people. Would he ever feel normal again? But, really, had he ever felt normal? Now that he knew what he was, he at least, had an explanation for his eccentricity.

As they drove, he watched the endless flow of people enjoying the springtime night, the smells of fresh green sprouts about to burst from the ground, and trees about to leaf out. Everywhere, the blossoms were eager to burst forth and bring joy to the normal people. He watched faces as they flashed by his vehicle, some laughing, some serious, but all very human.

Then, he froze. One of the passing faces locked his mind. It looked like Gretchen. He twisted to follow as her image passed behind. Then he turned, knees on the seat, to peer out the back window. It *was* her. The sight of her drained the life out of him. He wanted to yell at the driver to stop but, no, he couldn't. He had to wait the three years. That was the deal, and he always kept his word, especially when it was signed in blood.

Gretchen faded into the anonymous crowd as the van drove on.

Once in the underground garage, John fished out two more twenty-dollar bills. Larry accepted the tip with a smile and then screeched his tires as he drove off.

John stood there for a long time, just listening to the sounds of traffic, sounds of the city just beyond the dungeon-like garage. Then, he took a deep breath, gathered his wet, dirty duffle, his rifle, and his courage and took the elevator.

No one got on the elevator until he reached his floor. That was good. He looked like hell, he was carrying a rifle and he was too exhausted for explanations. He had lost the key but, he remembered the cypher lock combination to open his apartment door. It seemed so clean, so antiseptic, so ordinary.

He took a long shower and then, for good measure, a soaking bath. Warm water made everything better. He leaned back in the tub and tried to clear his mind. That was impossible. All he could visualize was the image of Gretchen walking along, shoulders hunched, head down, seeming lost in her thoughts. Over and over, the same few precious moments replayed in an endless loop inside his head.

Finally, he climbed out of the tub, toweled off and went to sleep between clean sheets in a climate-controlled room. It was wonderful. He gathered the sheet to his chin and curled into a fetal position. His last thoughts were of the Lycan tribe resting on their grass beds.

They were good thoughts.

Who Is Who and Who Are You?

John woke, panting like a child after a nightmare, unsure where he was. As he cleared his head, he saw two men in business suits standing at the foot of his bed. They had serious faces.

"Good morning, Mister Wagner. I'm Ben, and this is my brother, Bart. Mister Sypher wants to talk to you as soon as possible."

John shook his head. His neck hurt. "Sypher? Talk? How did he even know I was here?"

Ben snickered. "Seriously? He knew the minute you got within twenty miles. He has, as you might recall, Lycan senses."

"Okay, just give me a minute to shower."

Ben shook his head. "The boss didn't say to take your time and get prettied up. He wants to see you now, so put on your damned pants and let's go."

John felt a flash of anger as he threw off the bed covers and stood defiantly showing off partially healed red scars on his legs, arms, and neck. The two men in suits seemed unimpressed.

Bart, the quiet one, grabbed John's shoulder at a pressure point and squeezed hard. "Now! Mister Sypher said now!"

Pain shot through John's shoulder like electricity. He felt his chest and stomach knot up and grabbed at the bully's hand, but it was no contest. The thug was much stronger. He kept digging his fingers deeper and deeper into John's flesh.

Finally, John held up both hands in surrender. "Okay, okay. Just let me get dressed."

"Make it quick. The war council is waiting."

"War council?"

Ben shrugged. "That's what we call it. It's really the board of directors. They've been in the conference room, non-stop, since you went missing and the two Killer Monks were reported as dead."

Bart released his grip and pushed John back onto the bed with a dismissive sneer.

Ben tossed him a pair of pants that still had labels from the second-hand store.

John sat and struggled to pull them up. "How did he know about the monks?"

Ben sighed. "Did we mention that he's Lycan?"

John hobbled to the elevator, barefoot and shirtless. The pain returned, with vengeance. Every step felt like an electric shock. He felt like a puppy testing an invisible fence. His knees, hips, spine, and shoulders competed to see which could scream the loudest. He gulped air with each step.

The conference room was filled with milling men in suits. Many had taken off coats and ties and rolled sleeves as though settled in for the duration. Sypher sat at the head of the table with an angry scowl. He glared.

"Why didn't you tell us you were back?"

John felt wobbly and vulnerable as he stood, slightly bent and bare chested. "I hadn't slept for three days. I wasn't thinking…"

Sypher drummed his fingers on the table. "That would be a fine excuse for a civil service employee. You, however, are one of us, and we are being threatened. I expected more from you."

John straightened despite the pain. "I've killed three men for you. I've been shot, chewed up by dogs, and chased for days without rest. I'm sorry if that doesn't seem heroic enough to those of you sitting here in your padded leather chairs but I fought, damn it. I fought with everything I had."

Out of breath, John turned away from Sypher, hobbled to the closest empty chair, and collapsed into it. His breathing was quick and shallow.

Sypher leaned forward without acknowledging John's little speech. "Tell us about the Pures. How did you encounter them? What did you learn of them? Why did they attack the SWAT team?"

John tried to sit up straight. "Can I get a coffee?"

Almost instantly a china cup in a saucer was placed at his elbow.

He sipped and began. "Val and I received a message, probably from you, that we needed to get out of the safe house. I think someone in that little neighborhood must have turned us in. Just as we drove out of town, cops seemed to come from everywhere, but they went screaming by us. For a minute or two, we thought we were safe."

"But then, more cop cars showed up in the rearview mirror, and it became an all-out cavalry charge. They came after us with at least a half-dozen cars, all with lights and sirens going. We floored the gas, but they were gaining."

John sipped coffee and took a deep breath. "We realized

we couldn't outrun them, so we turned off onto a dirt road. But it led nowhere, just open pasture land and, to make things worse, a thunder storm let go with blinding rain. The downpour limited visibility to just a few feet.

"We thought that might help us escape so we sped up. Going full-throttle and with low visibility, we never saw the drop-off. We plunged over a cliff and fell almost fifty feet down. The impact wrapped the car around a tree like a taco shell. Val was killed. I was dazed."

John set down his cup and continued in the emotionless monotone common to disaster survivors. "Despite my injuries, I tried to get him free. His body was wedged inside the twisted wreckage. The bent metal had penetrated his torso, like a shark's jaws There was no way, no hope."

John sat silent, staring off into space with clenched teeth and, when he spoke again, he sounded bitter. "I grabbed the guns, ran away, and saved myself to fight another day. I wandered into the woods, evading the cops for a full day.

"Around dusk, I began to sense strange things, strange creatures. It was a clan of five Lycan Pures. They sensed me as well and seemed to intuitively understand my plight. They had actually come to help me. They led me to a house owned by Betty Mae, a human female, who runs a marijuana growing enterprise. She fed us all and made us comfortable for the night."

"I slept and, in the morning, woke to find they were gone; all of them, even Betty Mae. I was all alone, and I sensed imminent danger, so I took off. Barely made it out of the house before two teams of tracking dogs arrived. Those damned dogs pursued me through the entire day. Twice they caught up and attacked me. I killed several."

"After nightfall, the dogs gave up. I went back to the house seeking shelter. There I found two of the Bishop's monks waiting. I killed them and returned to the woods. Once again, the Pure Lycans came and took care of me, cared for my new wounds."

"Cared for your wounds?" Sypher sounded puzzled. "They had medical skills?"

"Yes. They seemed very knowledgeable, and their intuitive sense seemed to me to be greatly superior to ours."

Sypher was back to drumming his fingers. "The attack on the Madison Police SWAT Team, what can you tell us about that?"

"Not much, really. I left the Pures and wandered about until I found an abandoned farmhouse, where I took shelter. It seemed safe for a brief rest. I didn't want to stay in one place for long. When I heard someone coming, I ran back into the woods thinking the police must have been alerted."

"Somehow, the Pures must have again known of my plight. They came to find me and take me back to their cave. The three males remained at the house and didn't return until almost evening. When they came back into the camp in the woods, they behaved differently, kind of distant and less friendly. I think I saw blood on their fur, but I don't know exactly what happened. I assume they must have fought the SWAT cops."

John hesitated and tried to choose his words carefully. "After that, something changed with the Pure Lycans. They seemed different. They gave off a strange vibe, as though I was no longer welcome. Maybe something about their attack changed their attitude about me, made me seem a liability."

He thought for a minute, trying to recall events and keep his timeline right. "I left the cave and made my way to a small town where I called a cab... And, now, I'm here. Any more questions?"

The room was quiet.

Sypher moved papers around on the table with more force than necessary. Finally, he looked up. "So, you see yourself as a hero?"

"I see myself as a survivor, and a lucky one at that."

Sypher made a "humph" sound, not quite a laugh. "The monks you killed…how did you do that?"

"There were night vision goggles in the bag of goodies you left for us at the safe house. Using them, I was able to see the monks. I observed that they too had goggles, so I set a trap. I laid my goggles down in an open space, knowing that the light generated in the eyepieces could be seen over a long distance by others using night vision devices. Then, I waited until the monks came after the light source. When they were close enough to get a good shot, I took them out."

Sypher didn't seem impressed. "What about the SWAT attack?"

"I've told you everything I know about it."

Sypher nodded, but he was clearly not satisfied. He turned to the assembled men. "Questions? Anyone have questions for Mister Wagner?"

The analyst stood. "Yes, sir." He looked directly at John. "Can you tell us more about the Pures? We have some DNA we believe is theirs, but it's a real anomaly. All of us here in this room are genetically European Sapiens/European Lycan mix. The samples we took from the SWAT team bodies are different. We think they belong to…"

The man paused as though picking his words carefully. "They appear to be primarily Native American, ancient Native American at that. And there is Asian Lycan DNA. In short, they are dramatically different from us. Their alleles show a construction we have never before seen."

Sypher stood. "Did you get that? Did you hear what he said? These things are *not us*. You allied yourself with a pack of monsters. They may have cared for you, seemed to protect you, but they're just animals. We don't owe them anything. In fact, they may be a threat to us."

The analyst seemed taken aback. "Sir, there is no reason to believe—"

"To believe what? That these things are our soul-mates, our allies? No! They are a threat to us all. They are cartoon imitations of the Lycan breed." He stood with thin lips and eyes. Only after a long pause did he continue and then he spoke softly. "They must be destroyed."

The analyst looked startled and started to speak. Sypher's icy stare made him step back and look down at his shoes. John wanted desperately to defend the Pures, but it was obvious that Sypher was not willing to listen to dissenting opinions.

The Digital Nation CEO stood and looked straight ahead as though focusing on an image no one else could see. "I want a plan. By 5:00 tonight, I want a plan to eradicate these false Lycans before they are able to pollute our genetic pool and destroy our image. I want them dead, and this Betty whatever, the pregnant Sapiens... kill her, too."

The room was so still John could hear nothing but breathing and throat clearing.

———

No one announced the end of the meeting, but one-by-one, the men around the table stood, quietly gathered their papers and left. John managed to stand up on his tender bare feet. He was about to follow the other staff members but Sypher's voice made him freeze.

Louis Sypher, the boss, the head Lycan, the CEO, stood staring out his window and spoke in a quiet voice. "You think I'm wrong, don't you?"

John did not reply.

"You see, Mister Wagner, the world is made up of tribes. From them, we get our identity, our sense of being, our image of self. All that comes from the tribe. We exist as individuals only through our membership in our tribe. Once we lose that, we are just lonely animals without anchors to reality. Outside the tribe, there is no morality, no responsibility and no obligation. Alone, we are utterly immoral, capable of anything."

He sucked in a deep breath and clenched his fists. "We *must* protect our own. If we acknowledge these primitives, we debase our own breed. We cannot allow them to pollute our line."

John's voice was pleading, almost whining. "Sir, I beg you to reconsider. These are intelligent beings. They are our relatives, our friends. They saved my life."

Sypher turned and gave John an indulgent head shake. "You don't understand now, but some day you will. Our duty is to our own kind and no one else. That is the ultimate genetic imperative. We must protect all that is unique and special about us and that necessarily means eliminating others. That is our duty."

He sniffed. "Go, get cleaned up. A lot of people will want to talk to you."

———

Bishop Helsing was halfway up the cathedral front steps when Father Antonio caught up. The priest was breathless as if he had just run a sprint. He leaned forward, hands on his knees and spoke in spurts. "Do you know of the killings? The police have lost five men."

The Bishop made a slight dip of his head. "Yes, it's all over the news."

"Then you saw the body camera images. Previously, we have encountered the demons only in human form. Now they have attacked in their wolfen persona. I fear this is an escalation."

The Bishop stood tall and crossed his arms. He looked skyward and his tone was condescending. "So, have you lost more men? Your highly touted Killer Monks seem to be over-matched by the hellish beasts."

Antonio was taken aback. "The beasts have Satan on their side. This is more than a test of my men against the beasts of hell. This is a conflict between good and evil."

"Yes… Yes, it is. And in such battles, victory must go to the righteous. It is imperative that the followers of our Lord prevail. You must be stronger, Antonio. It is upon your faith the battle hinges. Go and commit yourself to prayer. The demons must be purged from my diocese, from my land, from my earth. Go back and slay the beasts."

Antonio bowed and backed away. Chastened, he turned and walked as he searched his soul for an answer. How could he kill the demons? *How?*

He remembered the stories from his youth. Once, back in Sicily, wolves had come nightly to kill sheep. The farmers used poisoned bait to kill the wolves. Perhaps that could work. But what bait would he use to attract demons? He would pray on it and perhaps the answer would come.

A Different Kind of Werewolf

J ohn was back in his room, dressed and bandaged, and feeling better after a couple of aspirin. At least, he was feeling better physically. His mind was a barrage of tumbling thoughts, conflicting emotions and a complete loss of personal identity. No matter how hard he tried, he simply could not think it through.

He was part Lycan, no question about that. He was part human, again not in dispute. He had always thought of himself as an honorable person, but where was the honor here? He was grateful to Sypher, but the man was showing signs of mental instability, like a gangster who wanted to wipe out opposing gangs. Humpty and his clan seemed to be decent, caring… what? People, animals, monsters, what? *Where should his allegiance be?*

There were no answers. He might have to just pick a side. That seemed callous and downright cowardly, and John Wagner was anything but a coward. He needed advice, guidance. Once he would have gone to his priest, but not after the pedophile scandal, or the local corruption scandal. Now, he had lost confidence in his church and its pastors.

Who in the secular world could possibly have meaningful advice? Only one name came to mind. He took the elevator and buzzed at the door. Mister Vrykolas was slow to answer. The old man finally cracked the door and spoke quietly. "Yes?"

"Sir, I am in need of your guidance and wisdom. Could you speak to me, listen to me, help me."

Vrykolas sighed and seemed to relax a bit. "Come in. May I offer you a cup of tea. It's my own blend, an old-world staple, not to the taste of most Americans. They prefer bland powdered teas, instant teas, or pods for high-tech machines. Mine is from imported leaves brewed in a simple pot."

John declined and the old man led him into the musty library of an office. Vrykolas sat down behind a great wooden desk stacked high with papers. There was a long moment of silence before John cleared his throat and began.

"Sir, do you know that Mister Sypher is planning to exterminate the small group of Pures who sheltered me? I think he sees them as a threat. They are not."

The old man just tightened his grimace. When he spoke, it was a slow and deliberate. "Louis Sypher believes he has a mission on earth, an almost holy mission. I suspect he sees the creatures not so much as a threat, but as a source of competition."

"Competition? They are living secretly out in the woods in very primitive conditions. They have no tools or weapons. How could they be a threat?"

"If they are what I suspect, their very existence is a threat to Sypher's ambition. You see, he is not just organizing a Lycan organization out of goodness of his heart. He has political ambitions. He wants to control, not only the Lycan, but

Sapiens as well. He wants to rule a kingdom of sorts and he is completely ruthless in that quest."

John's face contorted. "That seems ridiculous. The Sapiens outnumber us a thousand to one."

The old man smiled. "Actually, their number is much greater. But when did any tyrant ever see the fallacy of his own ambition? He has a plan. It will take decades but, eventually, he wants to amass enough followers to gain regional power and then become president – or maybe, king. His soldiers will eliminate opposition candidates, and he will create crises that stoke nationalist sentiment. Once elected, he will declare martial law and make himself dictator. If that actually happens, I expect he will create a police state where Lycans run everything and the weaker Sapiens become slaves."

John felt his heart rate increase. "Do you think this can actually happen?"

Vrykolas only shrugged. "Did people think Hitler would win an election? Did the masses welcome Communism thinking it would benefit them? I do not know. On this subject I have much knowledge, but little wisdom."

The old man stared out a window that had not been cleaned in years. "I do know this. Sypher has knowledge about your Lycan Pures, and he fears something about them."

"Fears? They are primitive, almost ape-like. They have no technology. They can't even speak."

"Ah, Mister Wagner, you are too much in the physical world. You have not yet learned to swim in the great sea of the mind. That is where the battles of the future will be fought. I do not know with certainty, but I suspect the wild Lycans may have superior powers to ours. I have seen the pictures of them killing police, and I was struck by how slowly the humans reacted. I wonder if they may have had their minds clouded and their reactions confounded."

John sat back and tried to remember his telepathic contacts with Humpty and his tribe. They seemed to know his every thought, but he received little back from them. He looked Vrykolas in the eye. "Have you seen any such creatures before?"

"No, but I do much research and I know of stories, many stories." He thought for a second. "Some tales of hairy men in ancient Manchuria sound similar. These Manchurian men lived solitary lives in the forest but came out regularly to demand tribute from the farmers and local priests, and when challenged, they used the power of their minds to drive people insane, even to suicide."

He shrugged. "Our analysis people here in the company tell us hair samples taken from the dead bodies of police show the ones we call 'Pures' to be a mix of Asian and American Indian DNA, but prehistoric, not from any currently living human sub-species."

John was confused. "So, what does that mean for our current conflict?"

"It means there are many unknowns. The forest people, as you called them, are the greatest unknown. The exact plan Sypher has in his mind is also unknown, but he is a driven animal, volatile and dangerous. He will kill without hesitation, and he cares nothing for those who do not bow before him. So, go gently and do not openly defy the man. You will not survive to see what evolves."

John rose and walked to the door. He looked back at the withered old man sipping his tea. He had learned much from Vrykolas, but he felt no certainty.

———

The trees were just coming out of their winter hibernation. Flowers peeked from cold, damp soil and promised to open soon. Even the grass had taken on some color. John walked among a crowd of people rushing to work, or to shop, or to do something in downtown Madison. No one noticed him, but he was paying attention to them.

In particular, he was exercising his sense, trying to tap into the thoughts of random people, to reach into their minds, to discover their private world, but with very little success. Concentrating hard didn't seem to help. Relaxing and trying to be open-minded didn't help either. He was getting really frustrated when he sensed something: danger maybe, violence, possibly, or just a silent cry for help.

He couldn't be sure what was about to happen, but he knew it had to do with the alley behind a nearby office building. Without thinking, or having any plan, he walked toward that alley. As he neared, he heard a commotion and knew, or at least sensed, that two policemen were feeling threatened.

John rounded the corner and saw them; two cops yelling at a homeless black man with a makeshift tent half-hidden behind a large metal dumpster. The tall cop grabbed a handful of dirty suit coat, but the old man fought against the cop's grasp.

In an instant, John understood the situation. He spoke with a tone of authority. "Officers, the man is not trying to be difficult. He doesn't want to leave the alley because his dog has just died, and he doesn't want to leave her body here for the rats. He is not a threat to you, or anyone."

The taller officer stepped over and got in John's face. "Yeah. Well, just who the hell are you and what business is it of yours?"

John remained calm. "Look behind the dumpster. He used his last blanket to cover her body. It would be an act of great kindness if you were to take him and his dog to a decent place where he could bury her. She was the most important thing left in his life."

The big cop seemed unsure. He hooked his thumbs in his belt and spoke out the side of his mouth. "Bill, go look behind…"

"Already there. He's right, the dog's dead. Looks like an older collie mix. Death is recent enough the body is still soft, no rigor."

The tall officer was about to speak but John cut him off. "Sir, if you don't want to help him, I'll be happy to call Animal Control and ask…"

Tall cop turned away and addressed the homeless man. "So, what's your dog's name?"

The man looked up with tired, teary eyes. "Her name is… or was, Sallie. I'm Samuel Pickens. I used to be an accountant but got laid off. Couldn't find any work at sixty. They want nothing but computer whiz-kids now-a-days. Wife had a stroke and died. Couldn't afford the ambulance and E.R. fees. Wound up losing my house and my car. I got a lawyer, but the lawsuit's going nowhere. So here I am, squatting in an alley, and can't even afford to bury my dog."

Bill, the shorter cop said, "Look, Jack, if you want to take him somewhere, I'm fine…"

Tall cop sniffed. "No. Mister Do-good here has volunteered." He turned to John. "Just don't bring him back here after, understand?"

John nodded.

The police got in their car and were gone with a screech of tires. He turned to the old man. "Mister Pickens, it will take me ten minutes to go get my car. I'll be back, and I'll help you find a place to bury Sallie."

Samuel Pickens wrapped his arms around himself, looked away, and nodded without emotion.

John left him and went to search in the underground garage. It had been days since he parked it there, and it took a while to remember the spot.

When he finally drove back to the alley, Samuel Pickens was standing on the curb, patiently waiting with his dog in his arms, still wrapped in her blanket.

Both got into the back seat, and John drove off.

He spoke loudly in case Samuel was hard of hearing. "I'm headed up toward the Wiles Conservation Area, I think that's what it's called. It's a beautiful place, peaceful and rarely visited.

Samuel still did not speak.

John saw him in the rear-view mirror, rocking and clutching his dead dog's body.

The drive was longer than he remembered, and the dirt road hard to find. But, after a few U-turns, John was sure he was back at the empty field where he and Val had crashed. This time, he avoided the cliff and drove down a gentler slope to the forest edge.

He shut down the car and opened the rear door. "I think that, just beyond these trees, is a beautiful place for Sallie can be put to rest. I'll just get my small shovel from the trunk."

Samuel nodded, and they set off walking. John offered to carry the pup, but Samuel did not acknowledge him.

They climbed down beside the stream. John remembered it being larger and swifter than it seemed now. There was a path of sorts and, twenty minutes later, they stood in front of Betty Mae's house.

John motioned for Samuel to sit on a lawn chair while he went and knocked.

No answer. John thought of breaking in but discarded that idea. Instead, he stood on the porch and concentrated, trying to open his mind to the ether. Within seconds, he felt it, the presence. He concentrated, trying to project, not words, but feelings. And he was rewarded with a flash of images. The Pures were close. He relaxed and placed a paternal hand on the Samuel's shoulder.

It took an hour before the first grunt came from the tree line. John stood straight and spoke in a low voice. "Do not be afraid. There are some very strange people coming. They are kind and gentle and caring, but they look like monsters."

"Afraid? I got nothing to fear 'cause I got nothing left to lose."

They waited until the nearby bushes rustled and Nurse stepped out.

Samuel might have thought he had no fear, but he let out a gasp of near-terror.

John tried to calm him. "It's okay. She's a friend."

"She? How do you know it's a she?" His voice was shrill.

"I know her. She and her people are my friends."

Nurse came close and bent to place her hand gently on the blanket and make a low cooing sound.

Samuel drew back from her and almost fell over. But, as she stroked the blanket and made maternal sounds, he relaxed slightly. That only lasted for a second.

Honey and No Name came crashing out of the woods. Again, Samuel sucked in air like a jet engine.

"It's okay," John repeated over and over.

Nurse placed her soft hand on Samuel's cheek. He seemed to find her touch calming. She stroked his face, and he began to cry, first in quick little sobs, and then with full shuddering anguish.

He began shaking and rocking back and forth.

Nurse keep looking him in the eyes and making her soft sounds. She reached out her arms and, reluctantly, Samuel allowed her to take his beloved dog. She cradled Sallie and rocked as gently as any human mother would.

Honey approached hesitantly and placed a hand on the old man's shoulder.

Samuel flinched at the touch but seemed to recover and then accept it.

Honey tilted his head toward the woods and motioned for Samuel to come with them. The old man seemed to understand.

John helped him stand.

He was elderly and weak, but did not resist.

Arm-in-arm, John and Samuel and Honey walked toward the shade of the trees.

Nurse and No-name led, but slowly, as though respectful of the old man's infirmity. In just minutes, they came to a knoll overlooking a bend in the stream. Humpty and the other female were waiting there. They came to Samuel, made quiet grunts, and placed gentle hands upon him.

The old man seemed overwhelmed but nodded appreciatively. John's challenge was to sift the flood of thoughts being emitted. He tried to respond but wasn't sure if it was working.

Nurse knelt and laid Sallie's body in the grass, where a single shaft of sunlight fell.

Now, John suddenly understood everything the Lycans had been trying to communicate to him. He spoke quietly. "They want to know if this is a good resting place?"

Samuel went over, bent down on weak knees, and laid out beside his dog, his friend, his companion. "Yes," he said. "Yes, this is a good resting place." He looked up at blue sky. "Bury us both right here."

———

Carlo, Bennie, and Dag sat in the shade of evergreens and drank the American coffee they considered watered down. The team leader spoke.

"We've lost him. Damn it, we've lost the man who killed Robert and has now killed Pierre and Hershel. This is not our way. We must be better than to let the demons defeat us."

Dag sat back and shrugged. "We must be honest, yes? These are not ordinary demons, like the ones in Ireland, or Romania. These are very - what is your word - savvy?"

Bennie said, "Yeah, that's a good word. A better one is that these assholes are just a lot more capable than anything we've gone up against before."

Carlo came back. "Well, we got terrible intelligence on them. Most of the information from Father Antonio has turned out to be false. Somehow, we must find out more about the demons, find out what is true. Obviously, they get excellent information about us. They knew about our hotel. They knew where Pierre and Hershel were. And they seem to know about our tactics and equipment. They are always a little bit ahead of us, and that usually means a leak. Who is their source? Who is selling us out?"

Carlo jumped in. "But how will we find this spy? We are operating in a strange land, our first Op in America. We don't know it like we know Europe. We have no way of knowing who to trust."

Bennie shook his head. "All our information has come from Antonio. He is beyond suspicion, so the big question is, who does *he* trust? Who gives him information? We need to follow his sources."

Carlo looked chagrined. "Check on Antonio? What is wrong with you?"

Bennie shrugged. "Hey, don't get me wrong. I trust Antonio with my life, but somebody is feeding him bad information. We need to find out who it is, and you know as well as I do; he'll never divulge his sources. So, what we gotta do is shadow him and find the trail back to whoever, or whatever, is compromising our operations. I hate it as much as you, but we both know it's gotta be done."

"Spy on Antonio? That's like spying on my own father."

Bennie made an exaggerated shrug. "Hey, Carlo, I know your old man. With all the shit he has going on, he *deserves* to be spied on."

Carlo almost laughed. "We must use extreme caution not to offend, or to be compromised. I think we should begin with his phone record."

Dag, who had been silent so far, cut in. "His phone? Are you saying we should hack the Monsignor's phone?"

Bennie looked a little pained. "Actually...I already have."

"What? Why?"

Bennie twisted a little. "I was worried about his safety and wanted a way to track him if he was like, abducted, or something. Also, if some bad shit happened to him, it would be a help to have his phone records to track down anyone involved."

Carlo was nodding. "I guess that makes sense. So, have you found anything?"

"Uh, no. I haven't even looked yet. I thought that would be kind of wrong without some good reason."

Carlo made an approving nod. "I think we have a good enough reason. So, let's have a check it out."

———

John used his small folding shovel, and the two male Lycans dug with their hands. It took fifteen minutes to make a hole large enough for Sallie.

By that time Samuel Pickens had calmed and given up demanding to be buried as well. He was kneeling with his hand on the fresh earth that now covered his dog, and he seemed very much at peace. He took a deep breath and almost whispered, "You were a very good girl."

Then, with the help of the two males, Samuel stood and dusted off his knees. He looked at John. "I feel funny, confused. There are all kinds of bizarre things in my head. I feel as though these creatures want me to stay."

John smiled softly. "You are perceptive. That is unusual in humans. These people are communicating with you, but you'll need to learn how."

"Learn how? That's not necessary. They really do want me to stay?"

John turned to Humpty and focused all his energy into a single thought. *Do…you…want Samuel?*

The answer came as an image of a campfire with the clan resting around it.

Nurse and the other female - *he needed to give her a name* - came and put their arms around Samuel, who choked up and then burst into a soft, whimpering cry.

Humpty came and made the females back away. The big Lycan took Samuel's hand and placed it on one hairy shoulder.

Then, he did something incredible. He said, "Good." The word wasn't exactly distinct, but it was recognizable. Suddenly, all the images of the past hour made sense. John understood and made a little laugh. "They want you to teach them. They want you to help them communicate with regular humans. Can you do that?"

Samuel looked perplexed. "Teach them? Why me? I have no experience, or particular talent, at teaching?"

John thought for a moment. "Tell me something. Have you been experiencing a stream of mental images just now?"

"Well, yes, but I thought that was just the emotion of the moment."

John turned to Humpty and tried to send a thought. He didn't really know how to do it intentionally, but it was worth a try. He thought the word 'good' over and over.

The big Lycan stood and once again made a sound like, *Goot.*

John turned to Samuel. "Did you sense that word just before I said it?"

"Yes, but…it must be…" He grew silent and then turned to Humpty with no sign of fear, or hesitation, and raised his hand, like an Indian saying *How* in the old movies.

Humpty mirrored his action, raising his hand as well.

"I think…I think they are telling me to stay near Sallie, my friend. I think they will care for me. I don't understand any of this, but I think I'm going to be all right. You can go now."

"But what about food and shelter and…"

Samuel had a peaceful look as he turned and almost whispered, "You may go now. I'll be fine here." He walked over to stand beside Honey.

All the others gathered around him, making their quiet hoots and mumbles as they reached out and touched Samuel.

Strange as it seemed, John thought there was something almost religious about the moment, like a rite of passage, or christening, or confirmation. He took a step back to give them room. They were stroking Samuel, grooming him.

Humpty left the cluster and came to John. He looked him straight in the eye and contorted his lips to make a new sound like "mow." John had no idea what that could mean. Humpty stretched an arm toward the group fussing over Samuel and again made the *mow* sound.

John concentrated as hard as he could but still didn't understand. Humpty repeated *mow* over and over. Each time, it became more distinct.

Finally, John said "More? Are you saying *more*?"

Humpty patted his chest and pointed to the old Sapiens man. *Mowah, mowah.*

"More? You want more what, more men?"

Again, Humpty slapped his hand on his chest. That might be a positive response, or not.

"Okay," John said.

Ohway, Humpty said and pointed back down the path they had come from.

John shouted to Samuel, "Are you okay?"

Humpty beat his chest and repeated, *Ohway*.

John received a thought. It was clear and precise, like spoken words. It was Samuel sending a thought. *I am an empath. I will be fine here with the Gors.*

He answered out loud, "Gors? Humpty and his people are called Gors? And why do you think you'll be all right?"

Another thought. *I knew the minute we walked into the woods that they were here, and they were good. They want me to teach them human ways. They want* me, *John. No one has wanted me for as long as I can remember. Here, I can be useful. Go, and leave me with my new family.*

"What about food, shelter…"

Another thought. *I will be fine. I will stay here until I die and then I will be buried near Sallie. I will be fine. Go, now, and let me begin to know of my new companions. Go.*

John hesitated, anguished over leaving Samuel. But then, where would he take the man, back to the alley? No, if he could be happy here, even for a short time, this was probably better than dying alone in the city. He stepped back and slowly raised a hand, as though saying, "Farewell."

Samuel and Humpty and all the others responded by staring and raising hands back at him.

John turned and left the old man in their hands. *God, I hope it's the right thing to do.*

The War Plan

He drove back to his apartment, undressed, and sat on the bed to inspect his many wounds. John was amazed that none were infected. He tried to remember what Nurse and the others had done to treat him. It was fuzzy. He recalled warm, muddy goo being rubbed all over, and smells of plant leaves wrapped over cuts and bites. He remembered warm, sticky stuff being poured over the leaves, but he still had no idea what they were or how they worked.

His thoughts turned to Samuel, the frail old man he left alone in the woods with a pack of hairy creatures. John made a deep sigh and wondered, was his judgment failing? It seemed as though he had made a lot of bad decisions that all started when he signed the contract with Lou Sypher. What would happen if he just left, took off and headed into the sunset?

That was a crazy idea. The Lycans were telepaths. They would find him and extract their vengeance. John sighed and went to the window to watch the endless flow of cars and pedestrians moving below. Could Sypher really enslave these people? They outnumbered his kind, and they would fight back, but he was clever.

A sobering thought, John was one of "his kind." He felt numb, trying to think clearly, to be reasonable. So really, would it be so bad to be on the winning side?

He put those thoughts aside. Nothing he could possibly do would affect the coming conflict. He just had to try and make the best of it. But his mind kept wandering to images of Gretchen. What would become of her? She was Sapiens. Would she be enslaved? Would he, could he, be one of her masters? The whole idea was too bizarre to even imagine.

———

For two straight days John was interviewed non-stop by officials of Digital Nation. Late on the second day, three new men entered the bare room, where he had been a virtual prisoner. They were clearly Sapiens, clearly tough-guy types. They wore cheap suits, blank expressions, and nervous eyes, probably cops. One had a coiled wire earpiece.

The oldest and fattest of the three pulled out a chair and sat. The exertion made him exhale like a big rig's airbrakes. He mopped his brow.

"Mister Warner, I believe?"

"Yes, I'm John Wagner."

"Very well, Mister Wagner, I am Madison Chief of Police, Mitchell. We have received permission from your boss, Mister Sypher, to interview you. I have been given to believe that you might shed some light on my wife's attackers. Is that true?"

John looked confused, and it was not an act. "I don't see how. I wasn't even aware she had been harmed."

"Do you know two men known as Ben and Bert?"

"No, sir. Those names sound vaguely familiar, but I can't

place them, and certainly not in the context of violence toward your wife. Do you know their last names?"

"No. We were hoping you might."

"Me? I don't have any idea why you think I…"

The chief beckoned to the cop with an earpiece, and they whispered. John could barely make out some of the words, "Verbal analysis…telling…truth."

Chief Mitchell scowled and turned back to John. "There is a foreign priest here working with the diocese. They have some crazy idea that there are covert anti-Catholic groups in the area who intend to conduct terrorist attacks on some of our sacred sites and high-ranking officials."

John became interested. "Why, sir, would they do that? Do they have specific grievances? And what would your wife have to do…"

The chief looked exasperated. "I don't know. This whole thing with my wife and the murdered SWAT team seems crazy. I don't even know who gave us your name as a suspect."

"A suspect! I am a suspect for what?"

The chief made a dismissive wave. "Oh, relax. It was an anonymous call, but it came direct to my private phone. I had it traced but it was a burner phone. The caller's location was somewhere near this building, so I thought I would check you out myself."

The police chief was a big man who probably hadn't been able to button his suit coat for a decade. He seemed to be sweating even in air conditioning, and his sagging posture in the overstuffed chair looked like that of a defeated man. John almost felt sorry for him. But, then, he remembered the police cars that chased him over the cliff and killed Val. He remembered the SWAT team, the dogs, and Killer Monks. All sympathy had evaporated.

When the interview, or interrogation, was over, the Chief and his elves left.

Sypher came into the room and made a slow, thoughtful nod. He smiled out of the corner of his mouth. "You handled yourself well. This man, Mitchell, seems very aggressive. Would you like to be the one who kills him?"

———

Samuel Pickens was quickly becoming comfortable with his new companions and his life in the woods. The Lycans proved capable students, and he was a patient teacher. The bond between them grew stronger every hour. He adjusted to the straw bed with pine bough covers; it was better than living on the street. He was fine with using a bush for a toilet; it was better than the stink of an alley. He was not so happy about a diet composed exclusively of wild game. Even garbage pickings had been better. So, he went to see Betty Mae. She agreed to a weekly shopping trip. Soon, he and the Lycan clan would have a much richer diet. Betty Mae seemed unconcerned with the cost. She had grown a bumper weed crop last year, and this season looked just as good.

Samuel liked her. She seemed a simple woman, without any agenda, who brought out his paternal instincts. An only child, he had married late. Both he and his wife, Joan, had wanted children, but she had problems and, after three miscarriages, they gave up and tried adoption, only to be told that they were too old. So, they settled for a dog, a gentle, loving dog named Sallie.

Samuel lost his job and his medical insurance just before the accident. The hospital bills were huge, and the creditors ruthless. He lost his retirement funds, his house, and even his car. The once middle class accountant had always been a conscientious saver, but Joan's medical bills were devastating. Suddenly, he found himself a widower, homeless and friend-less. He and Sallie were relegated to the street.

Now, even Sallie was gone. He had nothing, and no one, except his hairy companions of the forest. They were all orphans in a way; he and Betty Mae and the forest people. They had no one to turn to. It was an odd, but powerful, bond.

Samuel quickly learned the Lycan daily ritual and set up classes where he taught them simple English words, even the lip and throat actions necessary for speech. Then, he and Betty Mae demonstrated conversation, the give and take of human discourse.

The five Lycans were attentive students and were soon almost as proficient as a human toddler.

They practiced constantly. It made Samuel smile to hear them banter.

"Hewoh, how ah hue?"

"Guht en yhew?"

"Ahm guht tuw."

In time, they would get to the complex stuff. The conso-nants were much more difficult than the vowels. He made it a point to teach them critical statements like, "Don't be afraid, I won't hurt you," and "I am friend, do not shoot." That last one was a challenge, since the Lycans had trouble under-standing guns. All they knew was that guns hurt and must be avoided.

———

Father Antonio went to the chief of police and made his pitch. He was admitted to the office, but with Henry Dumas' warn-ing, "The chief is very busy. Make this quick."

Antonio did not like being told what to do and certainly not by some low-level functionary. He made a slight bow and a phony smile. "I shall, indeed, be brief."

As he entered the office, Chief Mitchell almost jumped out of his chair to thrust out a hand. His tone was solicitous. "Father Antonio, welcome. Please, come and sit and tell me what I can do for you and the Church."

"You are most kind, sir. My fellow servants of the Lord have requested that I ask for your help. I am reluctant to do so after you have already lost five good men to the creatures." He sighed and made a gesture as though holding an invisible ball in his hands. "They want to do a sweep of the wooded area where the creatures were last seen."

"A sweep? How many men are you requesting for this sweep?"

"Our thinking is twenty, more or less. You are probably better at judging such things. My men are now reduced to three. They would like you to act as herders, making noise and driving the beasts into a confined area where we can target and kill them."

"Hm-m-m. When do you want to do this?"

"The sooner, the better. We have no specific deadline."

Chief Mitchell sat back in his oversized office chair and looked as though he was chewing something. "I'll have to get with my people and establish a time that will fit with our other operations. I'll get back with you, but I've got to go and brief the mayor right now."

He rose and thrust out his hand again.

Father Antonio was gracious, as always. He left with courteous nods to everyone in the office. Once out in the hall, he grimaced and muttered, "I don't trust that son of a bitch, not even an inch."

———

It was Friday. Louis Sypher was pacing when one of his lieutenants knocked and came into the office followed by four others.

"Sir, you asked for a plan by today. We have one for your consideration."

"Okay, show me." Sypher tried but could not remember the man's name.

There was a small conference table in the office, and the lieutenant unrolled a three-foot map. "Here is the area where contacts with the Pures have been reported. The dog teams' travel paths are approximated with red lines. We could not, from their intercepted transmissions, accurately depict the police routes, but the actual encounters, as reported on those police radios, are shown as stars. The SWAT attack is the largest star."

He stood back and let Sypher study the map. The boss spoke slowly, thoughtfully. "So, if we take the known paths of pursuit, and the known points of contact, they form a rough circle. It seems reasonable to assume the Pures' base of operations is at the center."

"We agree, sir. In fact, we believe the most reasonable place would be the rock bluffs here." He placed a finger on a circled area. "We have overhead drone footage being analyzed as we speak. The initial satellite imagery looks promising, and we are launching additional drones to get low-level 3D close-up shots."

"Very good, *Wilson*." The man's name just came back to him. "When can I expect those pictures?"

"Later this afternoon, sir."

"I look forward to seeing them the minute they are available."

Wilson, *if that actually was his name*, left the map and departed.

Sypher studied it, noting the contours, the possible travel routes, the potential for hiding places. He visualized trying to get the perspective of someone on the ground.

After just a couple of minutes of staring, he placed a finger on the map and said out loud, "Here. That is where I would hide. It has shelter, probably good visibility to see attackers coming, several escape routes, and thick forest to ambush, or elude, pursuers." He paced, came back to the map, and seemed even more positive. "Yes, that is where we will find them, and *that* is where they will die."

Now, the next question. How big a team would he need, and how would he insert them? He didn't know how many Pures he would be facing. He wasn't worried about their armament, or their tactics. They were primitives who lacked foresight and the ability to make complex plans. They would probably attack in bold charges, suicide charges, easy targets for his team.

No need to go all-out He would use only as many fighters as he needed. Louis Sypher took a long, satisfied breath and called a meeting.

———

I am an empath, that's what Samuel said. That made sense. That is probably what drew John to the alley. That may have been what made John sense and then care about this forlorn, homeless man. That is probably how he knew so easily about the dead dog and the man's plight.

The Pures wanted more humans to live in their woods. Perhaps there were more empaths among the homeless. It was a long shot, but he was a gambler at heart. He drove until he sensed desperation. He even knew the direction of the thoughts. It led to a homeless camp under a bridge.

John got out of his car, stood with eyes clenched tight, and began to think. Over and over he thought, *Who wants to get out of here and go live in the woods where you'll be safe and well-fed?*

He was getting plenty of sensory input, but it wasn't clear. When he finally opened his eyes, there were four men standing and looking at him.

One spoke: "I'm willing to go into the woods, willing to go anywhere besides this shit hole. I'm willing to go anywhere there's a glimmer of hope." The others nodded.

John was almost overwhelmed by the flood of mental input from them. These guys *really* were empaths like Samuel. He never dreamed there would be so many just in one camp.

He looked them over. They were a rough bunch who might balk at living with the hairy forest people. But, as he explained the situation, they showed no fear, no hesitation. They didn't even seem skeptical of his wild proposal They just listened and shrugged.

When he and the four men arrived at the house, Samuel and Betty Mae were waiting with a cauldron of chili, bags of potato chips, and cases of soft drinks. They let the men eat and get comfortable before delivering the pitch. John did the talking.

"Okay, anybody ever heard of the Sasquatch, Bigfoot, or the Swamp Monster?"

They all nodded and made comments about stories they had heard.

"Well, they're real, but they're nothing like the stories. First off, they're not dangerous. In fact, they're good-natured and easy to get along with, and they're actually scared of humans." He paused. "There are some living right here in the woods, and they want to learn more about regular people."

Now he had their interest. A couple even put down their spoons to listen.

"We want you to work with them, live with them, teach them about people and how to get along. In return, you get three squares and a safe place to live and sleep."

A burly man, whose belly overflowed his ragged T-shirt, stood. The grime on his face was too thick to tell his race, but the accent was country. "So, let me get this straight. You brung us out in the woods to go camping with Bigfoot. Now, I'd like the three squares and a dry bed, so don't get me wrong, that's cool, but I ain't wanting to sleep with no monsters."

Samuel stepped up. "I said the same thing when I was on the street, but I have to tell you, these are good souls. They might look funny, and smell a bit off, but they are gentle, downright kind, and they want to be around people."

A thin man with the twitch of a druggy in need said, "What else? Does it pay?"

Now Betty Mae chimed in. "If you agree to work in the fields, you get ten bucks an hour, all cash, no deductions."

T-shirt still looked suspicious. "So, what about you, girlie? You feel safe around these things?"

"Well, I'll tell you mister, I feel safe *because* of these things. They are my friends, and they protect me, so you all need to understand; they're gentle as kittens, unless they see violence. That, they do not tolerate, and if you get their backs up, they can be some tough cookies."

The oldest of the group was a look-alike for Father Time. His wispy white hair and beard flowed onto his chest and back. "Food and lodging and some spending cash. I don't give a ding-dong about no monsters, I'm in. I don't want to spend one more night in the damned gutter."

Twitchy guy said, "I want to see 'em. I ain't signing up less I see 'em first."

Samuel nodded. "Fair enough." He went to the door and waved.

Nurse came slowly, tentatively glancing around, nervous as a cat in a dog kennel. She looked from man to man and went to clutch Samuel's arm. He patted her and smiled back.

"This is the female my friend John calls Nurse. She is good at healing, although I confess, I do not understand her methods."

It took several more hours, and a full case of beer, before they all agreed to the crazy idea of camping out with "Sasquatch." Nutty as that sounded, it was still better than the street. Only after the recruits had all attained a limber, relaxed beer glow did John introduce the other Lycans. There were sloppy salutes, drunken waves, and garbled giggling among the new guys.

Samuel spoke to John out of the side of his mouth. "I thought it would be a much tougher sell."

John leaned back. "It will be, once they wake up with a hangover and a bunch of furry new friends. We need to make sure the street people have no weapons."

Tribe of Lost Souls

Bishop Helsing was in a bad mood. He sat behind an enormous polished wood desk and toyed with a pen. When he spoke, he did not make eye contact.

"Antonio, I am frustrated that it is taking so long to solve our 'problem.' What must I do to facilitate your mission?"

"I apologize Your Grace, but these beasts of hell are proving far more cunning, and dangerous, than any we have ever encountered. They seem to anticipate our every move. It is almost as though someone is providing them with advance information."

The Bishop's face tightened. "Are you daring to accuse some of my people..."

"No, no, absolutely not! But many people know of our activities, some within the Church, some from the police, and others from support agencies."

"Support agencies? What agencies in particular are you speaking of?"

"There are many; the providers of our weapons, vehicles and lodging, as well as the reconnaissance drone people, the

DNA analytics firm, the contract dog handlers, and the government agencies who have been given just enough information to deconflict any of their activities."

"Government agencies, what government agencies?"

The priest grimaced as though caught in a lie. "Fish and Wildlife, the Park Service, town constabulary, and the county's water company."

"Good Heavens, Antonio. With so many people aware, how could we ever hope to avoid exposure?"

"I am sorry, Your Grace, but I am not familiar with your laws and customs. I felt it necessary to provide a cover story to these agencies to keep them from interfering. So far, they seem to have accepted our explanations and have not caused any problems."

Bishop Helsing sighed and shook his head. "Ah, but there is always someone with a grievance, or misunderstanding, maybe even a spy among them willing to subvert our plans. There is evil lurking everywhere, and Satan's minions are ever-alert, seeking ways to do us harm. You must use utmost caution, Antonio."

The bishop opened a desk drawer and produced four cardboard boxes, each about six inches by four inches, and set them on his desk.

"This may be a help to you in your Holy Mission. I believe your sidearms are all nine-millimeter; is this correct?"

Antonio was puzzled. "Yes, most are that caliber."

"Then, you must replace your ammunition with these bullets. They have been forged from silver by loyal, God-fearing members of the Church, and I have personally blessed each bullet. They should be deadly to the demons."

Antonio fought to restrain himself from saying he thought that was just mythology. Instead, he accepted the ammunition gracefully. The boxes were heavier than they looked.

"Thank you, Your Grace. These will be very helpful when we get face-to-face with the demons. I am hopeful that will be soon. I have made a proposal for a joint operation with law enforcement."

The bishop scowled. "But I thought you had been working together all along."

"Yes, yes, we have. But this will be a larger scale combined operation in the area near the site of the SWAT team massacre."

"Very well. Carry on, and go with God's blessing." There was little confidence in the bishop's voice.

———

Sunrise came with the smell of frying bacon and fresh-brewed coffee. The men from the vagrant camp slept inside the house in sleeping bags. The Lycan tribe slept outdoors but accepted mats and blankets. There was a lot of stretching and moaning from both groups as they woke.

The tension John anticipated had not materialized. Instead, the humans and Forest People seemed to find each other interesting, and not at all threatening. Having Betty Mae cruise among them with her large food tray made the bizarre situation seem normal, almost civilized.

As they ate, she announced loudly, "Okay, you boys from the city, we're going to have a morning shower schedule. There's a clipboard outside the bathroom, and a clock on the wall above. Each of you sign up for a ten-minute shower and don't hog the hot water. Later, we'll do laundry."

There had been little closeup interaction between the street people and the Lycans. They kept a cautious distance. But this morning, John saw the barriers begin to ease. They moved around each other, cautiously touching, tugging at hair and clothing, laughing a little while making noises and seeming to try to understand each other. This was working out better than John could have ever expected. He looked around and could not get over how similar it seemed to his childhood memory of the first day at summer camp.

Betty turned and shouted, "Forest People, let's clean up the porch. Roll your sleeping stuff, and pick up the trash you've left."

They listened and bobbed heads as though they understood every word. She demonstrated rolling up one blanket, herself, and then turned to them with a hand on her hip.

They imitated her, meekly clearing the porch and then patiently waiting for whatever came next.

Betty was still acting as the generalissimo. She continued directing cleanup and assigned duties, verbally to the street people, and with hand signals to the Lycans. The mood remained congenial.

The only hint of conflict came when the bearded man John called *Father Time* appeared to check out the Lycan called Nurse.

The old man tried to stroke her hair, and that brought an immediate charge from the one called Honey.

He jumped between them and rose to his full height to stare down at the oldster.

John shoved his way into the gaggle and spoke quietly. The moment passed.

Samuel found John and looked serious as he asked, "So how did you go about convincing these old homeless boys to come with you?"

John made an impish smile. "Well, you told me you were an 'empath,' remember?"

"Yeah, sure. So what?"

"Well, I never figured on finding a homeless man with the

gift. So, when I met you, it made me think. I thought that would be a good thing to have in any new members."

"New members?"

"Yeah, I'm thinking that the Lycan community is too small to accomplish much. They need fresh blood, but it needs to be people who can communicate. When we buried Sallie, I felt how you were in touch with the Forest People, sharing emotions and thoughts. Later, when I cruised around the camp under the bridge, I tried to open my senses and, damned if there weren't four men in just that one camp who had some degree of telepathic sensitivity."

"You could tell that from one drive-by?"

"Yeah. That was unexpected, but even more surprising, they were all willing to come with me."

Samuel took a deep breath. "That's not that surprising. Life on the street sucks. They were probably ready to do anything to get out."

John spoke very slowly, "Do you think they'll fight with us?"

Samuel seemed confused. "Fight? Fight who, and for what?"

John hesitated and ran his tongue over his teeth. "There are Catholic Monks hunting for these Lycans. They want to kill them, thinking they are unholy monsters."

"Well, what about you? How are you involved in all this?"

"I'm half Lycan. These are my people. I need to protect them."

"Well, this is a hell of a mess isn't it? And you think a bunch of street people will make good warriors?" Samuel thought for a second. "Actually, they are men with nothing to lose. They should make terrific warriors. I'm just not sure why you need an accountant."

John put a hand on the old man's shoulder. "Can you handle a gun?"

Samuel laughed deep in his chest. "Damned straight I can handle a gun. Let's go convince the other boys that this is a noble task. Most of them would do anything to claw back just a touch of the dignity of their old lives. Just give them a chance, the opportunity, the hope of doing something worthwhile. They'll fight all right."

The Fight Is Joined

Carlo got the call. "Yes, Father Antonio, we are ready, and yes, we have the bishop's silver bullets. We are simply waiting for the sheriff's men to call in-position. The police chief is quite anxious. He has been calling every few minutes. We are told the dog teams are all ready and, how do they say, *chomping at the bit*. This is correct, yes?"

He listened for a minute. "Yes, Dag and Bennie are well, and eager to avenge the death of their fellow priests. I understand, but we made an agreement with Chief Mitchell not to go in before he does. It's still early morning; we have a lot of light left in the day."

Another lecture. Carlo held the phone away from his ear. He had heard it all before. Finally, there was a pause, and he placed the phone back to his ear. "I shall keep you informed."

He hung up and exhaled, as though inflating a balloon. Then, a thin smile spread across his face. "Antonio is nervous."

Dag made his usual laid-back grin. "He should be nervous. These cops have no idea what they're dealing with, and we have no idea how they will react. I should not be surprised if they don't run at the first sight of a wolf-man."

The three monks shared a laugh.

———

Chief of Police Mitchell sat back in his tricked-out command-and-control vehicle. It had satellite dishes, external cameras, and (to use his word) a plethora of high-tech gadgets. It even had a phone. He reclined in his padded captain's chair and punched a button.

"Baxter, what's the holdup?"

A screech, then a breathless voice. "Dog handlers had some difficulty getting their critters to concentrate. We don't have a lot of the bad guys' trace material left for them to smell and track the scent. Also, the sheriff's deputies aren't on our frequency. That's making it difficult to get set up. We have to use cell phones."

"Damn it, Baxter, this should have been worked out in advance."

There was a silent pause. Both the chief and Baxter knew that the coordination had been so rushed there was no time for fine-tuning. "We'll manage, sir."

The chief bolted from his chair. "Drone images?"

A man from the back answered. "Yes, sir. They are airborne right now, flying rectangular search patterns. We used the site of the car wreck as our starting point. We've located the house in the middle…"

Chief Mitchell cut him off. "I don't need all the details. Just find these bastards."

"You don't want me to get close-up images of the house and surrounding…?"

Mitchell gave an angry look and did not answer. He did

not want the whole world to discover that his niece operated the biggest marijuana farm in six counties, and did it under his protection, in exchange for a sizeable cut of the profits.

The guy on a console next to Chief Mitchell yelled, "Contact. Drones have spotted five, or six, men with guns moving from the road into the woods. They are headed in the direction of the suspected camp."

Mitchell made a tight face. "What do they look like?"

"Uh, pretty normal. They're wearing camouflage jumpsuits, like hunters."

Mitchell was still standing. "Last damn thing we need is a bunch of civilians getting in our way." He thought those might be Antonio's men, the demon-hunting monks. But he knew there were only three of them left. That didn't square with the identification of five, or six, men. He chose not to share that information. It would be hard to explain why he knew anything about the monks.

Baxter reported in. "The dogs are ready when you say the word."

"Go, go, get going."

"Yes, sir." In the background, someone used a theatrical voice to shout, "Release the hounds."

Several people in the command vehicle smirked, but the Chief ignored them.

"All right, sir. The dogs are moving, on the hunt. They each have a GPS transmitter so we can see their position and direction of travel on our virtual map."

Mitchell nodded to himself before yelling at the men in the van. "Okay, tell Tactical Team Alfa to head due east toward the area we suspect they are camped. Tell Team Bravo to head a little south. Maybe we can encircle these...things."

The police, the sheriff's department and the demon-hunting monks were not the only one's monitoring the tactical radio frequencies. Sypher's team was also out in the woods, listening.

Ben and Bart and five others were moving cautiously through the old-growth forest. Under the great trees, shadows made their camouflage outfits difficult to see.

Bart had a tablet computer that mirrored the exact picture seen by police in the command vehicle. His smug little smile glowed in the screen's illumination as he shook his head and whispered, "Digital Nation must have some really top-notch IT people to intercept this signal."

Ben stopped, consulted his paper map and pointed. "Okay. Right up there is where Sypher thinks the Pures are hiding. The police and their travelling circus are all heading well south of that point. What do you think we should do?"

Bart thought for a second. "Let them beat the brush. We'll hold back and see what they find. They may do our job for us and wipe out the Pures. If not, we'll move in. But, for now, we'll just monitor the police while we keep watching for the Pures." He paused, "With all these people in the forest we're bound to flush them out."

———

It was a bright sunny day, and the houseful of men and beasts were feeling relaxed and lazy after a good breakfast and a night of good sleep. Betty, who seemed to communicate with Pures better than the others, made an announcement. "The Forest People want to take you on a tour, to show you around and make you more comfortable in the woods."

No one objected. In fact, the men immediately began shuffling about, suiting up for a field trip. Samuel came close and tapped John's arm. He looked sheepish. "I want... I want to thank you."

John gave him a curious look but said nothing.

"This morning... I laughed. I actually laughed. I haven't laughed in, I don't know how long, decades, probably. I want you to know that, whatever happens out here, I appreciate you saving me, and these other men, and my precious Sallie. I know she will rest in peace now, and I hope you will see fit to bury me beside her."

John could think of nothing appropriate to say, but it didn't matter.

Samuel walked away.

After a breath, John looked around the room. Men who, just yesterday, had been in the garbage pile of society, were busy cleaning house and picking up after themselves, and laughing. He only hoped this would all turn out well for them and for his Pure Lycan friends, and even for him.

Then, in one instant, everything changed. They all sensed it and froze. Every head, except Betty Mae's, turned to face east. All conversation stopped. Their senses alerted them to danger. Something was coming and it wasn't good.

Humpty stood and growled.

They all understood his message, even the new recruits, the homeless men.

John stepped up and shouted. "We need to leave. Humpty, will you guide us through the forest to a safe place?"

The answer was a rumbling growl.

John pointed outside. "Come. We must get away from Betty Mae's house so no harm comes to her."

At the sound of her name, Betty came out of the kitchen, humming and drying her hands on a dish towel. One look around, and her smile faded when she saw the activity, clearly preparations to leave. She understood that there was a threat and her tone became business-like as she spoke to John. "What's going on? There's something bad, something dangerous…"

No answer.

She grabbed his arm and said, "Last time, you were here you left a bag of guns. It's still in the basement. If you're leaving, you might ought to take them along…just in case."

John agreed and took the time to retrieve the heavy bag before he announced. "Okay, let's go." Then, he, along with the crowd of five Lycans and five street people, headed out the back door.

At the edge of the woods, they all turned and waved "goodbye" to the woman who sheltered and fed them. She waved back, but with a tight face. Then, she clutched her arms, and her eyes grew damp, as though this might just be an actual farewell, a forever farewell.

Trees dripped early morning condensation, but the gaggle of men and Lycans ignored the cold, wet vegetation and plunged ahead at a brisk pace.

———

Bart paused in a clearing, held up a hand, and stared at his tablet computer. "The Italians think they've found something. It looks like a campsite under a rock ledge. They're sending images and reporting evidence of very recent occupation."

Ben took a breath. "Okay, how far is it to that site?"

"I have to wait until they display some more info I can use to…Oh, wait. Here it comes." He focused hard. "I think it's just beyond…that hill." Bart pointed while still staring down at the screen.

Ben and Bart moved carefully, hardly disturbing a leaf.

The five other men on Sypher's Lycan-mix team followed, but they were less stealthy.

After a few minutes, Ben ducked down to peer through thick bushes. Ahead, he saw three men with rifles poking around and scanning. Still in a crouch, he motioned with a flat hand, and his five followers knelt quietly.

Ben made a whispering phone call. "Sir, we have the Italian monks in sight. They must think they've found a camp, or something. What should we do?"

He clicked off and turned back to Bart. "Boss said to watch them, see where they lead us."

"That sounds boring. We could take them out right now."

"What can I say? He's the boss."

———

John and his diverse band followed Humpty to the top of a ridge. From there, they had a wide view of the nearby hills and streams. Those with the sharpest eyes could make out several different bands of men and dogs snaking their way through dense woodland below.

John turned to Humpty. "They don't seem to be headed toward us. Do you know where they're going?"

Humpty looked him in the eye and wrinkled his forehead.

John got his message loud and clear.

Humpty thought that the hunters were headed toward the rock overhang, where the tribe had previously slept on straw piles.

The big male Lycan, leaned over the ledge and pointed.

John didn't understand.

Humpty pointed decisively once, then again, and again. "I'm sorry, but I don't…"

Humpty raised his hands, as though holding a rifle, and

made a "Bhom, bhom" sound.

"You think we should go and shoot them?"

Humpty grunted and folded his arms with determination. Again, he said, "Bhom, bhom."

"I'm sorry, Big Guy. I don't think that's wise. I think we should just let them exhaust themselves while we lay low."

Samuel had climbed a steep path to join the two of them. He paused with his hands on his knees, panting and exhausted. "The boys...the boys are getting...antsy. They want to know what you think..."

Humpty pushed by John, held up his imaginary rifle, and made the Bhom, bhom sounds.

"No," John almost yelled. "Come on, Hump, let's go talk to them, to the *boys*."

They were halfway down a steep rock face when the first shot sounded.

John ran, slipped, and slid until he was close enough to see his fellow fugitives all standing and looking down to the woods below.

He shouted, "Who fired that shot? Who..."?

Father Time stood silently and pointed down the hill.

John leaned out from a rock to see the valley below.

"It was one of them fellas yonder that shot. It weren't one of us." Father Time seemed adamant, even defensive.

John was about to question him when another shot echoed in the valley. Then, another and another. He tried to see through gaps in foliage, but that was hopeless. He couldn't see anything.

Samuel came in a breathless, bent-over run and regained enough control to say, "I have some vague feelings, premonitions, senses. I think there are others like you out there. They are near, and they mean to kill us." He looked pained as though it was difficult to get a clear mental picture.

John looked confused. "Others like me?"

"Yes, and others, regular people, not like you; and they, too, wish us dead. And there are yet others, but I cannot grasp their thoughts."

Humpty growled and pounded a fist on the ground. Perhaps he was sensing the same thing, but all his thoughts seemed to lead to anger and adrenaline. More shots.

John clenched his fists. "Who's shooting at who? What the hell is going on?"

Samuel said, "I think that should be 'at whom' my friend." He paused. "I'm starting to get a clearer picture. The seven men like you were fired on by three foreign men. The dogs are now loose but seem confused and directionless. There are many more men from many groups, but most seem disorganized, lost... and also afraid."

John controlled his breathing.

Samuel and Humpty, as respective spokesmen for the Sapiens and Pure Lycan members of their newly formed team, looked at him as though expecting guidance, leadership, even hope.

"All right." His voice was strong and steady, *he hoped*. "The woods are filled with groups of hunters, and they're probably all looking for us. I do not know exactly who they are, but they clearly mean to harm us. We must leave. Humpty, do you know a safe place where we can go and leave these fools to shoot at ghosts?"

Humpty crossed his arms and seemed to think for a minute before he made a long, slow growl and pointed.

All eyes followed his outstretched arm.

John shook his head and said, "Betty's house? No, I don't want to put her in danger."

Samuel was nodding in slow motion. "Maybe, just maybe, they've already been there and cleared the place. In any event, the hemp or cannabis or whatever is now several feet tall. Those fields could offer cover for an escape if the shooters return."

No one had a better plan so, without further direction, they began to follow Humpty as he tromped off. John still wasn't convinced, but Nurse came to him and took his hand in hers. The fur on the top of her hand seemed soft as a kitten's. With just a few light tugs, she got him moving and he, who had been the leader by default, became a follower.

———

Ben was angry. He turned to the five men from Digital Nation's 'defense unit' and yelled, "All right, who fired without permission?"

A thick fellow with a shaved head shot back, "I got a clear shot. We're out here to get rid of them damned Killer Monks. Ain't that right? I just did what we're supposed to do. What're you whining about?"

Ben moved close. He towered over the shooter. "Do you know who I am? Do you know what I could do to you?"

The shooter took a step back but bumped into Bart who stood behind him, immoveable as a great oak tree. The shooter looked from one of the brothers to the other and stopped breathing, and all his bravado evaporating. "Look, you got no reason to get down on me. I was just doing what I was told."

"What you were told, what you should have believed, is that we are in charge and you do what we tell you. Yes, we want the monks dead, but this is a bad position for the attack. They are on higher ground, and they have excellent shooting positions while we're down here in thick woods. Every move we make will rustle the leaves and bushes and possibly reveal our position."

The shooter couldn't control his thinking although he knew the brothers would pick up on it. "Okay, Sorry. I screwed up." He looked down at the ground.

Ben said out loud, "Okay then, that's done and over with. But now we're compromised. See how they have just moved into defensive firing positions? They're getting ready to repel a charge. I have a good sense of them now. They aren't scared. They're brave men, ready to die. So, let's accommodate them. You three go with Bart and make your way to ledge off to the left. You other two, come with me, and we'll work our way up the overgrown side of the hill. You'll all know when we're in position and we'll fire simultaneously. Questions?"

———

Carlo had a good feeling. He and the other two monks, Bennie and Dag, had the high ground. The creatures below seemed clumsy as they rambled through and shook the dense vegetation. He slid on his belly to get a view from the edge of overhanging rock and watched their movement. They were moving slowly, but he was patient. He lay flat for a long time, watching, taking in every slight motion of wind or creatures that disturbed leaves in the thicket below. But then…he lost them.

"Dag, they may have managed to go around our flank. See if you can wiggle your way up behind that big rock and survey the woods to the east."

Dag was a cheerful man; tall, blonde, athletic and outgoing. Carlo counted on him and never had a reason to doubt his skill, or his dedication. The climb up a smooth rock was risky, but Dag didn't hesitate. He pressed flat against the stone and almost slithered his way upward.

When he got to the rounded top, he popped up for one quick look and then pulled his head back like a turtle. He got out the words, "I don't see…

A hailstorm of bullets rained like pellets from a shotgun. The impacts chipped rock into little puffs all around him. Dag lay flat and still. His rifle slid out of his grip and down the rock face, bumping along the way.

Carlo swore in Italian; Bennie in South Boston English. Dag's lifeless body twitched as a slow trickle of bright red blood ran down the rock and dripped into a puddle. Neither of the two surviving monks spoke for a time.

Then, Bennie bolted toward the ledge swinging his rifle and yelling, "I'm going to kill the bastards…"

Carlo tackled him and wrestled him back to the ground. Both men were breathless, and not just from the exertion. "Look, Bennie, we can't let emotions…"

His speech was cut short by another barrage of bullets. Carlo was on top of Bennie as the first bullet ripped through his shoulder. He grimaced and let out a long yell through clenched teeth. He was sucking air, still trying to speak when the next shot went through his neck. For an instant, there was no blood, and then it came in spurts, one per heartbeat. In just seconds, the flow slowed.

Bennie began pounding on Carlo's chest trying to keep his faint heartbeat going, but Carlo's face had turned ashen and his arms limp. Bennie, the young thug who had been saved from a life of crime by his local priest, was now the lone survivor of his very special band of heroes. He fought back tears as he eased Carlo's body down to lie on the flat rock.

Then, he paused and brushed a hand to gently close his hero's eyes. Anger coursed through his body and his soul. He would not let his brother monks down. Bennie took in a breath, grabbed his rifle, stood tall and yelled like a Confederate soldier charging a Yankee line. He survived for three steps before the first bullet struck his forehead. He fell like a dead tree branch.

———

The radio man inside the command vehicle pulled back his headset and yelled, "Chief, there seems to have been a gunfire fight just ahead of where our guys are headed. Several shots have been heard, and drones show three bodies. Do you want our TAC Teams to hold back?"

"Hold back? Hell no, we're not holding back. Continue with the plan, a pincer-move around these beasts."

"Yes, sir." The man's voice seemed hesitant, as though he wanted to say more. He passed the chief's command to the dog teams, the police Tactical Teams, and to the sheriff's people. Then, they waited. There was a tense, jittery silence inside the mobile command post.

———

Bart was on his belly, inching forward to survey the woods below. "I see them just where you said they'd be."

Ben chuckled. "Well yes, it helps to be plugged into their computer's display. I can see the blips of the Sheriff's men's positions, about a quarter mile southeast of us. The Madison police are almost due east of them within a hundred yards of each other."

Bart stood tall. "Okay, listen up. Here's the plan. You two go down to the rock below us. You'll have a clear line of fire to the sheriff's team."

He turned. "And you three go over behind that outcropping and get a bead on the police. All of you stay back far enough that they won't be able to see where the shots are coming from. Got it? Okay, move."

Ben went back to his tablet. The blips were closer now, less than fifty yards apart. He peeked up over a flat rock and compared the landscape to his tablet display. Once satisfied, he said loudly, "You on the left, fire! You on the right…" he hesitated until he heard the first returned shots then yelled, "Fire! Fire on your targets."

Rippling shots echoed off the rock. Then, a moment of silence before gunfire below crackled in response.

Ben inched to the ledge and looked down. Just as he hoped, there was chaotic movement and firing. The sheriff's men were shooting into thick vegetation. The police were returning fire.

"Amateurs." He laughed out loud. "It worked perfectly! Those fools heard nearby gunfire and, now, they're blindly shooting back. I love going up against idiots."

Bart touched his earpiece. "The police chief is ordering his men to cease firing. No one is responding. The radios are saturated by screaming people. It's pandemonium down there."

Ben formed a smug smile. "I think we should quietly exit stage right and go have a celebratory cocktail. Well done, men, or should I say, fellow Lycans."

There were laughs all around as they began to sneak back from the ledge and away from the chaos in the woods below.

As they hiked, Ben made a phone call. "Sir, the three monks are dead, we got all of them. The police forces are busy shooting at each other, and I think our work here is done." He paused. "Thank you, sir. I'll pass that on to the rest."

As Ben and the team picked their way through dense growth, he turned to his brother and whispered, "One last task to deal with, the priest, Antonio."

Aftermath

J ohn, along with the troop of Lycans and vagrants, paused at the sound of distant gunfire.

Humpty grunted and motioned for them to keep moving deeper into the dark and dripping woods. Heavy tree canopy blocked sunlight and trapped moisture. Everything was wet. Slippery mud, and slimy vegetation from last night's rain, made walking precarious. To make things even more difficult, the forest floor was a tangle of vines and exposed roots. Every step could turn into an ankle-twisting disaster.

The Lycans seemed sure-footed, the men less so. But, in the cool cave-like cover of old growth trees, they were shielded from drones above, even those with infra-red sensors. Noises were muffled, and vision limited to just a few trees ahead. Even smells were diluted by the moisture and overwhelming scent of decayed wood. Dogs and their human trackers would have little chance in the dense woods.

The group wandered for two hours before breaking out into brilliant sunlight. It made them squint. Humpty grunted and led toward a gurgling stream. There, everyone knelt and drank from the fast-flowing water. The men splashed water on their faces and seemed refreshed.

John went to the big Lycan and said, "You have done well. You are a good leader. Where do we go next?"

Humpty looked into John's eyes and seemed to understand. He pointed to the far shore. Beyond that shoreline, steep hills rose into a forest of dense pines and cedars. It would a challenging swim and climb, but the day seemed to be getting warmer. Maybe it wouldn't be so bad.

The river crossing went smoothly, except for Father Time, who couldn't swim. He panicked, but Samuel and another man grabbed his arms to lead him. But the old guy became too frantic to even stand in the flowing stream.

Humpty watched for a minute and then came splashing over to them. He hoisted the old man onto his shoulder like a sack of potatoes, and calmly walked out into the current. Father Time fought and screamed, but Humpty was unfazed.

Once on the other side, he sat the man down. Father Time stood shivering and hyperventilating with his arms crossed tight. The rest of the group finished crossing and then waited until the oldster had recovered enough to continue their hike.

They marched in single file under the deep shade of tall trees. A thick layer of needles on the forest floor dampened sound and cushioned every step. It was eerily silent. No birds sang. No breeze disturbed the cathedral silence. With no sun, or shadows, John could not tell directions, but he trusted Humpty and followed without question.

———

Every ambulance in the county had converged on a little road close to the scene of the police shootout. Over a dozen men had been wounded in the fiasco of crossfire and the fist fight that followed. The sheriff's deputies blamed the Madison Police for firing first. The policemen were adamant that the first shot of the crossfire came from the deputies.

Chief Mitchell sat back in his command and control vehicle, watching the monitors as he pondered his future. It didn't seem bright. Try as he might, he could not think of a way to spin this. He picked up a phone and stated to dial his home number. But what could he say to his wife? He began to sag, took a deep uneven breath, and let the phone dangle.

He stared into empty space and reviewed the events of the past few days. First, his SWAT team had been wiped out. Now, his men were involved in a friendly-fire disaster. There was nothing good to offset any of it. He had been defeated by monsters. Call them Sasquatch or Bigfoot or demons; it didn't matter. They beat him and made him a laughing stock. He scanned the banks of video screens. The first news trucks with their big cherry-picker telescoping antennas were just pulling up. Reporters and photographers were forming little huddles, as though lining up for their next scrimmage.

All around the command post van, there was the chaos of medical workers, policemen, civilians and now, news reporters - damned news reporters.

He sighed. With the din of shouting people, vehicle engines, and blaring megaphones, no one even heard the shot from inside the van.

———

Father Antonio paced but kept his eyes locked on his phone that sat on a conference table like a bomb waiting to be defused. Finally, it rang. His voice was breathless as he blurted, "Yes Carlo, tell me what happened?"

"Oh, hey Antonio, this isn't Carlo. I'm just using his phone. He doesn't need it anymore."

The priest's voice became shrill. "Who is this? How do you have this phone?"

"Oh, Antonio, you're so slow to understand. You see, I am one of those demons you hate so much. We haven't actually met, but I feel as though we've known each other for a long time, so you can call me by my first name, it's Ben."

"Where are my men, my monks? What have you done?"

"Oh, come on, Antonio, no need to be so upset. They were warriors, and they died well, good deaths. You should be proud of them, say a little prayer for them as you thumb your rosary beads. That's what you guys do, isn't it, say a prayer when things turn to shit?"

Ben's voice turned mean. "Well, now, things really have turned to shit, at least for you. This really is the time to pray. Your hired killers are all dead. Their bodies are laid out in the sun rotting. Birds are picking at their eyes.

"So, they're all dead Antonio, and now, it's your time. Say your penance, or whatever. It's the big day you've always dreamed of, the day you meet your Maker. It's here. You, Antonio, are a walking dead man. We'll decide just when and where, but your life expectancy is down to hours Antonio...hours. Enjoy them, if you can."

The line went dead. Antonio stood like a statue, still clutching his phone. Ideas flashed through his mind, fleeting thoughts and images, but no clear plan. Where would he turn? Who could help him? There was only one person, Bishop Helsing.

———

The reporter was a handsome man with a commanding voice. He faced the camera and tried to avoid the temptation to make light of this monster story.

"We're here in rural Wisconsin at the scene of a wild shootout that left five people dead and at least four others wounded. Reports are confused, but it seems that the Madison police and the County sheriff's office were out hunting for the creatures that killed five Madison SWAT officers. Somehow, the two groups mistook each other and began firing."

He turned to a woman beside him and pointed his microphone. "What is your name ma'am?"

"I'm Betty Mae Jones, and I live right across the river from where all the shooting happened. It was the scariest damn thing I've ever experienced. I mean, how could they do that, just come out here and start shooting at shadows? Wasn't anybody in charge? Wasn't anybody thinking that there's folks living out here? All those bullets flying around; it's a damned miracle nobody else got killed."

The reporter touched his earpiece. "Ma'am, I have just been told the Madison Police Chief has been killed…"

"What? What did you say? My Uncle Mitchell is dead? How on earth…?"

"Chief Mitchell is your uncle? Did you know he was out here?"

"No." The look of shock seemed sincere. "No, I didn't know nothing about it. I just heard a whole lot of rifle fire and went down into my basement. I didn't come out until I heard all those sirens and the commotion and all."

She took a series of deep breaths.

The reporter said nothing. He just let the camera record her long moment of distress. Finally, she collected herself enough to clear her throat and say, "Who, who shot him?"

The reporter bit his lower lip as though choosing his

words. "It appears to have been a self-inflicted wound, ma'am."

"What? He shot himself? He'd never do that. He wasn't the kind of man..."

Betty Mae held up a hand, unpinned her clip-on mic, and turned away.

The cameraman followed her to capture the drama and emotion as she bent at the waist and began sobbing.

The camera panned slowly over the scene of ambulances, flashing lights, and uniformed men rushing urgently about. Then, back to frame the reporter's face as he spoke softly, respectfully.

"This is John Sanders reporting live from the Wisconsin woods where, today, a horrific scene of bloodshed and terror has played out. This disaster that has taken away a beloved family member of this poor lady, Miss Betty Mae Jones." He held out a hand in her direction and the camera dutifully followed his gesture.

Someone yelled, "Cut," and the reporter nodded with a slight smile. "Okay. Good material. Good job, guys."

———

Louis Sypher sat back in his leather chair and faced a full table of brutes in suits. "Okay, where do we stand?"

Williams, the youngest in the room stood and cleared his throat. "Sir, the news media are in a frenzy trying to cover the story. They have given no indication they have any suspicions about us or the Pures."

Sypher chuckled. It was a mean laugh, the kind that sent chills up the spines of tough men. When he spoke again, it was the voice of a battlefield commander.

"This is our opportunity to emasculate our opponents. I

want a story leaked. Fox News seems to be the most aggressive and, historically, they have not been as demanding of confirmation before they air a story." He was nodding and gesturing. "So, let's give them an epic tale."

A slight smile. "It will go something like this: The local Bishop is having mental problems and has even consulted with one of his priests, who is a certified psychologist. In his paranoia, Bishop Helsing contracted and paid for a team of assassins from Italy. He even gave them silver bullets. We obtained a box of those bullets to…to analyze."

Sypher was looking off into space as though visualizing. "These demon hunters, no, call them *Killer Monks*, came to the U.S. under false pretenses, were armed by the Catholic Church, and began a calculated program of killings. They even brutalized the police chief's wife in order to make him cooperate."

This was sounding good. Everyone in the conference room was leaning forward with rapt attention. "In order to create public support for their murderous plans, the monks staged that attack on the SWAT team. They wore costumes and used circus equipment to make them look like monsters with superhuman capabilities."

Sypher was nodding to himself, making it up as he went. "To add to the hysteria, they staged a murder of Vladimir Petrov…No, scratch that. It doesn't fit with the timeline. Make it, they talked the local sheriff into joining in their bogus monster hunt."

He looked pleased with himself. "With the woods full of armed men, the monks created an inciting event. While the police and deputies were thrashing around with little guidance and no clear objective, the monks fired on both groups from hiding.

"The sheriff's men and the police mistakenly returned fire,

but at each other. That led to an all-out firefight. No monsters of any kind were killed, only fellow law enforcement officers. Altogether more than ten men died, including the five Killer Monks, themselves."

He stood straight as though he'd just had a revelation. "Those silver bullets - give some to Ben and Bart. They can use them to add more confusion to this fiasco."

Several people at the table were scribbling frantically, trying to get the boss's words just right. Sypher stood and made a mean smile. There would be no discussion.

"Okay. Get moving. I want to see this on the six o'clock news."

He started toward the door but paused. "Oh, anybody know what became of John Wagner?"

No one responded.

A New Sovereign Nation?

The forest gave way to wide cultivated fields of corn just beginning to sprout. John came to Humpty with a quizzical look. "Is this where we have been heading?"

Humpty gave what might have been a smile. Then, he tilted his head back and bellowed, "Humf, humf, hum, hum."

For a minute, there was silence and then a distant sound like a repeat of Humpty's call. The non-Lycan men in the group looked tense. Who, or what, had answered the call? What were they all walking into? No one knew - but neither did they have any other plan.

Humpty, the big Lycan, gestured, and the gaggle of men and Lycans began to walk cautiously along furrows of freshly planted corn. When they were almost to the center of the wide-open field, Humpty halted and raised a hand.

John scanned, but saw no one. He kept his rifle ready. Out of the tree-line ahead came a hoot.

Humpty resumed walking and picked up his pace.

Samuel struggled to catch up to John and tug at his sleeve. Breathless, the old man said, "You have any idea what's happening, what we're headed into?"

John was honest. "Not a clue but, so far, Humpty has taken care of us. I'll follow him."

Samuel was panting, "I don't know… if I can…keep up."

Just then, more figures emerged out of the tree shadows. Shade prevented seeing details, but the new creatures were large and dark. At least six of them stood silent and still, patiently waiting.

As John and his group drew closer, he began to make out details. The new creatures were similar to Humpy's clan, large and hairy and slightly hunched. But their fur was a lighter shade of brown with tinges of gray.

The largest one, probably the leader, came forward and reached to put a hand on Humpty's shoulder. Clearly, they were friends.

John felt his stomach muscles relax slightly.

Nurse and her fellows clambered forward to pat and hug and chatter with the other clan.

John and the other men held back to watch with suspicion.

After a bit, the newly combined group of Lycans moved closer to the men. Those of the new tribe were curious, touching and sniffing and looking into the men's eyes.

Samuel cleared his throat and spoke quietly in a controlled voice. "I sense no hostility. We are oddities to them. I'm not sure why, but I think they want us to come with them."

One of the new group, a young female, by her looks, wandered back behind the men and suddenly became agitated, pointing and making shrill sounds, cries of alarm.

Humpty and the other Lycan leader rushed to her.

John sensed her fear and spoke in a near-shout. "It's the

guns. They fear guns. Everybody, lay down your guns and show them your empty hands."

Father Time clutched his rifle and started to speak. "I ain't giving up my goddamned…"

Samuel was on him in a moment. "Listen, you dumb shit, these creatures could kill us with a single punch, but they're being friendly."

The two men were nose to nose, eye to eye, breathing each other's breath. "Put the gun down, or you'll likely get us all killed, understand?"

Father Time looked like a petulant schoolboy. He clutched his rifle, sniffed, and looked around at the crowd of men and Lycans all staring at him. Slowly, reluctantly, he laid it on the ground, folded his arms, and looked away, like a chastened teenager.

Samuel put a hand on the old Father Time's shoulder in the same way Humpty had done, and said, "Thank you." It sounded sincere.

Crisis over, the two groups mingled and traded thoughts. The new group was curious, inspecting the men in a very hands-on way. Despite their initial reluctance, the street people relaxed a bit and accepted the indignity of fondling and stroking.

John turned to Samuel and said, "Thank you for that intervention."

Samuel only shrugged. After a moment he said, "I thought they would smell bad, but they don't. It's kind of a sweet, musky smell, like some exotic perfume a rich woman would wear."

John shrugged. "Well, *they* might smell sweet, but I know *I* stink. Even after that slosh through the stream back there I still smell like sweat and dirt—old, moldy dirt."

Samuel sounded quiet, but serious. "What do you think is going to happen here? What do these two groups have in mind? I'm getting very confused signals from them."

"Yeah, I know. All I can say is that there is no hostility in their thoughts. I think they want to help us, but aren't sure how."

"Well, as long as they're not cannibals."

John smiled, but it wasn't convincing.

———

Louis Sypher sat back in his chair and used the corded secure phone. "Yes, Ben, I have the updates. I understand you are now going after the Italian priest who brought the Killer Monks to America. That's good. Once he's gone, there's only one person left who knows of their operations, Bishop Helsing."

He listened for a moment. "No, Ben, we can't move on him now. With all the current publicity, that would create a wasps' nest of questions, and we might just get stung. No, we'll give him some time to sweat and then take him out in some inconspicuous way, maybe an induced heart attack, or some believable accident, I don't know. But, for now, he's not a threat. Anything he says would likely incriminate him."

They talked for a bit before Sypher asked, "So where is John Wagner? Have we lost track of him?" He scowled. "What? You think he is with the Pures who killed the SWAT boys? What is he doing there?" Sypher was drumming his fingers now. "Well, find out, damn it…and get back to me."

———

John and the former street people gathered under a shade tree apart from the Lycan group.

Samuel sounded earnest as he began: "We have to face some realities here. We're all grateful to be out of the city gutter, but survival in the forest will have its own challenges, and we need some sort of plan. We're going to need shelter, food, and a source of income. Once we establish those resources, we can set ourselves up as an independent community and live out our lives. Okay, let's hear some ideas."

The jittery man everyone thought was an addict was rocking back and forth and looking down at the ground. His voice was as unsteady as his movements. "I get a sense of a place nearby. It has empty buildings and some old equipment. There was a road, but it got washed out. Now, there's weeds growing up through the concrete and stuff. Maybe we could go there."

Samuel frowned. "Why should we go to some abandoned building? How will that help us?"

Jittery kept rocking with crossed arms. He looked like some sort of religious penitent. "I don't know. It's just… Well, the place is calling to me. It's like it's our destiny, or something like that."

John had been quiet, but now stood. "I don't know about destiny, but this idea is… Well, it's something. Anyone have a better plan?"

There was silence.

"Okay, let's go check it out. That won't hurt." He turned to Jittery. "What direction, and how far?"

"My name's Edward. They mostly call me Eddie Bugs. I think the place is over there behind that hill."

John made an approving nod. "Anybody have any objections…anybody? No. Then, let's go hiking and give it a look."

Without further comment, they stood, shook off the twigs,

and ground debris they had been sitting on and began the trek.

John shouted to Humpty, "We're going for a walk."

Samuel said quietly, "He already knows. He approves, but will not come. He wants to stay here with his friends."

The walk was long. As they began the second hour, Samuel came and almost whispered. "Do you trust this guy? I mean, his nickname is Eddie Bugs. He's obviously a tweeker, and probably unreliable. On top of that, we have no idea if he has really sensed something. Maybe he's just hallucinating."

John chuckled. "And, if he is, all we've lost is some time and energy. Now, I don't hold out too much hope but, like I said before…"

Someone shouted, "I see something."

Others crowded and peered into the dense foliage.

John and Samuel walked past the crowd. There was a really big wall, but so overgrown with vines that it was hard to make out its exact size, or shape.

John clumped his way through the tangle of jungle-like vegetation until he was close enough to reach out and poke his arm deep into the overgrowth on the wall. He felt around and then stood back trying to see the top and judge the size of it.

He turned and shouted, "It's stone. In fact, it feels like chiseled stone fitted to be a wall. It's a damned citadel."

The others all looked up, as though they might be able to see through the tangled growth. Eddie Bugs, grabbed hold of a vine and began climbing.

John shouted, "I don't think that's a good idea," but Eddie had already clawed his way up and almost out of sight. It took several minutes before his shouted report.

"I'm on the top of a stone wall, maybe twenty-five or thirty feet tall. Everything is thick with vines and weed, but I can see that there are four walls around a big open area with five buildings, all four stories high. I don't see a gate or entrance, but I can make out a stone road that leads back to the wall."

Samuel tried to shout but his voice wasn't very strong. John repeated for him. "Where does the road lead? Where should we look for an entrance?"

Eddie shouted back. "From where you are, thirty paces to your right, more or less."

Without anyone's direction, the group of five began to move. They stepped on and over tangles of vine and root and bush as they tried to approximate thirty paces.

Samuel was the first to notice. He bent to one knee and yelled. "Road! Underneath this thicket, there are finished stone blocks that I think are a road."

He turned and held out a hand in the direction of the wall. "The gate, if there is one, should be about there." They all went to probe and feel through the vines. Someone yelled, "I got something. I'm touching smooth flat wood. Could be a gate, or structural timber, or something like that."

John tried to poke through the growth. "These damned vines must be three inches thick. I don't know…" He paused and looked at the two largest vines, took hold of them, and made an animal-like yell. Flexing forward and then yanking back, he used his Lycan tensors to rip the vines loose from the wall. Three more yanks and a four-foot wide section of stone was laid bare.

Samuel was leaning to look. "Man, that is real craftsman-ship. Those stones must be almost a foot square, and they look hand-carved, but to very tight tolerances. Look, no gaps, no irregularities; they're perfect. Who could have done this?"

The rest of the crowd had spread out to start tearing away their own sections of vine. They lacked John's strength, but they were tenacious, and slowly the wall was becoming exposed. At least the bottom five feet of the thirty-foot-high wall was being exposed.

Then Eddie yelled, "Gate. I think I found a gate."

There was a stampede to come tear away the vines over his discovery. It wasn't so much a gate as a great wooden door.

John estimated it to be approximately six inches thick and six feet high. The wood was rotten and crumbling, but deeply rusted iron hinges, and a latch, were intact.

Samuel yelled, "All together, start pushing. Put your shoulders into it."

They grunted and sucked air and pushed.

Little by little, the wood crumbled until the great door fell back to crash in a cloud of dust and rotten wood. The opening it left was big enough that no one had to stoop to get through the tangle of vines that remained.

Once inside, they scanned the courtyard. It had an almost magical feel. Great vine-covered walls surrounded an open area like a parade ground all paved with blocks cut from the same type of stone as the walls. Stone benches faced a debris-filled fountain where a statue probably stood once upon a time. Corroded iron lamp posts looked like ancient gas lights.

Everything he saw convinced John this was a structure from the nineteenth century.

One of the homeless men found a large metal placard where it had fallen off the stone wall. He was furiously rubbing away quarter-inch-thick orange-brown corrosion. Finally, he dug deep enough to reveal a few faint letters.

He stood back and tried to get an angle that let him see the traces of cast brass letters. He shouted them out, "A-s-y-l... I can't read no more."

Samuel looked over his shoulder. "I would bet it said 'Asylum.' What else would those letters spell?"

Eddie stepped back and sounded rattled. "Asylum, you mean like a loony bin?"

John was thinking. "It doesn't really matter what it was. The question is, will it suit our needs? Let's split up and go snooping. We need to find out if it's safe and if it will provide adequate shelter. If so, we'll then have to evaluate whether it's defensible."

Samuel slowly scanned the perimeter wall. "I'll tell you this. It looks like this place could survive a nuclear blast. I'm anxious to see if its rooms are habitable. Come on, everybody, let's go hunting."

In just seconds, they were all gone on separate ways.

In the closest building, John found an arch that led into a hallway. Wooden doors were long rotted, but the stone walls were still sound. Old gaslight fixtures on the wall had rusted into nubs, but the floor was remarkably free of dirt and vegetation. Vines had intruded into some rooms, but others were completely free of growth. All furniture had long since crumbled to dust.

This was a damned castle, a fortress that could easily shelter his group. *But, what about food and other necessities?*

He walked out in the courtyard and yelled. "Let's assemble and report our findings."

It took a while for all five of the men to show up. Eddie was excited, bubbling and anxious to tell his story.

"I found a great big kitchen. The wood tables and stuff have only a little rot, but there's a big iron stove that looks like it will still work. And there's a cabinet made out of something, don't know what, but everything inside has survived and looks almost new. There's pots and tin plates and silverware. That kitchen can still work." He shrugged. "Except for there's no water. There's a handpump with a spigot, but it's rusted apart."

"That's great, Eddie, really great. Good job."

Another man said, "There's a dug well over there." He pointed. "Looks like it once had a couple of posts and a crank-type reel to haul up water buckets, but that's all gone."

"Good work." John was again trying to stay positive.

John saw that one last man who was being quiet as though holding back. "So, did you find any treasures?"

He nodded with no eye contact. "Tools. I found a bunch of rusted tools. Some could maybe still be used if we made new handles and such. There's axe heads and knife blades and hammer heads and a whole lot of farm stuff I don't know nothing about."

John went over and patted him on the back. "Good job. Well done." Then, he turned back. "Boys, this is terrific. If we wanted to, we could survive here forever." He paused. "At least, after we planted some crops. But, for now, this place offers safety from the crazy people who seem to be hunting us. I think we should go back and tell the Pures what we've found."

Samuel stood and said, "They already know. They'll be here in a few minutes."

As they waited, John turned to Samuel and said, "Any idea why someone would build such an impressive structure so far from civilization?"

Samuel looked across the courtyard. "Over there is a stone with '1837' carved into its face. I have no idea what this place was like back then. There could have been a town here. I know there was copper and iron mining in this area, and some trouble with the Indians, but that's pretty much all I know." He stopped to ponder. "The plaque that may have said 'asylum' makes it even more curious. What kind of asylum could it be?"

"Guess we'll never know, but it sure is a fortress. We'll be safe here, even if they send in Army tanks and Air Force bombers."

Both men laughed.

Humpty and the furry crowd arrived and looked around with suspicious scowls. They poked and climbed and sniffed.

Samuel, who seemed to have become their spokesman, said, "They want to know why you want to be here? They think there is something bad here, like spirits, or something. At least, I think that's what I'm getting from them.

Samuel touched his chin with his knuckles and grimaced. "Okay, they're coming around a little. They seem to like this place because of its strength. Maybe they will want to stay."

Samuel seemed thoughtful. "But I just don't see how we could manage so far from civilization. Now, don't get me wrong, this is a great hiding place, but for how long? We can subsist for a time on Betty Mae's generosity with food and money, but we can't take advantage of her forever."

Then, he retreated into his own thoughts. When he spoke again, it sounded as though he was just thinking out loud. "On the other hand, most of these men are on Social Security and Medicare, or even Medicaid. I could set up a post office drop for their checks. If Betty Mae would fund the renovations…"

John felt strangely awkward and walked off to leave the elderly accountant still thinking out loud. John wasn't sure why he felt uneasy, but he suddenly felt that he had to get away. After a brisk walk near the overgrown courtyard gate, he paused and bent over, breathing hard, almost shaking. He had to leave. He didn't know why, but he had to get away, to be by himself.

Behind him, he heard Eddie shout. "Water! I found water. In back of the kitchen, there is another hand pump, and this one is functional. The first ten gallons I pumped from it were thick and brown, almost sludge. But, then, it flowed nice and clear. We have water."

There was a child-like excitement in Eddie's voice.

John smiled, even as a dark cloud seemed to be coming over him. His mind was flooded by thoughts, senses, and ideas.

Everyone around him was sending signals, intentional, or simply as a byproduct of their thinking. He needed to clear his head and make room for his own thoughts and not be over-whelmed by sensory overload, confusion, and strangely…anger.

But why? *Everything was going just as I hoped. Why am I angry?* It made no sense. He looked all around at the activity. Men and Lycans were bustling around, checking, probing, consid-ering possibilities. Samuel and Humpty seemed to be guiding the activity, and doing it well.

They don't need me.

Until that point, John had not really considered the leader-ship role he had played. He was the decider, the boss Lycan. Now, others were assuming that role. He stood with clenched fists and teeth. He wanted to fight, but against who? He thought of the demon hunters, the police, the little lady back at the safe house. So many forces arrayed against him. He wanted to strike back at…who? A stray thought: Samuel would have corrected him for not saying "whom."

Then a moment of clarity. He understood his quandary. He understood that he had been a hero, a leader. Now, his power seemed to be evaporating. He had resisted being normal, being an ordinary Sapiens. But, now, he suddenly wanted it back.

Among the voices hammering away in his brain, there was one that came through clearly. It was Gretchen, and she seemed to be calling him. Why had he abandoned her? But he knew the answer. It was Sypher.

He wanted to get back at the man who took away his normalcy. He wanted to get away from Louis Sypher, cancel the blood contract, go back to being normal, at least, as normal as he could be. But, on the other hand, he still wanted to be in control, to dominate. He yearned to be the master.

He looked around at all the flurry of activity by both hairy and smooth creatures who had been banished by society. They were busy investigating their new domain. There was hopefulness in their actions.

They don't need me anymore.

Outcast - Loneliest Lycan

John walked through the woods. He didn't think about directions. He was being guided by some inner drive that he could not question. After two hours of picking his way through the brush, he was back at his car. He found the magnetic container under the wheel well with a spare key.

Then, John drove as though in a trance, steady and focused, but with absolutely no thinking. If he were honest, he actually knew his destination, but he drove on as though it were a divine revelation. He was headed for the Digital Nation headquarters building. Traffic was light, and he pulled into the underground parking lot in no time.

He took the elevator. At two different stops, waiting passengers declined to board with the filthy, stinking man who looked like a gutter bum. *Screw them*, he thought, but he did decide to go to his apartment and shower before...*before what?* He wasn't sure.

His key card worked and let him into an apartment that appeared untouched since he left. He showered and luxuriated in the warm water that cleansed his body. That body, when he looked down at it, was covered with still-healing scars and scratches and bruises. It had been a rough couple of days. He shaved and looked at the stranger in the mirror. *How could he have changed that much in a week?*

Once dry and dressed in clean clothes, he felt invigorated, but he still didn't know what he was being driven to do. Surely, he was not about to kill Louis Sypher. *Well, only one way to find out.* He got in the elevator and pressed the up button. *Up to where?*

It stopped just one floor above, and a man in a suit got in. Both he and that man had a flash of recognition. "Wagner," the man blurted. It was the Ben from the "Ben and Bart" team who had rousted John from his bed just a couple of days before.

The elevator had barely begun to move when Ben hit the emergency stop button. *This isn't going to be good.* John didn't wait to find out. He lunged to grab Ben by the throat, thumbs digging deep into the man's flesh.

Ben gagged and made gurgling noises as he tried to punch John, but they were too close for him to get a good swing. So, he grabbed at John's forearms but, strong as he was, he couldn't pull them away.

John made an animal growl and clamped his chokehold even tighter.

Ben's face was red, going to purple. His jowls were puffy, his lips swollen. Sypher's personal hitman kept making impotent punches and even kicks, but that just caused him to lose his balance and sag, dragging John's arms down with the weight. It was obvious to both that Ben wasn't going to get free.

John considered letting him go, but he didn't. He kept the Lycan tough guy in a death grip, clamping tighter and tighter until, finally, the thug struggled no more. When John finally did release him, Ben's head thumped against the elevator door. Clear fluid dripped from his mouth. One hand still twitched.

As John fell back against the wall to gasp; he realized that he had been holding his own breath. Almost as an afterthought, he frisked the dead man and removed two pistols, a snub-nosed revolver, and a Beretta nine-millimeter automatic. He popped out the Beretta's clip, intending to discard it but paused at the shiny bullets. That seemed really strange, but he had no time to waste on oddities. *Now, what to do with the body?*

He deselected the emergency stop button, and the elevator began to move. He got off at the next floor and hit the basement button to allow Ben one last elevator ride.

John was on the twelfth floor, near Vrykolas' office. If anyone had answers, he would be the one. John went cautiously, head down, no eye contact. No one seemed to notice him. He did not knock. He simply stood in front of the surveillance camera until the door buzzed open.

Vrykolas sat as before, half hidden behind stacks of papers and books. He looked up and made the closest thing to a smile John had seen from the man.

"Mister Wagner. You have certainly impressed many here at the office. How is it you have returned, and what do you seek?"

"Sir, I do not know what brought me back here. Something drove me to return, something that I do not understand, but am powerless to resist."

"Powerless?" The old man chuckled. "What drove you here, what drives you in everything you do, is not a lack of power; it is a lust for power. It is the alpha in you, the desire to rule. A dangerous and unpredictable force; it is also irresistible. I suspect it has plagued you for your entire life. Now, you have come back to what is the seat of power for our kind. You probably seek to challenge those above you, maybe even Sypher."

He exhaled and shook his head. "It is a fool's mission, Mister Wagner. Sypher is surrounded by…"

John blurted, "I just killed the one called Ben."

"You killed *Ben*? I don't know why I didn't sense that. Are you blocking me?"

Vrykolas was silent for an uncomfortably long time. "So, now you are making a big bet, the bet of a lifetime. Mister Sypher will not, indeed he cannot, allow that act to go unpunished. It would diminish his perception among the others. He must kill you, John. He has no options."

John Wagner felt an unaccustomed response, fear. "I did not mean to do anything… The bastard attacked me in the elevator."

Vrykolas inhaled deeply. "Yes, but that hardly matters. Here, Mister Wagner, here are your options as I see them. You could try to run, but your pursuers all have the same acute senses as you. They will find you, and then they will make an example of you. Or, you might negotiate. Unfortunately, I suspect you have little to offer in a deal. The last option, and the most likely to succeed, is to apologize, be contrite, throw yourself on the mercy…"

"I don't see that happening, sir."

"Nor do I, Mister Wagner but, honestly, what else can you do? You are, in the American vernacular, screwed."

John sat in silence for a while. Then, he rose, head down, moving slowly as he turned toward the door. He hesitated and stood, still looking straight ahead. "Has anyone ever challenged Sypher?"

Vrykolas shook his head. "Not for many years and, then, it was a very one-sided confrontation."

John nodded without eye contact and left, pausing to crack

open the outer office door and check up and down the hall. It was clear. He stepped out and began walking but he still had no plan, still being driven by the voices in his head, still didn't know what they wanted him to do.

He started to take the elevator, but Ben's body must have been discovered by now. There would certainly be a crowd gathered, and not a very friendly crowd. Instead, he took the stairs, carefully watching over the rail to see if there was anyone on the floors above or below. Luckily, not many people used the stairs, just a few physical fitness nuts.

The Contract Is Void

As he reached the eighth floor, he heard a commotion one flight below. Unsure what to do, he left the stairwell and tried to be inconspicuous as he walked down halls filled with busy people rushing from office to office. He was almost to the stairwell on the other side of the building when a woman with her sandy hair in a bun stepped into the hall, carrying a stack of papers.

It was Gretchen. He froze, nowhere to run.

She almost passed him without noticing, but something made her stop and look back. Her expression went blank and she said only the single word, "Jesus."

John tried to speak, but he could do no more than stammer.

Gretchen put one hand on her hip and said, "Well, this is just fucking wonderful. Not only are you not dead, you're stalking me at work. Whatever did I see in you."

John was taken aback. "You don't seem all that surprised that I'm alive."

"Really? I knew when they showed up with that..." She

paused and looked away. Her voice was bitter. "John, I sold you out. They paid me fifty grand and offered me a job, a good job, with good pay. All I had to do was play along with the dead fiancé act."

"Act? You were in on this?"

"Oh, sort of. They told me you were in trouble and had to get out of the country and, if I went along with the fake death, it would keep the FBI and Homeland Security from pursuing you on some sort of warrant. So, I did it." She looked him in the eye. "It wasn't that much of a sacrifice. The last two years with you were a mess, kind of like you were having an early mid-life crisis. I thought you might be happier without me."

Her eyes looked damp as though there might be a trace of a tear.

John stammered. "I always loved you, and I'm sorry for all the pain." A deep breath. "But, now, I know more about myself and…"

"You mean the Lycan thing? Yeah, they told me all about it. Tell you the truth, I thought it was kind of cool. You were such an unhappy human, I thought maybe you could do better as a wolf-man."

"You knew about *that*? You knew all along?"

"Well, no, not all the way. But they came to me and said you wouldn't be coming home and that it was in your best interest if I played along. I was upset, but I thought they might be right. You were so unhappy there at the end."

"I'm so sorry, Gretchen, but do you think there's any chance we could…"

She cut him off. "No! Don't even think about it. I'm with someone else, a normal guy who doesn't howl at the moon."

She turned and began a brisk walk down the hall, almost a run. John wore a stricken look as he watched her go. After everything he had done was for her, at least, he thought he was doing it for her at the time. Now, she was lost. He was alone. He didn't have much else to lose.

Screw it, he thought. He walked to the elevator and waited until the little ding announced its arrival. It was empty. He went into the little capsule. He was alone, and thought this might be a metaphor for his life; going somewhere with no reason and destined for a lonely journey, destined to die alone.

It was close to quitting time, and the elevator added people at every floor. It was getting tight, and he was crowded into a back corner. At least he had taken a shower. That thought made him smirk, just a little.

———

At the third floor, a large man in a suit boarded the elevator. He did not see John but, after a few seconds, that man lifted his chin, as though he just heard something, or maybe smelled something, or just sensed something.

John recognized him. It was Bart, Ben's brother, the other half of the hitman team. John slowly moved his hand toward a gun in his belt.

Bart seemed confused, concentrating, as though he knew something was wrong, but didn't know just what. Then, he turned and began to survey the fellow occupants.

John hunkered down, but a middle-aged lady beside him spoke loudly. "What're you doing down there? You some sort of pervert, or something?"

Bart had a sudden flash of recognition. He yelled and tried to claw his way over the crowd to reach John. But John Wagner had been through days of recent hand-to-hand combat, and was primed to fight back.

He met Bart's lunge with a flat palm under the chin that snapped the Lycan hitman's head back like a shaken rag doll.

Bart, the killer feared by so many, collapsed and fell back against several elevator occupants who screamed and squirmed and flailed. An old lady wormed her way out of the pile and smacked him with her purse. A man in a suit planted an elbow in his face. Bart's nose began to bleed. The big guy clawed his way clear, shook his head, and tried to stand, but the mass of people squirming all around him made that nearly impossible.

He was still surfing on a wave of elevator passengers when the bell dinged, and the door opened. People shoved their way past and jostled him along with the flow. Once out in the hall, the crowd dispersed leaving Bart and John alone facing each other. Bart wiped his bloody face and grinned. He was breathing hard, almost panting, and the look in his eyes was pure bloodlust.

John pulled the pistol from his belt and held it beside his leg.

Bart straightened, rolling his shoulders, getting himself together, and showing his teeth.

Without hesitation, John raised the pistol and shot him square in the forehead.

Bart the enforcer, the monster feared by so many, dropped to one knee, stared into space, and then fell forward like a freshly sawed tree. He lay with his head turned to the side, his mouth gaping and eyes focused a thousand miles away.

John tucked the pistol back into his belt, stepped over the body, and casually got off at the next floor.

A waiting crowd lunged to enter the elevator, saw Bart and then fell back screaming and cursing and knocking down people behind them. The pool of blood from the dead man's head was still spreading.

As he passed people in the hall, John forced a weak smile. No one seemed to notice him. At the stairwell entrance, he stopped and thought for a moment. Surely, Sypher would react to Ben and Bart's death by closing down the building. *But, if not the elevator, or stairs, what other option was there to escape?*

He slipped into a vacant office and tried a window. It was, as he expected, permanently sealed. He tried another and another, all sealed. Just as well, he wasn't thrilled about doing a Spiderman-type walk along a ledge. He went back into the hall, where he saw a firehose hanging on a wall. Behind the hose was an unmarked door.

No one paid attention to him. The dead man in the elevator was causing a logjam-like backup and, at quitting time, everyone was focused on finding a way out of the building, just as John was.

He tried the small door's handle. It was unlocked. Then, wearing his most nonchalant look, he slipped into a dark closet-like compartment. There was yet another door on the back side of the tiny compartment, a door that probably led to some sort of escape route. It was locked by a simple padlock held in place by four screws. He grabbed the lock, squeezed his shoulders forward and then yanked. The entire mechanism pulled out of the wall.

That door opened to an outside fire escape. It was a metal staircase that, just as he hoped, led him down seven stories and onto the flat roof of an addition to the main office building. There, he saw a smaller drop-down escape ladder to the street. In a few minutes, he was on the ground mixing with the crowd of workers on their way home.

John took a deep breath. Maybe killing Ben and Bart was not what drew him so strongly to the building, but it was satisfying, nonetheless. He boarded a city bus with no destination in mind. He just wanted to be somewhere else.

That seemed safe. He would be anonymous sitting on the back seat among the crowded commuters, but he wasn't. His mind was swimming with sensory inputs, so many that he couldn't keep them straight. One thing was clear. Sypher, and many others, knew he was there. One vague feeling overpowered all others, someone was coming, someone seeking him, and she would bring sorrow. It didn't take long.

A woman in an overcoat squeezed into the seat beside him. He tried to avoid eye contact but was overwhelmed by a rush of emotion so strong he wanted to scream.

She spoke softly but with a sharp edge. "Well, hello again, John."

All the air rushed out of his lungs. It was Gretchen... again. He couldn't look at her.

After so much adrenaline, he couldn't think clearly. He looked straight ahead as he spoke. "You need to get away from me. I'm being hunted."

She didn't respond. Both of them sat in silence, avoiding eye contact. Gretchen fidgeted with her hands.

Then, a whoosh of airbrakes made them lurch.

The bus driver turned and yelled. "Sorry, folks, a police car just blocked us. It looks like they want to board. Please, everybody, just stay calm. I'm sure this won't take long."

John turned, looked Gretchen in the eyes and whispered, "Take care of yourself and always remember that, no matter how odd or distant I seemed, and what terrible things they say about me, I have always loved you and always will."

With that, he went to the rear bi-fold bus door and ripped it open.

Two steps later, he faced four policemen in protective gear with guns drawn. John casually raised his hands and made an innocent little smile. "Gentlemen, there's no need to be frightened. I mean you no harm."

They were shouting, moving closer, pointing their guns at him. He pretended to stumble, but he was really just squatting, flexing his tensors. With a convulsive leap, he sailed high over the startled cops, well beyond their flashing cars. Landing on the sidewalk, he collected himself and broke into a furious run, a Lycan run. He was getting better at this stuff.

Two blocks and he stopped, once again, he was standing in front of the Digital Nation headquarters building. He suppressed a laugh. "Must be fate. But, what the hell, I have no place else to go." Then a shrug, "It really doesn't matter. I'll likely be dead within the hour."

But he was Lycan, and a Lycans would not die easily. He stood tall, walked in the front door, and fought against the stream of workers still surging on their way out. The police were herding people out the doors. The elevator door was crisscrossed with yellow *"Do Not Enter"* tape. So, he took the stairs. There was no reason to be sneaky. Sypher certainly knew he was there. John felt the man's thoughts in the same way you feel the first drops of rain before an approaching storm. This storm was going to be violent.

Sypher's outer office was huge and was decorated with enough paintings and statues to resemble a museum lobby. It was empty. All administrative people were gone for the day. John took a deep breath, squared his shoulders, and opened the boss's inner door.

Two bodyguards in suits were poised, waiting. Without hesitation, they charged at him. But these were run-of-the-mill tough guys. Compared to Bart and Ben, they were pussycats.

John dispatched them with a single blow each.

They lay sprawled on the Oriental carpet, not moving, not even seeming to breathe. He stood over them for a moment, just to be sure that they were really out cold and not playing possum. His thoughts went back to the two young gangsters back in that seedy apartment. That seemed an eternity ago, and a million miles away. But now, he went to Sypher's door and the reality of this moment hit home.

Louis Sypher stood with his back to John, as though unconcerned with the fight that just took place in his outer office. He puffed a cigarette, and smoke swirled around him like supernatural mist. Then he turned and gave John a hard look.

"I must say, you have performed well, John Wagner. I expected as much. I had such high hopes for you but then, you faltered. You befriended the Pures, those animals, those monsters that are our distant relatives. They are nothing to us, nothing but a threat. You just don't you see, they will make us appear to the Sapiens as an inferior breed, a lower class of animals."

He spoke through his teeth. "We are the dominators. We cannot be thought of as dumb animals. Those beasts, the Pure Lycans, must be destroyed. Understand? They *must* be destroyed." His tone sounded not just angry, but mean. "But, now…now you seem to think you are ready to be their master, their protector, their Alpha?"

Without warning, Louis Sypher knotted his fists, sank to his knees, and vaulted clear across the office like a cannonball. He let out a shrieking cry.

But John was ready, more than ready; he was younger, more agile, and toughened by recent combat. He easily side-stepped the attack and let the older man crash against the far wall.

Sypher picked himself up and turned back with a furious cry. He looked like an angry gorilla, ready to leap again, puffing like a steam engine starting up. With another scream, he charged John. They traded a flurry of punches, hard punches, punishing blows.

Louis Sypher backed off, panting and wild-eyed. The CEO

was showing his age. He spoke, and his voice was bitter. "I have never been beaten in combat, and I won't be now. Die, you traitor... Traitor to your own kind!"

John rolled his shoulders. "Well, you may never have been beaten, but there aren't any rules in this game."

John leaped.

Sypher leaped.

They crashed in midair. Clawing, punching, screaming, they slammed down onto the thick carpet and rolled, still entwined.

Sypher drew back and opened his jaws to reveal glistening fang-like teeth.

He lunged, but John was ready. His reflexes took over, just as they had with the rabbit back at the farm. He ducked the big man's thrust and then bit Sypher on the throat. It was a deep bite that tore away a good chunk of flesh.

The bigger man pulled back and used his hands to crab-walk away until bumping into an unconscious bodyguard's body. Sypher's face was pale. His expression seemed more confusion than pain. He ignored the blood spurting from the wound on his neck, even as it ran down his chest to drench his shirt, his hands, and the even the carpet. His breathing slowed, and he tried to speak. Nothing came out but gurgling blood and saliva. His eyes darted about before growing cloudy and still. He sagged into a heap. Air rushed out of his lungs in a long, final sigh.

John, too, was panting, gasping for air. He spit out the vile-tasting flesh and fought the urge to vomit. He sat there across from the three corpses for a long time, trying to control his breathing, and his thoughts.

Then, in a single moment, the realization came. He now knew what he must do. With a shake of his head, he drew his pistol and crawled over to Sypher, carefully placed the barrel of his gun into the ragged, torn neck, and fired once. The discharge blackened Sypher's throat wound and shattered the back of his skull.

Louis Sypher still slumped. Dead weight, his arms lay limp and tangled by his sides. His legs akimbo, his chin drooped on his chest, his mouth wide open and still dripping blood.

John stood and listened. There was no commotion outside. *Had no one heard the shot?*

He went to Sypher's private bathroom and vomited into the toilet, heaving long and hard, until he had no more fluid to expel. The piece of meat he spit out was much smaller than he imagined.

He felt exhausted, not just by the fight, but by all the events of the past month. But there was no time for rehashing the past. He had to clean up both himself, and the scene, and quickly. There was no telling what might come next.

He washed his face and hands then checked his body for blood. There was plenty. If necessary, he could explain it as having come into contact with Sypher, trying to resuscitate the dead man. John cracked the office door and peeked out into the hallway: empty - everyone gone for the day.

Then, one at a time, he dragged the two bodyguards to a garbage chute and hefted them in. If they were still alive, the eight-story drop would change that. A high-tech automated disposal in the basement would incinerate them with no human oversight.

"You have to love technology," John said with a grunt.

Back in the office, he wiped every surface that hinted of a struggle and placed furniture back in position. John also wiped the pistol and placed it in Sypher's lifeless hand and wrapped the fingers tight so rigor would make it difficult to pry them loose. He looked around trying to see the scene as a detective might. It was a plausible situation. No hint of external violence, a convincing suicide. The cops would probably not even think of the missing bodyguards.

John straightened, collected himself, picked up the office phone, and punched numbers. The answer was immediate. "Nine-one-one, what is the nature of your emergency?"

"Yes, hello. This is the offices of Digital Nation. My boss has just killed himself. I was about to leave for the day when I heard the shot and found him lying in the office. He's shot himself, shot himself in the head."

John listened to what was probably a set of routine questions. "Yes, I'm sure he's dead. Yes, it's the Digital Nation Headquarters, Eighth floor, room 801. Please hurry."

He walked to the door and looked all around. The entire floor was quiet, eerily quiet, like an empty cathedral. John went back to Sypher's office, unsure what to do next.

The desk phone rang, two rings, then three. He wasn't going to pick up, but something, a small voice in his head, told him, *Go ahead, answer it.*

He cleared his throat but didn't have a chance to speak. The old man's voice on the phone sounded weary, "So it is done. Sypher is no more. Do you feel ready to replace the man you have just murdered?"

There was a lengthy pause before John cleared his throat. "Replace him?"

He listened for a long, uncertain time, trying to be calm and take in everything. He had to keep it all straight. *Was he ready to move in and assume the CEO position? How many would accept him? Who would fight against his takeover?*

His mind was racing, images flashing, questions pouring at him. Then, he felt a surge of confidence welling in his gut. John looked at the crumpled body on the floor. Sypher probably meant well, but he was a monster who wanted personal power above all else.

Finally, John spoke with confidence. "Yes, Mister Vrykolas, I believe I am."

The old man replied, "Very well. I shall support you if, and only if, you agree to change the company's policy toward Lycans with higher percentages of pure blood." There was a hint of anger in his tone.

Vrykolas said, "The whole percentage idea has always been ludicrous. For a man of science, Louis Sypher allowed himself the arrogance of racist views. He would be the first to admonish underlings that the idea of describing DNA traits as a percentage makes no sense, and yet, he did just that. He knew perfectly well that different phenotypes frequently have exquisitely similar genotypes."

Vrykolas hesitated. He probably thought that John might not be all that knowledgeable in the field. "That is, we look different from those we have called 'Pures' but, at a genetic level, we are virtually identical. They are us, and we are they."

John sounded stern. "I, more than almost any other part-Lycan, understand. I have lived with them. I feel that I know them. They are intelligent, even though they do not speak…"

The old man interrupted. "I believe you. So, if you swear to me you will aid all of our kind, pure, and not-so-pure, I will help you. Now, tell me about the murder, and how I can portray it to the new chief of police."

"Sir, you have a relationship with the new chief?"

"Baxter? Well, yes. But it is a fragile relationship. John Dumas provided us a bio-sample, and Sypher identified him as roughly ten percent pure - *Sypher's percentages again*. We have met with Baxter and, after his initial doubts, won his tenuous cooperation. I've just finished speaking with him, and I'm hopeful he will help us. You, in the meantime, need to make sure there are no discrepancies in the crime scene or your story."

The phone went dead. John could no longer even sense the wise old man's thoughts.

He stood for a moment, looking at the big leather office chair, Sypher's chair. John touched the padded leather arm and spun it.

"The king is dead..." John spoke, almost in a whisper. Then he stiffened and spoke loud and defiant. "Long live the king."

No one in Digital Nation would dare oppose him now. The adrenaline rush was overpowering. He was the victor. Nothing else mattered.

He left the office to roam vacant halls. John felt the blood flowing through his veins, felt the power building inside him. He spread his arms wide, clenched his fists, took a deep breath and yelled to relieve tension. The deep sound of his voice reverberated in the vacant building as though in a cave.

He turned to a floor length mirror, snarled with tilted head and bared his teeth, pausing for a moment to appreciate the size and curve of his canines. They seemed to have grown larger. He blew out a stream of breath. *Yes, John Wagner, you are one badass Lycan.*

Who would dare stand against him now? *Who could?*

He turned back to Sypher's office. He had no reason to run or hide. It was *his* office now. He ducked under crime scene tape and plopped into the old king's leather-bound chair, his virtual throne. John swiveled around, like a child on a playground. He surveyed *his* new domain. It felt good.

He took a deep breath, steepled his fingers, and smiled. There were going to be some changes made with a new head Lycan. He, John Wagner, would take care of his kind, *all* those of his kind.

He laughed and spread his arms, an animal claiming his territory. Soon, everything would begin to change. The local community, the state, the nation, maybe even the world. A new age was coming, the age of the wolf.

———

The evening news began with a panoramic view of St. Raphael's church spire and the surrounding city.

Bruce, the male anchorman sounded serious. "Some bizarre goings on in normally sleepy Madison, Wisconsin. We've all heard of the Bigfoot attacks and the horrific friendly-fire incident that killed almost a dozen law enforcement officers and led the Madison Police Chief to commit suicide."

The commentators went silent as video showed the forest scene where ambulances and police moved in a chaotic hustle trying to help the wounded. Lights flashed, men shouted, sirens wailed.

"But, now, evidence of even stranger happenings. It seems that several of the dead in that police shootout were actually Italian monks brought to America as 'demon hunters.' Their leader, a Carmelite priest from Sicily, was found murdered in his hotel room just a few hours ago. The Bishop of the local diocese has declined comment except to say this is a period of mourning."

Bruce leaned into the camera. "And, if you thought it couldn't get any weirder, the CEO of a local company called Digital Nation seems to have killed himself, along with a couple of his employees."

Joan, the woman co-anchor sounded genuinely interested. "So how in the world are those deaths related?"

Again, the man paused for effect. "Silver bullets, they were all killed by silver bullets. That's right, *silver bullets*. What do you think Joan, are vampire or werewolf hunters now going after the Bigfoot mcnace, and how is a DNA processing company involved? You can be sure there's going to be a lot more to this story and it will unfold in the coming days."

Joan shook her head. "I'll bet Hollywood can't wait to get this one onto the screen... such a great setting: Sleepy, quiet, progressive Madison, Wisconsin; it's the last place anyone would expect such weirdness. I wouldn't be surprised if the town didn't become a magnet for monster-hunters, just as Roswell has been to Space Alien buffs."

Both laughed.

The Next Morning

THE NEXT MORNING

The senior staff assembled around the same conference table where John first met Sypher and Vladimir but this time, John sat at the head. Few on the Digital Nation staff had ever heard his name - at least few who were still alive.

He hadn't slept or shaved for days, and his suit, though clean, was still thrift shop. John stretched his hands onto the table and intertwined his fingers. He was about to speak when a large fellow at the far end took a took a deep breath and almost growled. "Okay, Vrykolas called us all here and said you are going to replace Louis. So, who the hell are you, and why should we be willing to trust a complete stranger?"

John collected his thoughts and then straightened to sit upright and stare back at the man. When he spoke, his voice was as deep as a cave echo. It sounded ominous.

"You will trust; you will follow; you will obey me; because you are Lycan, and we stand together. Loyalty is bred into our very souls. I did not seek this position. It was thrust upon me by events beyond my control. But, understand this; I have kept my bargain with Mister Sypher, and I now stand before you as his replacement. All who opposed me are dead."

He sounded as though reading a list: The bodyguards, Bart and Ben, the five Killer Monks, all the policemen and sheriff's deputies, the Chief of Police, and Louis Sypher -- all of them, dead."

He took a moment to look from man to man, staring hard into their eyes. Even the toughest of them flinched. John settled back into his chair but kept scanning their eyes.

"We're done talking about the past. We need to look ahead to the future, to the possibilities."

After a long, tense silence he continued. "Here is my guidance: We are but one subspecies of Lycans, but we are the most powerful. Therefore, it falls to us to protect and lead all of our fellows. In the past, we have looked with distain upon those we called 'Pures.' That will now change. We will establish a sanctuary for them where they can live and prosper and achieve to their capabilities."

Many around the table shifted uncomfortably. Some leaned forward with tight foreheads and jaws.

John continued without acknowledging their discomfort. "At the same time, we will enhance our own power within the Sapiens' world, eventually achieving dominance over them. I foresee a time when we shall be masters over all the world's humans. We will treat them fairly, but not allow their petty conflicts to distract us from our destiny."

The tall fellow at the far end made a dismissive sound. "That's a pretty damned grandiose statement. So just how do you intend to achieve this *dominance*. We have spent our lives in shadows, living covertly, pretending to be ordinary…"

John was nodding. "You're absolutely right. We've been pretending to be *normal*. That is, good little Sapiens boy normal. Now it's time to up the ante. We will take over the same way the powerful always do, by playing their game, the game of politics. We will use democracy to sell promises to make everyone happy. Then, like so many rulers before us, we will treat that democracy like toilet paper: use it once and discard."

There was an uncomfortable murmur around the table. Tall fellow couldn't restrain himself. "This is a pretty bold talk. I don't see any hope of it working. We have, throughout history, been persecuted, hunted, despised."

John was gaining confidence. "Yes, and, now, it's time for that to change." He looked from face to face. "We are in an excellent position to exert pressure on the system. People have lost confidence in their government and their institutions. Their leaders have been swayed by ridiculous team loyalties that led them to enact foolish policies. We can field candidates who will actually fix problems, make their lives better, and force them to treat each other with civility."

He let that sink in. "And, when someone opposes us...we'll kill them."

There was silence around the table. Even tall fellow seemed to ruminate.

John was feeling confident now, fully in control. He stood and thrust his shoulders back. His voice was strong.

"This is the Lycan way. This is our path to power and control. I want you all to go back and think of ways we can infiltrate and take over Sapiens' institutions. I want us to run everything, first in Wisconsin, then in America and, then... who knows?"

There was silence around the table before one of them leaned forward, shot a hard look at John, sucked air through his nose and then raised a fist. He began to pound on the table.

The pounding was slow at first. After a moment, another

joined in pounding…and then another and another. The slow cadence grew louder and faster becoming a thundering din. Objects on the table jittered. Pictures on the wall vibrated and tilted. The floor shook as they all joined, pounding and pounding, and then breaking into shrill cries.

John's heart throbbed in synch with the pounding. The pack was formed. He stood, threw back his head, and unleashed a long, fierce howl, the howl of a Lycan, the howl of a werewolf.

It had begun.

About the Author

A local Louisville author, Jim spins tales of knife-edged adventure, some with a bit of history, others with good old-fashioned *leap-out-of-the-darkness* horror. Come along as he takes you off the written page and into a world of far-away places and mysterious happenings where regular people wind up fighting their way through outrageous situations against great odds.

He's a pilot\ who's spent his life traveling to every continent and almost every exotic place you can name. Greenland, Pago Pago, Australia, China, Syria, Libya, Iran, South America, India: he's been everywhere and lived in Thailand, Japan,

Germany and Austria. You'll experience them in his stories and see them through his eyes.

As a veteran, he knows well the high-intensity emotions and real courage required in tight situations. He sees the world as full of mystery and deception, honor and malice, hard reality and dark forces that can turn everyday events into the great adventures of a lifetime. Now he turns experience into writing and invites you to share the fun.

The Terror series is written as J. Esker Miller.